W9-AWD-255

Praise for **Starship: Mutiny**

"[F]ew writers have Resnick's gift for pace and momentum, . . . his talent for producing a fast, smooth, utterly effortless read."

—*Analog Science Fiction and Fact*

"Resnick's reputation for writing two-fisted adventure has already been established, and *Starship: Mutiny* doesn't change that. Once again, the author demonstrates his ability to create characters several shades above stereotype, as well as fit them into a carefully conceived universe. Readers looking for an old-fashioned yarn will find this novel an auspicious start to a promising series."

—*Starlog*

"Mike Resnick is the king of intelligent space opera adventure. His future universe where the majority of his sf novels have occurred is superbly real, and characters, both human and alien, are the folk of legend. But despite this it never feels too out of the ordinary, and there is a definite realism (accepting the setting aboard starships that is). . . . This is a book that I believe cannot help itself when it comes to pleasing all of Resnick's many fans, and is one I feel should win him some new fans along the way. This is book one in the adventures of Wilson Cole and the Starship *Theodore Roosevelt*, and a fine start to the series it is. I want book two."

—*The Eternal Night*

"Prolific sf author Resnick ('Kirinyaga'; *A Hunger in the Soul*) launches a new series of military sf adventure with a solid introductory tale of one man's faith in himself and the loyalty of his comrades. A good choice for large sf collections."

—*Library Journal*

"When First Officer Wilson Cole challenges his incompetent captain aboard the starship *Theodore Roosevelt*, Cole must pay the price for mutiny in Hugo-winner Mike Resnick's rousing *Starship: Mutiny*, the first in a projected five-book series."

—*Publishers Weekly*

"The first of a proposed five-book saga set in his career-spanning Birthright Universe, Mike Resnick's *Starship: Mutiny* is just the kind of easygoing and unabashedly old-school space opera romp for which we've come to know and love him . . . whip-smart, fast-paced pure entertainment . . . simply pure escapism, impossible to resist by anyone who still remembers that good old-fashioned sense of wonder."

—*SF Reviews*

"Resnick's writing is effortless, full of snappy dialogue and a fast-moving plot. The real delight to reading this novel is the banter and jokes in the conversations between Cole and the crewmates he does get on with, the insults and sarcastic comments with those he doesn't get on with, and the real feeling of camaraderie and society it creates. It's very easy to imagine this as a real world and setting because the characters act so naturally together. . . . This was my first time at a Resnick book, so I had no expectations coming in. Needless to say, I was impressed. This is high-quality work. . . . There's a veneer of quality and above all believability that makes this heads above many space operas. . . . It's damn good fun."

—*SF Crowsnest*

Praise for **Starship: Pirate**

"What makes this novel so enjoyable is the dialogue; the majority of the story is told through the words of the characters. Snappy banter . . . proves entertaining. There are some omniscient narrative scenes, but most of the action and plot is relayed through the characters themselves. This allows the entire story to move along at a brisk pace, even more so with the brevity of the novel. As with *Starship: Mutiny*, Resnick puts a lot of story, ample amounts of action balanced with tension, in a short novel. With no words wasted, the story is very entertaining. While a very character-driven story, Resnick also brings in enough action to balance out the story. . . . With the two of five projected Starship novels published, Resnick is building a nice, thoroughly entertaining space opera."

—SFFWorld.com

"Continuing the story and characters started in *Starship: Mutiny*, Mike Resnick turns in a quality effort . . . a quick, fun read."

—SFSignal.com

"This sequel to *Starship: Mutiny*, set in Resnick's Birthright Universe, . . . shows the author's genuine flair for spinning a good yarn. Snappy dialog, intriguing human and alien characters, and a keen sense of dramatic focus make this a strong addition to most sf collections, with particular appeal to the sf action-adventure readership."

—*Library Journal*

"Resnick is writing good old-fashioned space adventure here, bereft of any complex themes or hard-science underpinnings, but he does it as well as it's ever been done. The 'DVD extras' in this book include, in addition to the chronology of the Birthright Universe in which Resnick sets most of his SF, the deceptively simple rules of two games mentioned in his stories, Bilsang and Toprench, which have been featured in various Resnick stories, revealed here for the first time anywhere. Fans of science fiction space adventures will be looking forward to *Starship: Mercenary*, the third book in this five-book series. Grade: B."

—*Sci Fi Weekly*

"[O]nce more [Resnick] has written a tale that gives so much to anyone familiar with his work, whilst (I would imagine) allowing someone new to his work instant access to this Universe. This series is Mike Resnick's first military sf. However, if you (like me) do not overly like military science fiction, do not be discouraged. This is very much Mike Resnick fiction. . . . If you like your sf to be space opera, if you like your sf gadgets to just work without needing an explanation of how, and if you don't need to worry about the vast interstellar distances getting in the way of telling the tale—then Resnick is an author you should read."

—*The Eternal Night*

"[T]he adventure that follows is enjoyable, action-packed, and funny. Resnick's style is effortless and full of humorous asides. The plot is enjoyable but it's the camaraderie and banter between the characters that really makes this a page-turner. The characters are larger than life but not in a clichéd way—the enigmatic alien fence David Copperfield is an exceptionally good character. This book is a light read and won't break any boundaries, but like most Resnick, it is absolutely unabashedly enjoyable. Sheer space opera entertainment is on the menu and it's a sweet dish. Pick the Starship series up and while away some enjoyable relaxation time in the Birthright Universe. You won't regret it."

—SFCrowsnest.co.uk

"Through these now many years the collected works of Mike Resnick have given me more pleasure per capita than those of any other writer; I read *Soul Eater* in manuscript in 1980 and pronounced that if he carried on Resnick would in a decade be viewed as the most important science fiction writer to emerge in the decade to come. An easy call as the rocketships then accumulated. *Starship: Pirate* is a wonderful novel, an expanse of color, light, and wit; its splendid rogues in space as fetching as they are wickedly memorable. It is a privilege to have lived and worked in science fiction during Mike Resnick's quarter century."

—Barry N. Malzberg

"Mike Resnick is one of the finest writers the science fiction field has ever produced, and *Starship: Pirate* is one of his very best works. A wonderful book."

—Robert J. Sawyer,
Hugo Award–winning
author of *Hominids*

"A memorable ride with a handful of Resnick's trademark oddball characters, a shipload of faster-than-light buccaneers, and a pirate queen to die for, all lightly seasoned by Charles Dickens. A rollicking good time."

—Jack McDevitt

Praise for Starship: Mercenary

"While the novel is fast paced and entertaining, Copperfield's character adds a great deal of humor and comedic relief to the story and grows into more than strictly comic relief by the novel's end. . . . So the bottom line is this: if you've enjoyed the first two Starship novels, there is no reason not to continue on with the story."

—*SFF World*

ALSO AVAILABLE BY MIKE RESNICK

IVORY

NEW DREAMS FOR OLD

STALKING THE UNICORN

STALKING THE VAMPIRE

STARSHIP: MUTINY
BOOK ONE

STARSHIP: PIRATE
BOOK TWO

STARSHIP: MERCENARY
BOOK THREE

MIKE RESNICK

STARSHIP:
REBEL

BOOK FOUR

an imprint of Prometheus Books
Amherst, NY

Published 2008 by Pyr®, an imprint of Prometheus Books

Inquiries should be addressed to
Pyr
59 John Glenn Drive
Amherst, New York 14228–2119
VOICE: 716–691–0133, ext. 210
FAX: 716–691–0137
WWW.PYRSF.COM

12 11 10 09 08   5 4 3 2 1

Library of Congress Cataloging-in-Publication Data

Resnick, Michael D.
　　Starship—rebel / by Mike Resnick.
　　　　p. cm.
　　"Book four."
　　ISBN: 978–1–59102–695–2 (acid-free paper)
　　1. Cole, Wilson (Fictitious character)—Fiction. 2. Space ships—Fiction.
3. Space warfare—Fiction. 4. Dissenters—Fiction. I. Title. II. Title: Rebel.

PS3568.E698S738 2008
813'.54—dc22

2008030717

Printed in the United States on acid-free paper

To Carol, as always

And to Eric Flint:
        Friend
        Collaborator
        Co-editor
        Boy genius

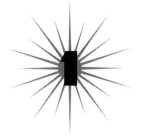

Wilson Cole sat alone at his table in the small, cramped mess hall of the *Theodore Roosevelt*, sipping a cup of coffee, when he received the transmission from the bridge.

"We're all in position, sir," said Christine Mboya, the slender black woman whose image suddenly appeared before him.

"Has Mr. Briggs analyzed their capabilities yet?" asked Cole.

"Level 2 pulse cannons, Level 3 lasers."

"Okay, nothing to worry about. Let me speak to the Valkyrie."

An instant later the face of his Third Officer, an exceptionally tall redheaded woman, appeared above Cole's table.

"What is it?" she asked.

"Pass the word, Val. I want all of our ships except this one to stay out of firing range."

"Why?" she demanded. "Are we here to engage the enemy or aren't we?"

"They can't do the *Teddy R* any damage, but they can pierce most of the smaller ships' defenses."

"Not if we destroy them first."

"Just do what I tell you to do," said Cole. "With a little luck we won't have to destroy anyone."

"Some war!" she snorted, and broke the transmission.

"Christine?"

"Sir?"

"Is Four Eyes down in the Gunnery section?"

"Commander Forrice is on his way there," she answered. "One moment, sir." Pause. "He's arrived."

"Let me speak to him."

The image of a burly member of the tripodal Molarian race appeared, surrounded by computerized controls for the ship's armaments.

"Everything's ready," said Forrice. "Just say the word."

"How big a crew have you got down there?"

"Four, counting myself."

"That'll be enough if we need it," said Cole. "No one fires except on my express order."

"Even if we're under fire ourselves?"

"Even so. They don't have anything that can damage us."

"You're the Captain," said Forrice.

"Thanks for remembering," said Cole dryly, ending the transmission.

He finished his coffee, considered going to the bridge, decided there was nothing he could do there that he couldn't do where he was, and contacted Christine Mboya again.

"Sir?" she said.

"Have we pinpointed Machtel's headquarters yet?"

"No, sir. They're maintaining radio and video silence."

"Can't say that I blame them," said Cole. "If it was me, I wouldn't want to let a superior force know where I was holed up either." He shrugged. "Okay, negotiating in private would have been easier, but it's time to get this show on the road. Put me on audio and video, broadest possible bandwidth."

"Done," she announced. "Start whenever you're ready."

He chose one of the cameras that monitored the mess hall and stared into it. "This is Wilson Cole, Captain of the *Theodore Roosevelt*. This message is for Machtel, or, if he is no longer in charge, whoever is running his organization. My fleet has been commissioned by the government of the Pirelli Cluster to rid it of the warlords who have taken it over. I'm sure you are aware that we have already deposed the Cluster's two other warlords—the human Chester Braithwaite and the Canphorite Grabius. You are all that remains."

He paused for almost half a minute, long enough for them to start getting nervous wondering if he was going to speak again or if he'd said his piece and was about to start firing on them.

"You have nine ships on the ground and three more docked in orbit. I'm sure you have analyzed our strength, but just in case you haven't, let me inform you that you are facing a fleet of forty-three ships, many of them with greater firepower than any of your own."

He broke the connection and poured himself another cup of coffee.

"That's *it*?" demanded Val, whose image popped into view again. "That's all you're going to say?"

"Of course not," replied Cole. "But let them worry about it for a few minutes."

"Right now they're probably getting us in the sights of every weapon they own."

"Right now they're counting our ships and analyzing our defenses," answered Cole calmly. "In another minute they'll realize I wasn't lying, and then we'll continue the conversation."

"It's been a pretty one-sided conversation so far," noted Val.

"I haven't asked them to say anything so far."

Suddenly Malcolm Briggs's voice came over the ship's intercom, though not his image. "Incoming! Pulse and laser fire!"

"Solely at us?" asked Cole.

"No, sir. They're also targeting Mr. Sokolov and Mr. Perez."

"I trust they're out of range?"

"Yes, sir."

"Okay. Tell Christine to wait thirty seconds and then put me on again."

"I've pinpointed the source of the pulse fire," announced Forrice from his post in the Gunnery section. "You want me to take it out?"

"I want you to do nothing without an express order from me," said Cole.

"That's what I was requesting—an express order."

"No."

"You're on in five seconds, sir," said Christine.

Cole cleared his throat, counted to five, and began speaking.

"This is Wilson Cole again. I trust you've convinced yourself that you're not about to inflict any damage on us. The corollary is that we can annihilate you in less than a minute."

A brief pause.

"However, we have no desire to cause you any damage or loss of life. We are not conquerors, we are not warlords, and we are not criminals. We are a mercenary force, hired by the authorities of the Pirelli Cluster to put an end to your aggressive and illegal domination of the local star systems. And I should note that in this instance we are an *overwhelming* mercenary force.

"We have now reached the point where decisions must be made," he continued. "We are confiscating the three docked ships. Any of you on the planet can surrender and pledge your allegiance to my fleet. If you do so, you will not be harmed—but you will not be left in control of your ship. Two of my men will be installed as Captain and First Officer until such time as you have proven your trustworthiness, and any disloyalty will be punishable by death. Those of you who choose this option should take off immediately and put your ships in orbit around the fifth planet in the system. If you do not wish to meet us in combat or join us as an ally, fly your equivalent of the white flag and leave the cluster immediately, via the Landrigan Wormhole, and you will not be fired upon . . . but you will never be allowed to return. Your third and final alternative is to remain where you are and meet us in combat. You have ten Standard minutes to make your decisions, after which combat will commence."

He broke the transmission, considered having yet another cup of coffee, decided not to, and took an airlift up to the bridge, where Christine Mboya, Malcolm Briggs, Val, and the alien Domak were manning their stations.

"Any response yet?" he asked as he arrived.

"Five ships have signaled that they want to join us," answered Christine, "and are heading to the fifth planet."

"Tell Jacovic to monitor them, and take out any ship that heads that way and *doesn't* go into orbit."

"Two white flags, sir," announced Briggs.

"Tell Sokolov to take a couple of ships, follow them to the wormhole, and make sure they enter it," said Cole. "What's left?"

"Two ships, sir," said Domak, a warrior-caste Polonoi, her muscular body covered with natural armor. "I've identified one as belonging to Machtel."

"Got him in my sights," said Forrice's voice.

"Forget it," said Cole. "He's not going to stand his ground."

"He hasn't moved yet," said Forrice.

"He's just proving how tough he is. He's got a couple of minutes left."

"The other ship is heading to the fifth planet, sir," said Briggs. "That leaves just Machtel."

"He's probably not the type to take orders," said Cole. "I'll give plenty of ten-to-one that he heads for the wormhole rather than the fifth planet."

"He's not heading anywhere," said Forrice.

"He will," said Cole. "This isn't *his* planet. Every other ship has already left. He won't prove anything by dying. We're just doing to him what he did to whoever was here before him, and we're doing it a lot more humanely."

"A humane war!" snorted the Molarian.

"Whose life do you want me to trade for Machtel's?" asked Cole. "Yours? Val's? Mine?"

"You don't have to trade anyone's life," said Forrice. "*We* can kill him. *He* can't harm us."

"Whether we kill him or let him escape, we accomplish our mission," replied Cole. "And by doing it this way, word will spread to future opponents that they don't have to fight to the last man, that we're not in the punishment or retribution business, that we're just as happy to achieve a bloodless victory."

"Sir?" said Briggs.

"Yes?"

"Machtel just took off. He's heading for the wormhole."

"Good. Tell Jacovic to take eighteen ships out to the fifth planet, put our new members in a tight formation, englobe them, and escort them back to base. That ought to discourage any foolhardy heroes among our new recruits."

Val looked up from her control panel. "You really want to give this asshole a free pass?"

"Machtel? I promised him one."

"He's just going to be more trouble in the future," she said. "The other ships have already entered the wormhole. We could take him out and no one would be any the wiser."

"And when he didn't show up at the other end, you think the others won't know what happened?"

"So what if they do?" she persisted.

"Then before long far more powerful forces than his would know they could never trust our word again."

She shrugged. "All right—but if you change your mind, we've got thirty seconds before he reaches the wormhole."

"How the hell did I manage to assemble such a bloodthirsty crew?" Cole said wryly. "I feel a need to speak to someone who's glad that we didn't blow nine ships to hell and gone." He walked over to a bulkhead and tapped his fingers against it. "Come on out, David."

The bulkhead slid open, and an odd-looking creature of vaguely human proportions, but dressed like a Victorian dandy, stepped out onto the bridge. His eyes were set at the sides of his elongated head, his large triangular ears were capable of independent movement, his mouth was absolutely circular and had no lips at all, and his neck was long and incredibly flexible. His torso was broad and half again as long as a man's, and his short, stubby legs had an extra joint in them. His skin may have possessed a greenish tint, but his bearing and manner were properly upper-class British at all times.

"Is it over?" he asked.

"It was a nonevent," said Cole.

"The bigger our fleet becomes, the more nonevents we can expect to have," said the alien approvingly.

"We just added eight more ships," Cole informed him. "Five from the planet, three that were docked in orbit."

"So we're up to fifty-one?"

Cole nodded. "If they all work."

"You're going to make it harder and harder for me to solicit contracts that will cover all our expenses."

"The burdens of success," replied Cole. "I suppose we could attack a Republic convoy. That ought to put a huge dent in our expenses by the time we escaped."

"It's unkind of you to make fun of me, Steerforth," said the alien.

"I'm open to suggestions," replied Cole. "Who would you like me to make fun of?"

"Why are you being like this?" asked the alien.

"I apologize, David," said Cole. "It's just that we should *all* be celebrating a victory where we didn't have to fire a shot—but I get the distinct impression that most of my senior officers would rather engage in armed conflict."

"Well, you *are* a military ship and crew," noted the alien. "War is what most of you have trained for all your adult lives."

"No sane man wants to go to war," said Cole. "These aren't expendable chess pieces under my command. They're living beings, and it's my job to keep them alive."

"I agree," said the dapper alien. "You have to be quite insane to face the possibility of losing a battle."

"Which is why you sit them out hiding inside a bulkhead," noted Cole.

"Resting, not hiding," shot back the alien. "I'm the *Teddy R*'s business agent, not one of its lieutenants—and as a rational and foresightful business agent let me predict that there will be no more pitched battles in our future. Our fleet is growing larger and more powerful almost by the week."

"Yeah," agreed Cole sardonically. "Eight or ten million more ships and we can meet the Republic on even terms."

"Make fun of me if you wish," said the alien, "but I'm telling you that you will not see another armed conflict or my name isn't David Copperfield."

"I hate to point it out," said Cole, "but your name *isn't* David Copperfield."

"How can you say such a thing, Steerforth?" demanded David.

"Possibly because my name isn't Steerforth."

"Details, details," said Copperfield. "People take the names they want on the Inner Frontier. I took David."

"I didn't take Steerforth," said Cole.

"It is my gift to you, courtesy of the immortal Charles."

"You and Mr. Dickens can have it back," said Cole. "I just hope you're more accurate about your military predictions than your name."

Cole had the uneasy feeling that some nameless god of the spaceways grinned sardonically and silently mouthed the words: *Well, you can hope.*

It wasn't home—that was the *Teddy R*—but it *was* headquarters.

It was Singapore Station, perhaps the most remarkable structure on the Inner Frontier. Its genesis went back some eleven centuries, to the 883rd year of the Galactic Era, when two small space stations, built midway between the Genoa and the Kalatina systems, were splitting the business in a sector that could support only one station. In desperation their owners decided to form not just an economic partnership, but a physical one as well. The two stations were moved to a midpoint between the systems by space tugs. Workmen and robots labored for three Standard months, joining them physically—and when they reopened they found that business was booming.

Others saw and learned and copied, and by the fourteenth century G.E. there were dozens of such super-stations across the Frontier. They found that the bigger they were, the more services they could provide—and the more services they could provide, the more clientele they could attract, so they kept combining and growing.

By the time Cole and his crew first docked at it, almost two hundred such stations had combined into one super-station—Singapore Station—that was as heavily populated as any colony world, and measured some seven miles in diameter. It consisted of nine levels, with docking facilities that could handle almost ten thousand ships, from huge military and passenger vessels to the little one- and two-man jobs that were commonplace on the Frontier.

Singapore Station was well named and well located. An interstellar gathering place reminiscent of the fabled international city back on old Earth, it was halfway between the Republic and the huge black hole at the galactic core. Warring parties—and there were *always* wars going on in the galaxy—needed a Switzerland, a neutral territory where all sides could meet in safety and secrecy, where currencies could be exchanged, where men and aliens could come and go regardless of their political and military affiliation, and Singapore Station filled that need.

It was also a wide-open venue. Whorehouses, catering to all sexes and species, abounded. So did bars, drug dens, casinos, and huge open "gray markets." (By definition no item was illegal or contraband on Singapore Station, so there couldn't be any black markets.) There were elegant hotels, comparable to the finest on Deluros VIII. There were gourmet restaurants, side-by-side with slop houses, as well as alien restaurants catering to more than one hundred non-human species.

Four of the nine levels possessed what had come to be known as Standard gravity and atmosphere, though no one knew if that was Earth Standard or Deluros VIII Standard (and since they were almost identical, no one really cared). There was a level for chlorine breathers, one for methane breathers, another for ammonia breathers, and one small section with no atmosphere at all, where space-suited men and space-suited aliens could meet as uncomfortable equals. A middle level provided automatic transport for all.

Cole had chosen Singapore Station as the headquarters for his rapidly growing fleet of ships the first time he set foot on it a year earlier. It was the one place on the Inner Frontier where he trusted the security, where he could replenish his supplies, and where he could make contact with those who might be interested in hiring the services of the *Teddy R* and its sister ships. Though David Copperfield still negotiated Cole's end of the contracts, he didn't have enough contacts to solicit sufficient work to keep Cole's small but growing navy busy—

but there was one man who did, and that was the man who ran Singapore Station. Known as the Platinum Duke for his multitude of platinum prosthetics—not much of the original man remained on the exterior except his tongue, lips, and sexual organ—he had formed a partnership with Cole that had proved profitable to both parties.

The Duke also owned a large casino known simply as Duke's Place, and it was the unofficial hangout of the *Teddy R*'s crew. The Duke himself kept a large table at the back of the casino where Cole and his officers were always welcome, and where there was no tab for food or drink.

Cole entered the casino and walked past the human and alien games to the Duke's table, accompanied by his Chief of Security, Sharon Blacksmith, and David Copperfield. Val had accompanied them as far as the entrance, but made a beeline for the gaming tables the moment she entered. The Duke's security system alerted him to their presence, and he emerged from his private office, looking far more robotic than human, to greet them as they reached the table.

"I hear you took care of Machtel without firing a shot," said the Duke. "That's, what, three in a row?"

"It makes more sense to assimilate the ships and crew than destroy them," said Cole, pulling a chair out for Sharon and then seating himself. A robot approached, and he ordered drinks for himself and Sharon. "You want anything, David?"

"A bottle of Cygnian cognac," replied the dapper little alien.

"Come on, David," said Cole. "Your metabolism can't handle our stimulants."

"I know," replied Copperfield. "But I don't have to open it. I'll just let it sit here on the table in front of me for atmosphere."

"Fine," said the Duke. "If you don't open it, I can sell it later."

"You'll have to forgive him," said Cole. "He gets a little more obsessed every day. I can't believe he hasn't visited one of the whore-houses here."

"David Copperfield would never frequent a brothel!" said the alien heatedly.

"I stand corrected," said Cole.

"How many of Machtel's ships and crew did you confiscate?" asked the Duke.

"Eight ships, fifty-seven Men and aliens," answered Cole.

"That's quite a fleet you're accumulating," said the Duke. "You're going to run out of challenges before too long."

"We've *faced* challenges," replied Cole. "Trust me, they're overrated."

"Besides, we can't go getting him shot up now that I've finally got him trained," said Sharon.

"Decorum forbids me from asking what you'd got him trained to do," said the Duke, his human lips smiling in his platinum face. He looked over at the Valkyrie. "You'd think she'd stop by and say hello."

"She will, after she's beaten your table or blown all her money," said Cole. "You know her."

"I still wish she'd hire on right here. I never saw anyone who could spot a cheater quicker, and I've never seen the human or alien who could beat her in a fight."

"She's quite remarkable," agreed Copperfield.

"I need her right where she is," said Cole.

"You wouldn't be happy with her anyway," added Sharon. "Wilson's the only person she'll listen to."

"Why is that?" asked the Duke.

"Because he's never wrong," said Copperfield. "Except when he dis-agrees with me."

"Funny," added Sharon with a smile. "I was about to say the same thing."

"Ah!" said the Duke, looking across the room. "I see Commander Jacovic has joined us."

"He was a little late getting in," replied Cole. "I had him escort the new ships back, just in case one of the them tried to pull anything funny." He waved his hand to catch Jacovic's attention, and the tall, thin Teroni walked across the room and joined them.

"Welcome back, Commander Jacovic," said the Duke.

"I am just Jacovic now," replied the Teroni. "I am no longer an officer in the Teroni Navy."

"Commander of the Fifth Fleet, to be exact," said Cole.

"That's in the past. We are no longer enemies, and neither of us is a member of any Navy."

"Except our own," said Sharon. "The only difference between you and Wilson is that the Teronis haven't offered a ten-million-credit reward for you, dead or alive," said Sharon. "The Republic's Navy is somewhat less enamoured of our Captain."

"Out here that's a badge of honor," remarked the Duke. "In fact, it makes you a hero. The fact that you were justified, that you actually saved millions of Republic lives by forcibly replacing your captain, doesn't quite detract from the fact that you are the most wanted criminal in the galaxy."

"How comforting," said Cole dryly.

"And by the way, the reward is now up to twelve million," added the Duke.

"Whoopie," said Cole unenthusiastically.

The Duke studied Cole's face. "Our hero looks neither pleased nor proud. Why not?"

"We both know the Navy's not going to send a major fleet to the Frontier after the *Teddy R* as long as they're in a war with the Teroni Federation," answered Copperfield. "But if they keep making the reward bigger and bigger, then sooner or later, despite your security, Singapore Station is going to be crawling with bounty hunters."

"It won't happen here," the Duke assured him. "Whoever accepts the contract will want to live long enough to spend it."

"You can stop one killer," continued Sharon. "But what if twenty of them form a partnership? That's still better than half a million a man."

"Enough," said Cole. "The risks go with the job."

Sharon was about to reply when they heard a cry of triumph from across the room.

"She beat your *jabob* game," noted Cole, referring to the alien gaming table where Val was holding up a fistful of cash.

"It would be so much cheaper to have her work for the house than play against it," muttered the Duke.

A robot delivered a bottle of whiskey to Val.

"Not to worry," said Cole. "She'll chug-a-lug a couple of bottles of booze and probably wind up losing it all back to you."

"Remarkable lady," said the Duke.

"She's got her share of rough edges," agreed Cole. "But when the chips are down, she's the one I want protecting my back."

"Just so long as she leaves your front alone," said Sharon.

Suddenly the Duke summoned a robot. "Where are my manners?" he said. "What will you have to drink, Commander?"

"Just Jacovic," the Teroni corrected him. "And if it's all right with you, I think I would prefer to eat."

"My kitchen is at your disposal."

"Meaning no disrespect, but there is a restaurant three levels down that specializes in Teroni food," said Jacovic. "I just stopped in to tell Captain Cole that we returned without incident, and to say hello to you." He got to his feet.

"You'll be back later?" asked the Duke.

"Yes."

"Give me the name of the restaurant and I'll see to it that there's no charge."

"Thank you," said Jacovic, "but I prefer to pay."

He turned and headed to the door.

"A little anti-Man sentiment there?" asked the Duke.

"No," answered Cole. "A little pride." He shrugged. "Besides, out here he's got nothing to spend it on."

"We have *that* in common," said a familiar voice.

Cole turned and saw Forrice, his First Officer, spinning toward the table with his remarkably graceful three-legged gait. The burly Molarian, whose tripodal structure made sitting on chairs crafted for humans all but impossible, waited until a robot brought him a seat that had been made especially for him.

"I thought you were busy spending all your money, Four Eyes," remarked Cole when Forrice finally seated himself.

The Molarian's reply was a guttural growl.

"What happened?"

"Guess," muttered Forrice.

Suddenly Cole grinned in amusement. "Wrong time of year?"

"It's not funny!" snapped Forrice. "You and Sharon have sex whenever you want, which is altogether too often if you want my opinion, but Molarians are different. Our females are seasonal."

"And the Molarian whorehouse didn't have any in season?"

"Not one!"

"Poor baby," said Sharon sympathetically, and neither Cole nor Forrice could tell if she was sincere or teasing him.

"So what do you do now?" asked Copperfield.

"It all depends," said the Molarian. "Have you and the Duke gotten us another assignment yet?"

"No," said Copperfield. "Steerforth wanted to give the crew a week's shore leave. Well, Singapore Station leave, anyway."

"Then maybe I'll borrow one of the shuttles," said Forrice. "There's supposed to be a Molarian whorehouse over on Braccio II. I could be there and back in three days' time."

The Duke shook his head. "You don't want to go anywhere near there, Forrice," he said.

"Oh? Why not?"

"There are a couple of hundred Navy ships in the vicinity," said the Duke. "At least, they were there two days ago."

"What the hell are they doing out here?"

"The usual," answered the Duke. "Forcibly recruiting cannon fodder. Plundering agricultural planets for supplies. Appropriating fissionable materials from a trio of mining worlds. Pacifying a couple of worlds that have somehow annoyed them. And then explaining that they were doing it all for our own good. You know the Navy."

"We *all* know the Navy," said Sharon. "We were in it. That's why we can never go back to the Republic."

"Anyway, I hate to put a damper on your love life, Forrice," continued the Duke, "but I'd stay away from there until we get definite word that the Navy has left."

"It's a damned lucky thing Molarians don't believe in God," muttered Forrice. "Because if we did, I'd be sure He hated me."

"He's probably just having a little fun at your expense," said Cole. He put an arm around the Molarian's shoulders. "Come on, Four Eyes. It's just another week. You've waited half a Standard year, you can wait a few more days."

"I know, I know," said Forrice glumly. He got to his feet. "I'm going to wander the streets feeling sorry for myself. If I'm lucky, maybe some mugger will attack me. I've got a *lot* of extra aggression tonight."

He turned and headed out of the casino.

"Poor bastard," remarked Cole. "Nature played a hell of a trick on the Molarians. The females are seasonal, but the males are always ready."

"You're very fond of him, aren't you?" asked the Duke.

"He's been my closest friend for, I don't know, twelve or thirteen years."

"I find that surprising."

"Why?" said Cole. "Molarians are the only race besides Man with a sense of humor. He's smart, he's witty, he's brave, he's loyal, and"— Cole smiled—"he leaves Sharon alone, even at times like this."

"Well," said the Duke, "how about dinner?"

"Yeah, we could use some real food after all those damned soya products on the ship," said Cole. "What have you got tonight?"

The Duke recited the day's menu, Cole and Sharon made their choices, David Copperfield ordered a steak that they all knew he wasn't going to touch, and a few minutes later the meal was served.

And five minutes after that, Val walked over and sat down with them.

"Ah, the lovely and remarkable Valkyrie!" said the Duke by way of greeting.

"Can it," she said. "I'm not in the mood."

"You lost it that fast?"

"Shut up and give me something to eat."

"She lost it that fast," Cole confirmed with a smile.

Val glared at him, and Sharon decided he was the only living entity in the galaxy who could have said that without being decapitated two seconds later.

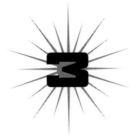

Cole made his way to the *Teddy R*'s security section, where he found Luthor Chadwick, Sharon Blacksmith's second-in-command, sitting in front of a bank of monitors, keeping a watchful eye on all crew members who remained onboard the ship.

Chadwick snapped him a salute. "Hello, sir," he said. "What can I do for you?"

Cole resisted the urge to tell him to stop saluting. "Is your boss in her office?"

"Yes, sir."

"Alone, or still interviewing our new recruits from Machtel's crew?"

"I believe she's alone, sir." He checked a monitor. "Yes, sir. She's finished the last of them a few minutes ago."

"Good. That's what I want to talk to her about."

Cole approached the door to Sharon's office, which instantly read his retina and bone structure, and irised to allow him to step through.

"How's it going?" he asked.

Sharon leaned back on her chair. "I'd call them a mixed lot."

"You want to expand on that?"

"They're outlaws and cutthroats, Wilson."

"So are we, except for the cutthroat part," replied Cole. "How many can we work with?"

"Well, you've got three who are borderline psychopaths and one who crossed that border years ago. I suppose we can fit the rest in."

"Okay," said Cole. "That's still fifty-three more crew members. Give me the names of the four crazies."

She ordered her computer to print out the four names.

"Thanks," he said, taking it from her. "The sooner we get the bad eggs off the ships, the less contamination we risk."

"I'd be *very* careful handling them, Wilson," she said. "You've got a couple of real killer-dillers there."

"Well, if you're going to keep a few systems under your thumb the way Machtel did, I suppose you need some real killer-dillers."

"What do you plan to do with them?" asked Sharon. "We can't just turn them loose on Singapore Station."

"I know," said Cole. "I suppose I could just have Val beat the shit out of them twice a day until she's broken their spirits."

"Seriously."

"Seriously? We'll confiscate their weapons and dump them on some world that's got a competent police force. If I can't turn them loose in Singapore Station, and I agree that I can't, I sure as hell can't turn them loose on some little pastoral farming world. They'd rob and kill the first family they came upon and swipe their ship."

"Well, when you decide exactly where you're placing them, let me know so I can notify the authorities."

"Will do," said Cole. "In fact, I suppose I'd better get the ball rolling. Lunch later?"

"Here or the station?"

"The station has real food, the *Teddy R* has soya products. Which do you think?"

She smiled. "I'll meet you at Duke's Place in a couple of hours."

"Fine."

He turned and left her office, walked out of the security section to a nearby airlift, took it down two levels, got off, and approached the smallish room that had been turned into a very undersized gymnasium. He entered it and found himself facing Eric Pampas, a muscular young man, and the Valkyrie. Both were lifting weights, weights Cole was sure no one else on the ship, even some of the sturdier aliens, could budge.

"Good morning, sir," said Pampas, putting his barbell on the floor and saluting.

"Good morning, Bull," replied Cole. "Are you two just about done?"

"Another five minutes," said Val. "What's up?"

"Sharon's interviewed the new crew, had the computer run psych tests on them, and she tells me we've got four serious nutcases."

"Only four?" said Val, lifting her weight again. "That's better than last time."

"I've got a list of their names. Jacovic is keeping an eye on all the new crew members aboard the *Silent Dart* until they receive their ship assignments. I want you to pull these four out and—"

"—beat a little obedience into them?" concluded Val. "Good. Bull needs the exercise. I'll lend a hand if he needs it."

"Try not to understand me so fast," said Cole. "I want you and Bull to load them into the *Red Sphinx*. Stay with them until you land, make sure they're not in the middle of a desert or a wilderness, give them back any weaponry they'll need to defend themselves but nothing powerful enough to cause any serious problems to the local constabulary—I'll leave it to your judgment—and then have Perez bring you back to Singapore Station."

"We could kill them right now and save a lot of trouble," said Val. "You set 'em loose on some third-rate world and they're likely to feel betrayed and resentful."

"Why?" said Cole. "We could have destroyed them back in the Pirelli Cluster, but we let them live."

"If they were sane enough to take that into account, you wouldn't be dumping them, would you?" replied Val.

"Val, we're not cold-blooded killers," said Cole. "Well, *some* of us aren't," he amended. "Just do what I tell you to do."

"I hope they decide they don't want to go," she said.

"Bull," said Cole, turning to the young man, "if that's the case, make sure it was *their* decision and not *hers*."

Pampas, finding himself between the Captain and the Third Officer, nodded an agreement but didn't salute, which seemed to satisfy both of them.

"Okay," said Cole. "Finish up, shower, and get over to the *Silent Dart* in an hour. By the time you transfer them to the *Red Sphinx*, Perez will know where you're going."

Cole left the room and took a different airlift up to the bridge, where he found young blonde Rachel Marcos sitting at the computer complex.

"Good morning, sir," she said, standing and saluting.

"Good morning. I've lost track of the time. When is Christine back on duty?"

"It's still red shift for another two hours, sir. She'll come on when it's white shift."

"I need some information sooner than that," said Cole, frowning. "Hunt up the three nearest nonagricultural oxygen worlds possessing organized law enforcement and reliable medical and transportation facilities."

She spoke a code that he didn't understand, and a moment later the computer threw up a holograph of the sector, with Singapore Station and three reasonably close worlds brilliantly highlighted.

"Any immigration restrictions on any of them?"

Another coded statement. "Yes, sir. Niarchos IV is currently closed to human immigration."

"Which of the other two has the larger police force?"

She asked the computer, and suddenly only one planet was flashing. "Mirbeau III, sir."

"Thanks. That should do it."

Cole walked over to stand beneath the half-sling half-cocoon that held Wxakgini, the Bdxeni pilot whose race never slept and whose neural circuits were wired into the ship's navigational system.

"Pilot," said Cole, who had long since given up trying to pronounce Wxakgini's name, "are there any wormholes between our present location and Mirbeau III? You can get its coordinates from the computer."

"Yes," answered Wxakgini, whose response to Cole's inability to learn his name was to never call Cole "sir." "The Yoriba Wormhole will let a ship out near the fourth planet of the Mirbeau system."

"Transit time from Singapore Station?"

"Utilizing the wormhole, four hours and seventeen minutes," replied the pilot. "Through normal space at light speeds, just under four days."

"Okay, thanks," said Cole. He turned back to Rachel. "Contact Mr. Perez. Tell him he's about to be visited by Val, Bull, and four of Machtel's men. Have him warn his crew that the men are highly dangerous, and to keep clear of them. He's to utilize the Yoriba Wormhole and drop them off on Mirbeau III."

"Should I clear it with the planetary authorities first, sir?" asked Rachel.

Cole shook his head. "What if they say no? Tell Sharon to alert them *after* Perez has dropped off his cargo and is heading back to Singapore Station."

"Yes, sir."

"By the way, has Four Eyes returned to the ship yet?"

"I believe he's in the mess hall, sir."

"Thanks," said Cole, heading off to an airlift. He descended to the mess hall, entered it, saw Forrice sitting alone at a table, and joined him.

"Up to a little work this afternoon?"

"We don't have afternoons in space," replied the Molarian.

"I know, but it's easier to say than 'Up to a little work this white shift?'"

"What did you have in mind?"

"Val and Bull Pampas are about to separate the psychos and put them down on an innocent, unsuspecting planet," said Cole. "I'd like you, Jacovic, Domak, and Sokolov to take the remaining recruits and their ships out and put them through some more exercises and see what they can do. We know they can terrorize innocent planet-dwellers; let's see if they can take orders and execute military maneuvers."

"I suppose it makes sense," agreed Forrice. "If there are anymore washouts, we might as well find out now."

"I want you aboard that class-K ship, the one called *Hummer*."

"Any reason why?"

Cole nodded. "It has an all-human crew. I want to make sure they'll take orders from a member of another race."

"What they do now and what they'll do when they're under fire may not be the same thing," noted Forrice.

Cole shrugged. "Perhaps not, but we've got to start somewhere."

"All right," replied the Molarian. "I'll let Jacovic devise the exercises. He's got a command of military maneuvers that even impresses me."

"That's why he was in charge of the Fifth Teroni Fleet. At one time I think he had over ten thousand ships under his command." Cole paused. "We haven't needed him yet, knock wood, but when we finally do, we're going to be damned glad we've got him."

"We fought against each other for years," remarked Forrice. "I'm surprised he doesn't feel any animosity toward us."

"Do you feel any toward him?"

"No," admitted the Molarian. "The way I view it, we were all just soldiers doing our job."

"There's your answer," said Cole.

"Also, the one time we confronted him, he had us dead in his sights, and he behaved like an honorable being," continued Forrice. "There aren't a lot of those in *any* race."

"You never know where an honorable being will crop up," agreed Cole. "Or even a competent one."

"Maybe we can spot one during the exercises this afternoon," offered Forrice.

"I doubt it," said Cole. "If he was honorable, he wouldn't have been working for Machtel, and if he was competent, he'd have deposed Machtel and taken over his operation by now."

The Molarian stared at his old friend for a long moment. "You know," he said at last, "I just hate it when you make sense. So many problems were simpler when they only had me thinking about them."

"I apologize."

"Damned well better," growled Forrice.

"You're a little ray of sunshine today."

"Guess why."

"The Navy will clear out in another day or two, and you can spend a week fucking your brains out on Braccio II."

"Two weeks."

"I don't want you coming back so thin that we have to carry you to your post every day."

"You've been sharing your bed with Sharon for almost two years, and it hasn't cost *you* any weight."

Sharon's image popped into view. "That's because he just lies there and I do all the work."

"You were listening?" asked Cole.

"I'm the Chief of Security. It's my job to be nosy."

"I've changed my mind," said Cole. "Four Eyes, if you want her you can have her."

"If the Navy sticks around another week," replied Forrice with a hoot of alien laughter, "I may take you up on that."

After the Molarian had finished his meal and left, Sharon's image appeared opposite Cole again.

"You know," she said seriously, "I'm hardly shy, and I haven't been virginal in a long time—but I find the crew's constant obsession with brothels disquieting. Not just the men. I know Val frequents that one that supplies male androids. And here's dear old Forrice unable to talk about anything else. Don't you find it all rather . . . I don't know . . . tawdry?"

"You have to put it in perspective," answered Cole. "Look at our situation. We can't go back to the Republic. We can't have families and settle down. We live in a sexual universe, and we have sexual needs. You and I lucked out and found each other, but whorehouses are what most of them have to settle for. When you're an outlaw ship—an outlaw *fleet* now—with prices on your heads, the last thing you want are long-term relationships with any planet-dwellers. So you make your accommodation."

"You know," she said after a moment, "I think I agree with Forrice."

"About what?"

"I just hate it when you make sense. You take away all my distaste for a clearly distasteful situation."

"I was planning on taking you to that elegant new restaurant that just opened up on the sixth level of the station," said Cole. "They're supposed to have mutated bison imported from Pollux IV. I suppose we should each pay our own way to avoid another distasteful situation."

"I can live with that one," she said promptly.

"You're sure?" he asked with a smile.

"Easier than you can live a celibate life for the next six months," she replied. "Your choice."

"Let me see a menu and check the prices and then I'll make a decision."

She laughed, he laughed, and both of them decided they were very fortunate not to have been born Molarian.

It would be a few days yet before they knew *how* lucky.

Cole and Forrice walked past the gaming tables of Duke's Place and sat down at the Platinum Duke's table.

"I got word that you wanted to speak to me," said Cole.

"How soon can you be ready for a major action?" asked the Duke.

"That all depends. Define major action."

"The biggest outlaw on the Inner Frontier is the Octopus . . ." began the Duke.

"Human?" asked Forrice.

"I don't know," admitted the Duke. "I don't think anyone does, except his lieutenants."

"Okay, so he's the biggest outlaw on the Frontier," said Cole. "Go on."

"I'm surprised you haven't heard of him."

"Why should we?" asked Cole. "We're not exactly long-term residents. The *Teddy R* goes out after selected targets, and then it comes right back to Singapore Station."

"I'm sure someone on the ship has heard of him," said the Molarian. "After all, we've added more than four hundred to our various crews. Maybe the original members of the *Teddy R* don't know who he is, but beings who've lived most of their lives on the Inner Frontier probably have."

"I repeat: What about him?" said Cole.

"There's a consortium of some forty-three worlds that would like to put a stop to his activities."

Cole shook his head. "Not good enough. Spell it out."

"They want him killed or imprisoned, and his fleet demolished."

"How come no one's asked us to do this sooner?" asked Forrice. "We've been a mercenary fleet for just short of a Standard year now."

Cole shot him a look that said: *Dumb question.*

"They never thought you were strong enough until now," replied the Duke. "Word has spread that you prefer to assimilate enemy ships and crews rather than destroy them, so they figure every time you score a major victory you're that much bigger and more powerful for the next assignment."

"What's the bottom line?" said Cole.

"They'll pay you the sum of—"

"That's David's bottom line," interrupted Cole. "I want to know what we're up against."

"I don't have exact numbers," answered the Duke. "It's estimated that he's got between three hundred and four hundred ships."

"I don't think much of your notion of fair odds."

"When you hear what they're paying . . ."

"Later," said Cole. "Tell me what kind of armaments they're carrying."

"I haven't the slightest idea."

"How many planets do they control?"

The Duke shrugged. "I told you: forty-three."

Cole shook his head. "That's how many are willing to pay us. How many does he control—planets that are too afraid to join the consortium?"

"I'll find out. Don't you want to hear the price?"

"After you find out what I want to know, then we'll talk price," said Cole. "Although right at the moment, I'm inclined to tell you to forget it. They outnumber us six or eight to one, maybe more. We've got a lot of small class-G and class-H ships. If they've got any Level 4 thumpers or Level 5 burners and commensurate defenses . . ."

"So you'll lose a few ships," said the Duke. "You'll replace them with the ones you assimilate."

"Those ships you shrug off are filled with people who depend upon me to keep them alive, or at least give them a fighting chance to survive."

"You have to expect losses. This is war, Wilson."

"Not if we don't declare it," said Cole. "And war has nothing to do with dying bravely and nobly for your side. Our job is making the other guy die bravely and nobly for *his* side."

"You really don't want to hear the price?"

"Not now."

The Duke shrugged. "Okay, but if I can't make my commission, at least go place some bets at the tables."

"You don't know our Wilson," said Forrice. "He never gambles." A hoot of alien laughter. "That's probably why we're willing to follow him."

Cole noticed Val approaching them from the alien *jabob* table. "She's smiling. I guess she won her money back."

"How can she drink like a fish and stay so beautiful?" asked the Duke.

"A better question is how can she abuse her body the way she does and stay so fit and powerful?" said Forrice.

"She's certainly not like any other woman I've ever met," agreed the Duke.

"She's not like anybody anyone's ever met," said Cole. "Give me fifty like her and I could probably conquer the Republic."

"*If* she felt like it," noted Forrice. "That's always the wild card."

"She always feels like conquering things," replied Cole. "The problem is that she doesn't always feel like obeying orders . . . though I must admit she's getting better at it."

Val reached the table, pulled up a chair, and ordered a bottle of brandy from a robot waiter.

"You're going to share that with everybody, right?" asked the Duke with a smile that said he was gently teasing her.

"With my shipmates," she replied seriously. "You own the stock. You can order your own bottle."

"You know," said the Duke thoughtfully, "I'll bet *she's* heard of him."

"Of who?" asked Val.

"The Octopus."

"Ugly son of a bitch," she said contemptuously.

"You've met him?" asked Cole.

"Not lately. I knew him, oh, about ten, eleven years ago."

"Is he human?"

"Sort of."

"What does that mean?" asked Cole.

"He's either a freak or a mutant," answered Val. "He doesn't wear a shirt, and he's got six misshapen hands sticking out of his sides."

"Can you tell us anything else about him?"

"He's smart," she said. "Almost as smart as me. Physically he's not much."

"With six extra hands?" said the Duke.

"They're not arms, just hands."

"It's still impressive."

"He tried to grab my ass with one of them, so I coldcocked him," replied Val. "He never tried again."

"Doubtless why he's still alive," said Cole wryly.

"Damned right," said Val seriously. "Why all the questions?" Suddenly she turned to the Duke. "You got us a commission to take him out."

"It's still in the negotiating stage," said Cole.

"That means you won't agree until you know what he's got," said Val decisively. "I can't help you. Like I say, it's been ten years."

"There's no rush. Forrice and Jacovic are still working our new ships and crews into shape." He turned to Forrice. "Any potential command personnel there?"

"Too early to tell," replied the Molarian. "I think we should leave our people in place there for the time being."

"Does Jacovic agree?"

The Molarian shrugged. "You'll have to ask him, though I can't imagine he doesn't."

"All right," said Cole. "When we put our people permanently in command of the new ships, take the personnel from Perez's and Jacovic's ships. I'm getting to where I don't know half the crew of the *Teddy R.* I want to keep the ones that I still have."

"That shouldn't prove a problem," said the Molarian. "I'll make the transfers when we go back to the ship." He stood up. "And now, if there are no objections and there'd better not be, I think I'll take my leave of you and go over to the Glowworm, where I plan to try my luck at the *stort* table."

He headed off toward the door in his graceful spinning three-legged gait.

"I don't know what he enjoys about that stupid alien game," remarked Val.

"*Stort?*" repeated Cole. He smiled. "He wins at it."

"Big deal. He ought to try the *jabob* table right here."

"You were lucky, my dear," said the Duke. "It's got a fifteen percent break for the house."

"That's what makes it so challenging," she said. "Most places it's only two percent."

David Copperfield waddled over and sat uncomfortably on a chair that was made for humans.

"Where have you been?" asked Cole.

"I thought someone ought to find out what's going on in the galaxy," replied the little alien.

"The Republic's still at war with the Teroni Federation," said Cole. "You didn't have to go to a subspace radio for that. It's been going on for twenty-odd years."

"Trivial stuff," said Copperfield with a contemptuous sneer. "Spica II won the divisional murderball title. The Deluros VIII stock market is up three percent. And there are now thirteen books, disks, cubes, and holos about the mutiny aboard the *Theodore Roosevelt*."

"Each more inaccurate than the last, no doubt," said Cole with no show of interest. "Did you learn anything useful?"

"Not on the radio," admitted Copperfield, "but a cargo ship that just landed reports that the Navy decimated six more worlds on the Inner Frontier."

"Why would a naval commander obey an order to wipe out six neutral Frontier planets?" said Cole disgustedly.

"Not everyone is a mutineer," said the Duke with a smile.

"Oh, well," said Cole, "if they're done, maybe we can clear Four Eyes to make a quick trip over to Braccio II." He got to his feet. "I'm going back to the ship now. David, I'm sure the second I'm gone the Platinum Duke is going to tell you about all the trillions we can make for no effort at all if we accept the assignment he's working on." He paused. "First, you do not have the authority to negotiate or accept it without my approval, and second, you are not subtle enough to slyly introduce it into the next ten conversations we have as if it just came up spontaneously."

"Steerforth, you cut me to the quick."

"Just remember what I said, or I'll take a butcher knife and go hunting for your quick."

"I'll come with you," said Val, getting up and grabbing her bottle.

"I thought you'd want to spend the night celebrating your win," said Cole.

"I do," she said. "But I want to hide half the money first, just in case my luck turns."

"I can hold it for you."

She considered it for a long moment, then thrust a wad of Republic credits, New Stalin rubles, and Maria Theresa dollars into his hand.

"I wouldn't trust anyone else with it," said Val.

"I appreciate that."

"Where will you be if I need it back in a hurry?"

"If you think you'll need it back to cover some losses, why not just keep it?" said Cole.

She shook her head. "I've got to at least go through the motions."

"If you come by for it later, I could just refuse to give it to you."

"No," said Val seriously. "If I'm liquored up and you won't give me my money, I might kill you."

"You won't."

"I don't *think* I will, but you never know . . ."

"I've never seen you that liquored up," said Cole. "I'll take my chances. You can have the money back when we take off on our next mission, whatever it is."

She stared at him, then nodded and took her bottle back to the Duke's table.

Cole made his way to the *Teddy R*, where he found Rachel Marcos waiting for him.

"What's up?" he asked.

"We just finished the damage report from the Machtel operation," she replied.

"What damages?" demanded Cole. "Not a shot was fired."

"Some space debris damaged the *Longshot* and the *Penny Dreadful* inside one of the wormholes."

"I assume their structural integrity hasn't been compromised, since they made it back to Singapore Station."

"They seem okay," she reported. "But if the abrasions aren't fixed, the ships *could* begin developing problems."

"It is anything Slick can't handle?" asked Cole.

Slick was the *Teddy R*'s only Tolobite, an alien who along with his symbiote, which acted as a second skin, was able to work long hours in the airless cold of space.

"He's seen the holographs of the damage and thinks he can fix it, sir," said Rachel.

"Okay," said Cole. "Run the reports and holos by Mr. Odom"— Mustapha Odom, the *Teddy R*'s engineer—"and if he agrees, tell Slick to go to work on them."

He went to Sharon's office, waited until she was through with her work, and took her to dinner on Singapore Station, where he ran into Forrice.

"How did you fare?" he asked.

"I broke even," replied the Molarian. "Tricky game, *stort*. Just when you think you've got it figured, you find out that it's more complex than you imagined. Must have been invented by a Canphorite." Suddenly he smiled. "But I heard some good news: The Navy has stopped killing everyone and is going home."

"Until the next time," said Sharon.

"Until the next time," agreed Forrice. "If you have no objections, I'll take one of the shuttles and head off to Braccio II in a few hours."

"I suppose it's okay," said Cole. "But there's no reason why you should be the only happy Molarian on board next week. Take Braxite and Jacillios with you."

"I'll take Jacillios," replied Forrice. "But Braxite messed up one of his legs somehow when we were running the new ships through their paces. He's in sick bay with some pressure bandages on it."

"So give him some crutches and take him along anyway."

Forrice shook his massive head. "Men can get along fine with one leg and a crutch or a prosthetic, but Molarians have to have the use of all three. Believe me, he'll be in so much discomfort that he won't be able to partake of what's awaiting us on Braccio II."

"Well, you're the guy who'd know," said Cole.

"I'm off to get my gear together and alert Jacillios to the fact that we're leaving shortly. I'll see you when I get back."

"Have a good time," said Cole. "And be careful."

"I won't do anything you wouldn't do with our esteemed Security Chief," answered the Molarian, "but I'll do it with far more finesse and élan."

"I'm sure you will," said Cole. "But I meant, be careful in case there's still a Navy ship or two lurking in the area."

"If I run into one, I'll give it your exact location in exchange for an extra day on Braccio II," said Forrice with a hoot of laughter.

"Don't say it," remarked Cole as Forrice swirled off to the *Teddy R*.

"Don't say what?" asked Sharon.

"Tawdry."

"I wasn't going to."

"Good."

"Sad," said Sharon.

"Why?"

"We don't have any Molarian females aboard the *Teddy R*," she replied. "How would you like to face the knowledge that you were on a ship with no women, and you could never go back to your home world?"

"I'd probably develop a crush on Vladimir Sokolov or Bull Pampas," answered Cole.

"Say that once more and you can spend the night with them," said Sharon.

Cole decided not to say it once more.

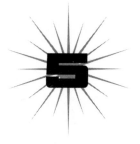

The next two days were uneventful. Jacovic supervised the training of the new members of their makeshift team, and the rest of the crew spent their time enjoying the various attractions of Singapore Station. For the bulk of them it meant drinking, gambling, and eating real food (as opposed to soya products). Most of them avoided the plethora of drug dens, because Cole had made it clear from the day he'd arrived as the *Teddy R*'s Second Officer that he disapproved of them and the people who used them.

There were other attractions as well. Sharon found a pair of art galleries. Christine spent long hours discussing computers with a dealer in black-market machines. Rachel Marcos and Luthor Chadwick stopped by a small theater, watched a revival of a millennia-old Shakespeare play, decided they enjoyed it, and saw four more plays in the next thirty-six hours. No one knew quite what Val did when she wasn't in Duke's Place, but she usually returned with a satisfied smile, as well as an occasional split lip or bruised knuckles.

As for Cole, he spent his time wandering through the alien levels of the station with no set purpose in mind except to satisfy his curiosity. It was on one such excursion that he was walking down a broad corridor, idly glancing into store windows, when a Lodinite brushed against him.

Cole didn't think much about it at the time, but later, as he was ascending to the human levels, it occurred to him that he and the Lodinite had been the only two beings in the corridor, and that the Lodinite could have—*should* have—missed him by a good twelve to fifteen feet. On a hunch, he began rummaging through his pockets, and sure enough he came to a folded piece of paper.

He opened it, saw that it was in a language he couldn't read, assumed it was Lodinite, and instantly contacted Sharon, who was in one of her art galleries.

"What's up?" she asked as her image suddenly appeared in front of him.

He held up the note. "Recognize the language?"

She shook her head. "No. Why?"

"Someone wants me to read it. A Lodinite passed it off to me, but he could just have been a messenger."

"Christine's busy watching Oedipus get his eyes plucked out," said Sharon, "but Malcolm Briggs is on watch back on the ship for another two or three hours. He's almost as good with a computer as she is. You might have him take a shot at it."

"Okay, thanks," said Cole, ending the connection. He decided not to transmit the note's image again until he knew what it said, just in case there were any electronic peepers around, so he summoned a robo-cart and instructed it to take him out to the *Teddy R*, which was moored half a mile out on Docking Arm 7. Even if Sharon was mistaken and Briggs wasn't on duty, he wanted the note translated on the ship, where the *Teddy R*'s security systems would prevent anyone not on the bridge from reading it.

As it happened, Briggs *was* on duty.

"How long should this take?" asked Cole, explaining what he wanted and handing the young officer the paper.

"The difficult part is identifying the language," answered Briggs. "Once we do that, it should take about half a second."

"Try Lodinite."

Briggs had the computer scan the message, then uttered a command.

"No, sir," he said a moment later. "Definitely not Lodinite."

"There can't be a lot of races using this particular scrawl," noted Cole.

"You never know," replied Briggs. "More than eighty races use the character we use for 'o,' and another fifty use some form of 't' and 'i.'" He uttered another command that sounded as alien to Cole as Molarian or Lodinite. The computer began humming to itself, then replied to Briggs in the same mathematical language.

"Got it, sir," said Briggs. He frowned. "It's in Pnathian."

"Pnathian?" repeated Cole. "What the hell is that?"

Briggs shrugged. "I've never heard of it."

"Ask the computer."

Briggs did so. "Pnath is a thinly populated planet at the far reaches of the Republic, as you near the Outer Frontier. Population estimated at four million. They pay their taxes, refuse to serve in the military for religious or ethical reasons, were late to develop interstellar travel, possessed a barter economy prior to joining the Republic . . ."

"Enough," said Cole. "What does the note say?"

Briggs had the computer print a hard copy and handed it to Cole.

The Octopus extends his greeting and felicitations to Captain Wilson Cole of the Theodore Roosevelt, *and requests a private meeting with him that may prove to be to our mutual advantage. Conditions being what they are, I recommend neutral ground, and that each of us be accompanied by only one subordinate. If this is acceptable to you, bet five Maria Theresa dollars on the Level Three Blue Empress in the* porchii *game at Duke's Place before 2200 hours, Station time. This will signal your acquiescence, and before 2400 hours a time and place will be proposed. You will signal your acceptance by making the very same bet.*

"No signature," noted Briggs when Cole showed him the note.

"He already told me who it's from," answered Cole.

"Are you going to take him up on it, sir?"

"I'll have to think about it, but yeah, probably I am. If he's got Singapore Station covered that thoroughly, I think it's worth a pair of five-dollar bets to learn what he's got in mind."

"It could be a trap," said Briggs.

"It could be," agreed Cole. "But I doubt it. After all, if he wanted me dead, the Lodinite could have backshot me this afternoon just as easily as it passed me the note."

"I'd like to be the one to accompany you, sir," said Briggs.

"I appreciate the offer, Malcolm," said Cole. "But in case it *is* a trap, I'm taking the Valkyrie."

Briggs tried unsuccessfully to hide his disappointment.

"Try not to look like I just shot your pet or your best friend," continued Cole. "You're very good at what you do, and in all immodesty, I'm pretty good at what I do. But I've never met anyone as good at what *she* does as Val. When I need my back protected—or my front, for that matter—she's the one I want protecting it."

"I know, sir."

"In fact, while I'm thinking of it, let's see if we can track her down." He checked his timepiece. "It's about 1900 hours Station time right now, so it wouldn't hurt to alert her."

Briggs spent the next ten minutes trying to locate or contact Val, but without any success.

"Her communicator must be broken," he said at last.

"The hell it is," said Cole.

"Sir?" said Briggs, puzzled.

"It's okay," said Cole. "I know where she'll be." He began walking to the airlift, then stopped and turned to the young lieutenant. "That note remains secret until I say otherwise."

"Security will be able to find out, sir. They have access to every-thing I do up here."

"Sharon and Chadwick are both off the ship. The likelihood is that they'll stay off past 2200 hours, and even if they don't, there's no reason why they should retroactively monitor every command you gave the computer. If they find it, they find it. Just don't volunteer any-thing."

"May I ask why, sir?"

"I don't want a bunch of earnest but uninvited bodyguards scaring the Octopus away."

Cole went back to the airlift, took it down to the shuttle bay, and emerged onto the enclosed docking arm, where he summoned a robo-cart and was soon in the interior of Singapore Station.

He walked past Duke's Place, past his favorite restaurants, and eventually came to a halt in front of a nondescript building that had a single small glowing sign above the door: GOMORRAH. He paused for a moment, then entered it.

A shining metal robot stood behind a small counter in a foyer that was far more opulent than the building's exterior hinted at. "Greet-ings, good sir," it said in silky tones. "Welcome to GOMORRAH, the most unique brothel on the Inner Frontier."

"All of your employees are androids, right?" said Cole.

"We prefer to think of them as perfect specimens of humanity, indistinguishable from yourself except in the area of performance, where they exceed all expectations and comparisons."

"Okay, this is the place, then," said Cole. "I need to speak to one of your clients."

"I'm afraid that is forbidden, sir," said the robot. "Our guarantee is that no patron will be disturbed during the length of his or her stay here."

"Before we get into an argument, at least tell me if she's here," said Cole. "Her name is Val, though she's got about fifty others she uses on occasion. Big woman, close to seven feet tall, redheaded, damned good-looking though I imagine that would be lost on you."

"I cannot release that information, sir," said the robot.

An instant later the robot was staring down the muzzle of Cole's burner. "I suggest you make an exception."

"This is pointless, sir," said the robot. "I have no sense of self-preservation, so threats are useless."

"Do you have a bouncer here?"

"A bouncer, sir?"

"Someone to keep the customers in line if they start acting in"— he searched for a term the robot would understand—"antisocial ways?"

"Each of our robots is more than capable of subduing any living human, though of course such force is almost never required."

"So you're the only nonprostitute on the premises?" said Cole.

"Other than the patrons, yes, sir."

"And clearly it is your duty to preserve their privacy and their dignity."

"That is correct, sir."

"Then I think we may reach a meeting of the minds after all," said Cole, his burner still trained on the robot's head. "Pay attention, now. If you don't tell me what I want to know, I fully intend to melt what passes for your head until it is nothing but a metallic puddle."

"I told you before, sir," said the robot. "I have no sense of self-preservation."

"I know," said Cole. "But you've also told me that you have a sense of duty. If you don't tell me whether Val is here and, if so, what room she's in, I will melt your head down to a molten lump, do the same to any other android who stands in my way, and I will then break down every door in the house looking for Val, and I will have absolutely no respect for your patrons' privacy. Is that quite clear?"

"That is unacceptable," said the robot.

"Then I suggest that it is time for you to make a value judgment. Is it better to answer my question or to end your existence while not protecting the privacy of most of your patrons and the property of your owners?"

The robot stood absolutely still for almost ten seconds. "The patron known as Val is in Room 16."

"Can you summon her?"

"No, sir. You must contact her yourself."

"I have a feeling she doesn't like to be hampered by clothing *or* equipment," said Cole. "Can you summon the robot she's with?"

"The *android*," the robot corrected him. "She is with two of them. I can contact them, but I cannot summon them."

"Can you patch my voice through one of them?"

"Your message, yes. Your voice, no."

"All right," said Cole. "Here's my message: Val, this is Cole. You've got an hour to wear out your partners and finish up your fun. Then I want you to report to me over at Duke's Place. We've got a job to do, and it can't wait."

The robot was motionless again for a few seconds. "The message has been transmitted."

"Fine," said Cole. "May I make a suggestion?"

"What is it, sir?"

"She's going to be in a foul mood when she comes out of that room. If I were you, I'd develop a sense of self-preservation in the next hour and be somewhere else when she emerges."

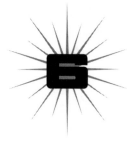

Duke's Place was crowded, as usual.

Cole sat at the table the Platinum Duke had reserved for him and his crew. He was joined by David Copperfield, Sharon Blacksmith, and the Duke himself. They spoke about the art galleries, the theater, and the murderball results from the Quinellus Cluster, and finally Sharon could stand it no longer.

"Damn it, Wilson!" she said at last. "You've been indulging in small talk for forty-five minutes, which is half an hour longer than you've done it in all the time I've known you. What the hell's going on?"

"Nothing," said Cole. "I'm just relaxing."

"And glancing at the door every ten seconds," she continued. "Who do you think is going to walk through it?"

"You never know," said Cole.

"You know what I think?" said Sharon.

"I have no idea what you think."

"I think you're chatting away about all these things you couldn't care less about so you don't inadvertently talk about what really interests you!"

"You want to talk about sex and food, I'll talk about sex and food," he said.

"Bah!" Sharon got to her feet. "I'm going to get a breath of air. You'll tell us when you're ready to."

"The air's the same out there as in here," said the Duke.

"True," said Sharon. "But out in the corridors I don't have to listen to his bullshit."

She turned and began walking away.

"If you run after her, I believe you could catch her before she leaves the casino," offered Copperfield.

"She's a free agent," said Cole.

"Ah!" said Copperfield, his alien face alight with excitement. "You're having a lover's quarrel!"

"I'm not quarreling with anyone."

Val entered the casino just at that moment.

"Excuse me, gentlemen," said Cole. "I have to speak to my Third Officer. I'll be right back."

"Have her come over to the table and speak to her right here," suggested Copperfield.

"She's got a crush on you, David," said Cole. "I wouldn't want her making a fool of herself in front of all these people."

"She has?" asked the little alien, his face lighting up. "Really?"

"Would I kid you?" said Cole, getting up and walking across the room to intercept Val before she could reach the table.

"What is it?" she said ominously. "And it better be good. I'd paid for four hours, and they wouldn't give me a refund. You owe me five hundred Far London pounds."

"I'll pay you when we're back at the ship," said Cole. "But I'm going to need your help first."

"Doing what?" she demanded.

"Keep your voice down and listen," said Cole, and something in his tone made her instantly alert. "In about an hour and a half, I'm going to bet five dollars over at the *porchii* table."

"That's an alien game," she said. "No human can keep all those rules straight." Then: "It's a signal."

He nodded his head. "It's a signal."

"To whom?"

"An old friend of yours," said Cole. "The Octopus."

"What does he want?"

"A meeting. We each bring one protector. You're mine."

"Damned right I'm yours," said Val. "I'm worth five of Bull Pampas and ten of anyone else you've got on board."

"And modest, too."

"Modesty's for those who have something to be modest about."

"Anyway, the man's fleet has us outnumbered five or six to one, and he's infiltrated Singapore Station to the point that he could single me out and pass word to me about the meet without anyone else seeing or knowing about it. He'll have someone we don't know at the table, ready to spot whether or not I make the bet." Cole paused. "Based on all that, I think he sounds like a good man to know."

"*I* know him," replied Val. "'Good' isn't exactly the word I'd use for him. He's the biggest warlord on the Inner Frontier."

"And I'm the most wanted criminal in the Republic," Cole reminded her.

"He probably heard about the offer the Duke got, and figures he might as well kill you now and maybe he won't have to waste any ships going up against us. Or maybe he just plans to turn you in for the reward. It's got to be one or the other."

"That's why you're coming with me," said Cole.

"I hope he tries," she said grimly.

"I trust you don't mind it if I hope he doesn't?"

"All right," said Val. "Have we got anything else to talk about right now?"

"No."

"When do you place the bet?"

"At 2200 hours."

"Ship's time or station time?"

"Station."

"I'll see you at the *porchii* game then," she said. "In the meantime, I'm going to try my luck at the *jabob* table. If I have a run of bad luck, I assume you'll honor my marker for up to five hundred pounds?"

He nodded. "I said I owed it to you."

"Good," she said, flashing him a smile. "You get to live long enough to place your bet."

She was on her way to the gaming tables before he could answer.

"Get your business taken care of?" asked the Duke when he returned to the table.

"Yeah."

"Good. I've bought a controlling interest in a discreet little restaurant at the far end of the station, just above the transport level. Why don't the three of us go over there and see if I've made a wise investment?"

"Later," said Cole.

"It's got mutated beef from Greenveldt," said the Duke enticingly.

"I'm not hungry now. I'll catch up with you later."

"Your loss," said the Duke, getting to his feet. "David?"

"I'll wait until my old school chum is ready," answered Copperfield. "He shouldn't have to eat alone."

"But it's all right if I do?" said the Duke, amused.

"You're a capitalist swine," explained Copperfield. "We're merely consumers."

The Duke laughed. "How can I argue with that? I'll see you later."

"You should have gone with him," said Cole.

"I wanted to stay and see how they contact you."

"What are you talking about?"

"Come on, Steerforth," said Copperfield. "I was the biggest fence on the Inner Frontier. Covert contact is my forte. You sit here, you have nothing to say, you practically chase Sharon away, you speak to the Valkyrie where no one can overhear you, you turn down a free meal at the Duke's new restaurant. What else could it be? You're waiting here to be contacted, and Val has something to do with it. Probably she's your protection."

Cole stared at the little alien for a long moment. "You didn't get *that* out of Charles Dickens. You're *good*, David."

"Why, thank you, Steerforth," said Copperfield. "Who are you meeting?"

"I'll tell you later."

"Let me know if he really has eight hands."

"Why should you think it's the Octopus?"

"You can't be bought off, and right now he's got the only fleet powerful enough to scare you off," answered Copperfield.

"Oh, I don't know," said Cole. "I scare pretty easy."

Copperfield emitted a strange sound, his equivalent of a snort of disbelief. "So am I right or wrong?"

"Yes."

"Yes what?"

"Yes, you're right or wrong," answered Cole. "And now the subject is closed."

"But—"

"You heard me."

"Yes, Steerforth."

Cole sipped a drink and watched the customers, wondering if the Octopus's representative had arrived yet and which one he might be. Finally, with about five minutes remaining until 2200 hours, he wandered over to the *porchii* table. Val arrived a minute later, standing at the far side of it, not even acknowledging his presence.

Finally, when the moment came, Cole announced that he was betting five Maria Theresa dollars on the Level Three Blue Empress. The Mollutei in charge of the table took his money, spun wheels, rolled dice, turned up cards, and did four or five other things to prepare for the move. When he finished there were cheers and curses, some bets were paid off, others kept, pieces were moved higher and lower, forward and back, left and right—but Cole wasn't watching the pieces or the table. He was looking to see if anyone, human or alien, turned and left the moment he made his bet. As far as he could tell, no one did.

A moment later he began walking back toward the Duke's table, and Val joined him.

"Spot anything?" he asked softly.

"Whoever it was is still there," she said.

"No sense continuing to watch it," said Cole. "If he didn't leave the minute I placed the bet, there's no way to tell who he is. He could be the first one to leave the table now, or the tenth."

"That's why I'm here," said Val. "Let's dip into the Platinum Duke's drinkin' stuff while you're waiting for them to contact you."

"Sounds good to me," agreed Cole.

They reached the table, and found that Sharon had returned and that she and David Copperfield were waiting for them.

"Are we on speaking terms?" asked Cole as he sat down.

"Oh, shut up!" snapped Sharon.

Val chuckled.

"What's so funny?" asked Copperfield.

"She's on speaking terms with Cole, but he's not on speaking terms with her," said Val. "Good for you, Sharon! I find that proper and fitting."

Sharon stared at Cole for a moment, then shrugged. "Screw it," she said at last. "I'd rather talk to you than look at you."

"Lord knows most men are easier on the eyes," agreed Val.

"Shall we seal our renewed romance with some Cygnian cognac?" asked Cole.

"Why not?"

Cole summoned the robot waiter, ordered a bottle, and sent him off to the private room where the Duke kept his finest stock.

"I saw you at the *porchii* table," noted Sharon. "I didn't know you knew how to play."

"Evidently I don't," said Cole. "I lost five dollars."

"That's a big bet for him," put in Val.

"Maybe you should try that game Forrice has fallen in love with," suggested Sharon.

"You mean *stort?*" asked Cole.

"I think that's the name of it."

"Four Eyes is a fool," said Cole. "The damned game has a fifteen percent break for the house."

"Then why does he play it?"

"Because until one of the frail flowers at his favorite house of good repute comes into bloom, he's got nothing else to do with his time," answered Cole.

The robot returned, set the tray down on the next table, opened the bottle, and filled each of four glasses halfway, then passed them out.

Cole and Sharon sipped theirs, Val downed hers with a single swallow, and David Copperfield simply stared at his.

"Don't worry, David," said Val. "When you're all through pretending you like it, I'll drink it for you."

"Thank you," he said gratefully.

Cole took another sip, then frowned.

"What is it?" asked Sharon.

"Val, give me your glass," said Cole.

The Valkyrie passed him her empty glass, and he poured his cognac into it.

"He's good," said Cole, impressed. "I'll give him that. He even got to the robot to make sure I got the right one."

"What are you talking about?" asked Sharon.

Cole stared into the bottom of his glass, and read the message:

"Alpha Benedetti, third planet, smallest moon, 1600 hours tomorrow. You know the conditions."

Below it was a drawing of a stick figure with eight arms.

"So where do we set down?" asked Val, studying the cold, dead moon on the *Kermit*'s viewscreen.

"They invited us, they'll let us know," replied Cole. "There's got to be a structure somewhere. There's no atmosphere, and I figure the temperature is a couple of hundred degrees below zero Fahrenheit."

"We're sitting ducks out here, orbiting the moon," said Val. "We should have taken the *Teddy R* to back us up."

"They'd have spotted it from a light-year away, and they'd have cleared out before we got here," replied Cole.

"You don't know what kind of reception he's prepared for you," said Val.

"I know if he wanted me dead, he could have killed me back at Singapore Station," answered Cole.

"Then why am I here?"

Cole smiled. "He could always change his mind."

A strong voice came to them over their radio: "Captain Cole, I am delighted that you accepted my invitation. Home in on this signal and you'll figure out where to land."

The voice stopped, but the transmitter remained active. Cole instructed the *Kermit* to lock on to the signal, and a moment later the shuttle readjusted its orbit, heading toward the little moon's geographic south pole. The signal got stronger, and the ship closed in on it.

"There it is," said Cole, as a small building and hangar came into view.

He manipulated the shuttle down to where it was skimming just a few feet above the moon's surface, slowed it down to a snail's pace as it approached the hangar, and gently maneuvered the *Kermit* into it.

"The hangar's attached to the building," said Cole. "So let's give them a couple of minutes to make it airtight and fill it with oxygen."

Val made no reply, but began checking her weapons: a burner, a screecher, a pulse gun, and a knife in each boot.

"Remember," said Cole, "you're here to discourage the Octopus's muscle, not to hurt anyone unless I give the order."

"Or die," she added.

"I know you are not enamored of the Octopus, but try not to be so optimistic," he said wryly.

She glared at him and made no reply.

He waited three minutes, checked the hangar's readings, and finally opened the *Kermit*'s hatch. "It'll be a little chilly until we get into the main building," he announced, "but you won't die for lack of air."

He stepped out into the hangar, followed by the tall, statuesque redhead.

"No greeting party," noted Val.

"Why should *they* freeze their asses off?" said Cole. "They know we're coming inside."

He walked to the only door and waited until it transmitted his image to some interior command post. Suddenly the door irised to let him and Val pass through, then snapped shut after them.

They found themselves in a large room, paneled with some alien hardwood, illuminated by unseen light sources, with a plush carpet that rippled gently beneath their feet. There were a few chairs, a sofa, and a kitchenette at the far end.

Two men were facing them. There was no question as to which was the Octopus. He stood almost as tall as Val, with a bald head, dark piercing eyes, and a waxed mustache that seemed to have four spokes pointing off in each direction. He had broad shoulders, and six hands, some quite misshapen, jutted out of his torso, three on each side. He wore no shirt, and Cole doubted that his skintight pants concealed any weapons. The other man was short, burly, heavily muscled, and even more heavily armed.

"Captain Cole!" said the Octopus, walking over and extending his hand—one of the two that were attached to arms. "How good of you to accept my invitation." He turned to Val. "And the delectable Salome—or did you finally change it to Cleopatra as you planned to?"

"That was eighteen names ago, or maybe nineteen. I'm Val now."

"For Valentine?"

"No," said Val. "Talk to *him*. I'm just here to make sure all you do is talk."

She walked across the room and stopped in front of the small muscular man. It was obvious that she didn't intend to move unless he did.

"Too bad," said the Octopus, looking at her. "I had hoped the years might have mellowed her." He turned back to Cole. "Can I fix you something to drink?"

"Perhaps later," replied Cole. "First I'd like to know why you've summoned me here."

"I should have thought the answer would be obvious," said the Octopus. "Just as you are the most wanted man in the Republic, I am the most wanted man on the Inner Frontier. Surely you don't believe two such men could meet in any public place?"

"I was wondering why we should meet at all," said Cole.

"Great men like to converse with other great men," said the Octopus.

"To say nothing of great egotists," replied Cole.

The Octopus threw back his head and laughed. "I *knew* I was going to like you, Wilson Cole!"

"I'd say the feeling was mutual," said Cole, "but you haven't given me any reason to like you yet."

"That's why you're here," said the Octopus. "You and I are going to become friends. Are you sure I can't give you something to drink?"

Cole shook his head. "Later, perhaps."

"Or eat?"

"Why don't you just tell me why I'm here?"

"You're here because you have a healthy curiosity, and because you know that having a price on your head has more to do with circumstance than character."

"Brief and to the point isn't exactly your style, is it?" said Cole.

"I'm infatuated with the sound of my own voice," admitted the Octopus. "It's one of my multitude of sins."

"I would never have guessed," said Cole as the Octopus laughed again. "If it's all the same to you, I think I'll listen to the rest of this sitting down."

"That's what chairs are for," said the Octopus. "Well, unless you're our redheaded friend over there, in which case they're for breaking over people's heads."

Cole sat down. "It's been a long day. Nudge me when you get to something interesting."

The Octopus pulled a chair up, sat down next to Cole, and tapped him gently on the shoulder.

"What was that for?" asked Cole.

"I'm nudging you."

"Okay, I'm listening."

"The Inner Frontier," said the Octopus.

"What's so interesting about it?" asked Cole.

The Octopus smiled. "The fact that you and I could own it." He leaned forward. "I am not without my sources. I know that you have gone out on several missions at the behest of the Platinum Duke and the alien that calls itself David Copperfield. Your fleet is now the second largest on the Inner Frontier, behind only my own. If the Platinum Duke and the alien have not yet received an offer for you to try to meet me in combat, it is only a matter of days or weeks before they bring such an offer to you."

"It's conceivable," said Cole noncommittally.

"I think if I were to attack your fleet today, I have the firepower to defeat you," continued the Octopus, watching him closely.

"Probably."

"But I won't," said the Octopus. "Consider that."

"I assume you have a reason?" said Cole.

"Of course I do! Why should the two greatest outlaws in the galaxy go to war with each other?" said the Octopus. "Why not combine forces? Between us, we could literally rule the Inner Frontier and plunder it six ways from Sunday."

"What's Sunday?"

"An antiquated word from an antiquated calendar," explained the Octopus with an impatient shrug. He stared intently at Cole. "Your expression doesn't give much away."

"It's not supposed to."

"But you're considering it, aren't you?" persisted the Octopus.

"Not really."

"But you *should*," urged the Octopus. "Our united forces would be powerful enough to discourage any usurpers. I am a formidable enemy, but the same traits would make me a wonderful partner. I know I have a reputation as a cold-blooded killer, but I have never killed anyone who didn't deserve it, or anyone who was willing to walk away rather than fight. I have never assimilated a planet into my little empire if the populace was willing to fight to retain their independence. I know that

most people view me as a villain, but in truth I am simply an entre-
preneur. I have no desire to interfere with the daily lives of the worlds
that I control. I offer them protection, they pay me a tribute in
exchange for the comforting knowledge that they can function in
absolute safety, and everyone's happy."

"Except the planetary governments," suggested Cole.

"That's where you're wrong," said the Octopus. "As long as they
pay us, we don't interfere with them, and they still get to pretend
they're important leaders of men."

"And if they don't pay you?"

"Why speak of such depressing things?" asked the Octopus. "If
they don't pay me, their successors do."

"It sounds efficient."

"It is," the Octopus assured him. "And if you will join me, we can
gradually expand our sphere of influence to the entire Frontier. I've
studied you, Wilson Cole. I know that you prefer assimilation to anni-
hilation. Now you can do it on a massive scale. Within ten years we
could control perhaps a thousand worlds."

"So you'll get tributes from a thousand worlds instead of a hundred," said Cole. "What will you spend it on?"

"Why, whatever I want," said the Octopus, puzzled.

Cole shook his head. "I assume you can't enter the Republic and
spend it there."

"Alas, no," replied the Octopus. Suddenly he smiled. "You may be
the most notorious criminal in the Republic, but you are not the only
one. I was born a freak, even in a galaxy where mutation is not
uncommon. You might say that my life has been an unending exercise
in overcompensating for my feelings of inferiority. I developed my
body, I actually have two college degrees, I am not without a certain
measure of skill in the bedroom—and despite all that, I was still

shunned like a freak. So, after appropriating what I considered to be start-up costs from a number of banks, I left the Republic in rather a hurry and came out here where a man is judged by his abilities. My crimes against the Republic may not equal your own, but they are mine and I take an enormous pride in them."

"You still haven't answered my question," said Cole. "If you can't spend your ill-gotten gains in the Republic, can you enjoy them in the Teroni Federation?"

"Not if we're still at war with them."

"We are," said Cole. "So where will you spend your money?"

"The answer is obvious," replied the Octopus. "I'll spend it on the Inner Frontier."

"But if you're the warlord of the whole Inner Frontier, why buy what you can just take?"

The Octopus stared at Cole for a long minute, then laughed again. "I *like* you, Wilson Cole!" The laughter suddenly ceased. "Where do you spend *your* money?"

"We've only been out here for three years," said Cole. "So far most of it has gone into fuel and repairs to the ship, and wages to a crew that can never go home again."

"I thought that just you alone were on the Republic's wish list."

Cole shook his head. "My crew broke me out of the brig while I was awaiting my court-martial. They may not have my notoriety, but every last one of them is wanted by the Navy."

"You don't strike me as a power-hungry man," said the Octopus. "Certainly not as power-hungry as I am. Why in the world did you depose your ship's captain in a war zone?"

"She was about to take an action that would have cost about five million Republic citizens their lives."

"Ah! A genuine hero!"

"The Navy views it differently," replied Cole.

"Besides," said Val from across the room, "if he was a hero, do you think I'd be serving with him? He's a mutineer and an outlaw."

"A telling point," agreed the Octopus.

"She's turning into a fine officer," said Cole. "Her only problem is that she can't hold her admiration for my virtues in check."

The Octopus stared at him. "I've heard that you turn down as many assignments as you accept."

"More."

"Why?" asked the Octopus. "I've got the only fleet you have to worry about."

"For our first half-year as mercenaries, I had a fleet of one," answered Cole.

"So you did," said the Octopus. "I seem to remember hearing that you couldn't cut it as pirates, so you went into the soldier-for-hire business."

"I don't think I'd have worded it quite that way," said Cole ironically. "But, in essence . . ."

"So why have you turned down any assignments at all since you started putting together a fleet?" persisted the Octopus.

"We'll help anyone with a legitimate grievance," said Cole. Suddenly he smiled. "What we won't do is help someone who wants to become another Octopus."

"I think if I were you I'd reevaluate my priorities," said the Octopus. "An ethical mercenary doesn't figure to last much longer out here than an ethical pirate."

"I'll take it under advisement."

The Octopus stared at him for a long minute. "Captain Cole, it has been a pleasure to finally meet you. This interview is over." He reached out and shook Cole's hand again. "I hope we never meet in battle, but I cannot work with a moral man."

"We have nothing further to discuss?" said Cole.

"That's right."

"Good. Then I'll have that drink."

They got to their feet and walked to the kitchenette, which doubled as a bar.

"Should I pour one for Cleopatra, too?"

"Might as well," said Cole. "If you don't, she'll just take the bottle from you."

"Damned right!" Val chimed in.

"It's a pity," said the Octopus, pouring three Antarean brandies. "We could have been great friends."

"You show me why you're better for the worlds you control than the men who want to pay me to drive you away, and we can still be friends," said Cole.

"So you *have* had an offer?"

"Almost. I decided not to listen to it until we were closer to equal strength."

Val took her glass. "Anything for *him?*" she asked, jerking a thumb in her opposite number's direction.

"He doesn't drink," said the Octopus.

"Does he talk?"

"He used to. Then one day he was arrested and talked to the wrong people. When he got out his friends made sure it never happened again and he emigrated out to the Frontier." The Octopus shrugged. "That was a long time ago, and of course we all have to learn to live with the consequences of our actions."

"Even you?" she asked.

"Even me," the Octopus assured her. "Though in my case, I expect to be able to put those consequences off for another half century, and with any luck at all I'll be dead by then."

"Another optimist," muttered Cole.

They finished their drinks, Val had a refill, and then it was time to leave.

"It's been interesting," said Cole.

"That it has," agreed the Octopus. "You have many qualities, Captain Cole. I think under other circumstances we could have been wonderful allies."

"If we actually merged our fleets," replied Cole, "there's no one left out here to be allies *against*."

Which just proved that Wilson Cole was as fallible as anyone else.

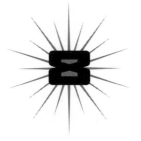

David Copperfield scurried into the mess hall, where Cole was nursing a beer.

"Any word from Forrice yet?" asked the little alien.

"David, it's only been four days. I gave him and Jacillios a week. Now go away and let me drink my beer in peace."

"But we may be going into combat soon," said Copperfield, "and we need our First Officer." He learned forward intently. "I've got the details."

"Take some antacid," said Cole. "Maybe they'll go away."

"This is very unbecoming of you, Steerforth," said Copperfield. "You were never this flippant when we were schoolmates."

Cole sighed deeply. "David, we were never schoolmates. I grew up on Pollux IV and Lord knows where the hell you grew up."

"We *were* schoolmates!" insisted Copperfield. "You must never lose touch with history!"

"I think you're losing touch with reality," said Cole wryly. "Okay, David, what details do you feel compelled to share with me?"

"Whatever the Octopus told you about his fleet, he exaggerated."

"We never spoke about his fleet."

"Of course you did," insisted Copperfield. "He was trying to scare you off, of course. He could have no other reason to meet with you. But the Platinum Duke has found out much more about him. I think we should take the commission."

"David, you never saw a commission you didn't want to take," said Cole wearily.

"Do you want to hear what we learned or not?" demanded Copperfield.

"If I listen politely, will you go away when you're done?"

"I don't understand this attitude, Steerforth," said the little alien. "But to get to the point, it is true that the Octopus has three hundred and sixty-two ships. However, at least three hundred of them are two-man and three-man jobs."

"That's still a lot of ships," said Cole.

"None of the small ships have anything stronger than a Level 1 pulse cannon or a Level 2 laser cannon."

"That leaves sixty-two ships, David. What have *they* got?"

Copperfield swallowed hard. "Nothing we haven't seen before."

"I'll just bet." Cole studied the dapper little alien for a moment. "Come on, David. Out with it."

"Seven of the ships have Level 4 pulse cannons, and it's possible— but not certain, not certain at all—that the Octopus's ship has a Level 5 laser cannon."

"And just where do you think we've seen that weaponry before, David?" said Cole.

"The *Pegasus* had a Level 5 laser cannon."

"The *Pegasus* was Val's original ship, the cannon was never installed, and the ship's in a junkyard," said Cole. "What about the Level 4 thumpers? Where do you think we've seen them?"

"Aboard the *Teddy R*," said Copperfield with a sickly smile.

"How many have you seen here?"

"Two."

"And how many does the Octopus have?" persisted Cole.

"I don't have the exact number."

"*That* many?"

"Why are you embarrassing me, Steerforth?" demanded the little alien.

"Would you rather be embarrassed or outnumbered, outgunned, and destroyed?" asked Cole.

"But—"

"Go back to the Platinum Duke and tell him we'll pass on this one."

"But they're paying—"

"I don't give a damn what they're paying," interrupted Cole. "You have to survive to be able to spend it."

"I can't believe we're going to turn tail and run!" said Copperfield.

"We don't have a tail and we're not running," answered Cole. "We're just not accepting the assignment. Besides," he added, "I've got a sneaking fondness for the Octopus."

"How can you like someone like that?"

"I like you, and you've probably broken at least as many laws as he has."

"Nevertheless, I am sorely disappointed in you, Steerforth."

"I'm desolate," said Cole. "Perhaps you should leave me to drink my beer in miserable isolation."

"Bah! You're impossible when you're like this!" said the little alien, heading off to an airlift. "I'm off to report to the Duke, and drown my disappointment in an Antarean brandy."

Cole resisted the urge to point out that his system couldn't metabolize alcohol. He knew Copperfield wouldn't drink it, but merely order it for show—though after two years he still had no idea who the alien thought he was posturing for.

"Did you hear all that?" said Cole when he was alone in the mess hall.

"Of course," said Sharon as her image popped into view. "Your old school chum can't understand why you won't face Billy the Kid and Doc Holliday armed only with a flyswatter."

"I have no intention of facing him, period. He outnumbers us seven to one, and more to the point, he's probably no worse than the

governments that were running his little empire before he got there."
Cole took a final swallow of his beer. "I've been thinking . . ."

"Just when things were so peaceful," she replied.

"I'm being serious," said Cole. "I think the reason the Duke has
been having trouble getting us assignments lately is that we usually
outnumber the enemy almost as much as the Octopus outnumbers us,
and clients don't want to pay for ten times the necessary firepower."

"So?"

"So maybe we'd do better breaking into smaller units. Put ten or
twelve ships each under Jacovic, Perez, and maybe Sokolov or Domak, and
keep about fifteen or twenty under the *Teddy R*. There are probably a lot
more assignments to be had that way. Right now the Duke is trying to
get commissions that cover the expenses of close to fifty ships. We didn't
have this kind of trouble getting work when we were a smaller fleet."

"It seems logical," she agreed. "There's not really much sense
having this big a fleet if you're not going up against the Octopus."

"I think I'll talk to the Duke about it next time I go over to the
casino." He paused. "By the way, how's Braxite doing?"

"He's still in sick bay. The medic says he's got cartilage damage, but
he's no expert in Molarian physiology. Because of that he can't do arthro-
scopic surgery, and if he opens the leg up it could mean a four-month
recovery and a permanent limp, so he's just prescribing bed rest and some
anti-inflammatory medication until we can find a Molarian doctor."

"Too bad," said Cole. "Still, we can't have a different medic for
every race aboard the ship. Is Braxite in much pain?"

"Mostly psychic pain," replied Sharon with a grin. "He's thinking
of all the fun Forrice and Jacillios are having."

"Speaking of Four Eyes, has he contacted us yet about when he
plans to return?"

"He's probably too exhausted."

"What the hell," said Cole. "He deserves it. And think of the fun we'll have teasing him when he gets back." He stood up and stretched. "Another dull day in port. I think I'll take a nap."

"I'll wake you in a few hours for dinner."

"Sounds good," he said, heading off for the airlift as her image flickered out of existence.

It felt like he'd only been asleep a few minutes when he heard an insistent female voice.

"Captain Cole? Are you there, sir? Captain Cole?"

He sat up groggily. "Is it dinnertime already?"

"This is Christine Mboya, sir. I'm on the bridge."

He opened his eyes and found himself looking at her holograph. "What's up?"

"We're getting a transmission I think you'd better see, sir."

"From who?"

"It's from the Braccio system, sir."

"Four Eyes?" said Cole. "When's he due back?"

"No, it's not from Forrice, sir," said Christine. "Take a moment to wake up and gather your wits about you, sir."

"I'm dressed. I'll be right up to the bridge. By the time I get there, I should be reasonably alert."

Cole got to his feet, rinsed his face off, left his cabin, took an airlift to the bridge, and stopped cold.

A life-size holographic transmission filled the far end of the bridge. Forrice was strapped to a chair. His face was a bloody mess, one of his four eyes clearly gouged out. It was obvious that two of his legs and one of his arms had been broken, the fingers of one hand mutilated. His torso looked like a piece of raw hamburger.

Standing next to him, staring into the camera, was a human male wearing the outfit and insignia of a captain in the Republic's Navy.

"How long as this been going on?" asked Cole.

"The transmission just reached us about three minutes ago, sir," said Christine. "It's being sent all over the Frontier on the broadest possible wavelength. I'd say fully a third of the Frontier worlds possessing subspace receivers can receive it."

"So this is the notorious Commander Forrice of the outlaw ship the *Theodore Roosevelt*," said the officer. "The Republic has posted a three-million-credit reward on his head, which I will be happy to deliver after I have severed it from his body. The fee will be split with the establishment that thoughtfully and patriotically informed me of his presence here."

Forrice had been gasping for breath when Cole arrived, but now his breathing was becoming so shallow Cole could hardly notice it.

"Nothing will free this traitor, but one thing can keep him alive. I have asked him to give me the location of the mutineer Wilson Cole and the *Theodore Roosevelt*. As you can see, he proved less than communicative, as did his companion." The camera panned to the lifeless body of Jacillios, so badly beaten as to be almost unrecognizable. "I will ask him one more time. If he refuses again, you will all get to see what the Republic does to criminals and traitors." A pause. "If Wilson Cole is monitoring this transmission, you can save your friend by contacting me in the next Standard minute and giving me your coordinates. After that, we'll just have to find you ourselves."

Christine turned to Cole. "Sir?"

Cole stared at the transmission, his face an emotionless mask.

"Sir?" she repeated. "Should I make contact?"

Cole shook his head. "He's dead already."

"No, sir," said Christine. "He's still breathing."

"Even if they don't touch him again, he's gone in two minutes, three tops."

"Sir," said Briggs from his console, "I've pinpointed their ship."

"Call all the crew members back from the Station. They've got fifteen minutes. If they're not back by then, we're leaving them behind. Then coordinate with Pilot," said Cole. "That ship doesn't leave the Frontier before we reach it. I don't care what it takes."

"Yes, sir."

Cole continued staring at the holograph of his friend.

"Captain Cole," announced the officer, "your time is up." He placed a screecher next to the Molarian's head. "Commander Forrice, so is yours."

He fired the sonic weapon. Forrice managed a single grunt of pain. Blood poured out of his ears, his body convulsed once, and then he was still.

"That's it," said Cole. "Kill the picture."

"Yes, sir," said Christine, breaking the connection.

"Pilot," he said to Wxakgini, "we take off in fifteen minutes. I don't care how much fuel you use, how much strain you put on the engines, what kind of wormholes we have to traverse, just get us within range of that ship before it's back in the Republic."

"It doesn't look like it's going anywhere, sir," said Briggs.

"You heard me." He turned back to Wxakgini. "Give me an ETA."

"If it remains in the vicinity of Braccio, and the Mishwalter Wormhole remains stationary, ninety-seven minutes from takeoff. But it will put an enormous strain on the engines."

"Just do it," said Cole. He looked around. "Where's Val?"

"Probably sleeping," said Christine. "This is red shift."

"Wake her and tell her to get down to Gunnery. Same with Bull Pampas, wherever he's at."

"Yes, sir."

"Now I want to talk to Mr. Odom."

Mustapha Odom's image instantly appeared a few feet away from Cole.

"Yes, sir?" said the engineer.

"We're going to put a lot of stress on the engines," said Cole. "Your job is to keep them working for the next two hours and not to warn me about the long-term damage it might do. And on my command, I'll want all power diverted from our screens and shields to our weaponry. Is that clear?"

"Yes, sir," said Odom. "But—"

"No buts," said Cole harshly. "Is that clear?"

"Yes, sir."

Cole broke the transmission, then turned to Briggs. "Mr. Briggs, you've got one hour to identify the ship in question, and hunt up the name of her captain. Christine, alert the crew and have them take up battle stations one hour from now." He turned and headed to an airlift.

"Where will you be, sir?" she asked.

"In my cabin. I'll be back before we're out of the wormhole."

When he reached the cabin, he found Sharon waiting for him.

"I'm so sorry, Wilson," she said.

"I know."

"It was just a fluke," she continued. "The Navy was never going to waste time hunting for us, we've proved that over the past two years. Some bastard spotted him and thought he could get a piece of the reward."

"Some bastard is going to regret it," said Cole grimly. "He was an ugly four-eyed Molarian, but he's been my closest friend since I entered the service."

"Do you want to talk?"

He shook his head. "There's nothing to say."

"Would you rather I left you alone?"

"Makes no difference," said Cole. "I'm going to spend the next hour mourning my friend, and the hour after that avenging him."

Sharon took a good hard look at his face and saw something beneath the pain and the sorrow that made her think that the one person in the galaxy she would not want to trade places with was the captain of the Republic ship.

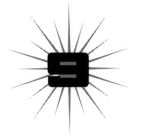

Cole emerged from his cabin one hour later. He stopped by the mess hall, got a cup of coffee, and took the airlift up to the bridge. The makeup of the crew hadn't changed, except for the addition of Domak at the computer controlling the ship's defenses, and he walked over to Briggs.

"Are we getting close?" he asked.

"We'll be out of the wormhole in another six minutes," answered Briggs.

"And is our target still in the area?"

"I'm not sure, sir. The instruments say so, but they're inaccurate from inside a wormhole."

"Sir?" said Christine.

He turned to face her. "Yes?"

"While you were in your cabin I told Commander Jacovic and Mr. Perez to join us. If you don't want them, I can order them to return to Singapore Station."

"Who told you to invite them in the first place?" asked Cole.

"You weren't available, and Commander Forrice is dead. I'm next in command, we're up against a class-M ship, and I thought—"

"You were right," he interrupted her. "And yes, we can use all the help we can get." He paused. "Has anyone identified the ship yet?"

"Yes, sir," said Christine. "Its registry number was embedded in its subspace messages. We are after the *Endless Night*."

"Its captain?"

"Manfred Baltimore."

"Mr. Briggs, do we know what its defenses are?"

"I assume they're standard for a class-M warship, sir," replied Briggs.

"So its weakest point is its shuttle bay?"

"I would assume so, sir," said Briggs. "But of course they won't have anyone posted there, and these modern class-Ms can seal off any damaged area in a matter of two or three seconds."

"I know."

"Then it seems to be counterproductive to attack the shuttle bay, sir," continued Briggs.

"We're just considering possibilities," said Cole. "Christine, didn't you or Briggs say it was covering a goodly portion of the Frontier with its broadcast?"

"Yes, sir."

"Isn't that transmitter also located in the shuttle bay?"

"Let me check on that, sir," said Briggs. He had in his computer case a three-dimensional schemata of a class-M ship. "Yes, sir, it seems to be wired throughout the shuttle bay."

"Good," said Cole. "Now see if you can identify a class-M's sensors."

Briggs uttered a brief command to his computer, and three small protrusions on the ship's exterior began blinking.

"I see three sets of sensors. Are there any more?"

"No, sir," replied Briggs. "Or perhaps I should say, there aren't supposed to be any. That doesn't mean that Captain Baltimore hadn't jury-rigged some."

"Three minutes," announced Wxakgini.

"Pilot, once we're back in normal space, how long until we reach the Braccio system?" asked Cole.

"Six minutes at full speed," replied Wxakgini.

"Christine," said Cole, "as soon as we're out of the wormhole, get me Perez and Jacovic on a scrambled channel."

"They're in the wormhole right behind us, sir," she said.

"Then we should have no trouble communicating, as long as we're all inside it, right?"

"That's correct, sir."

"Fine. Contact them right now."

A few seconds later images of Jacovic and Perez appeared a few feet away from Cole. They weren't as clear as usual, but both captains saluted and waited for Cole to speak.

"Unless it's decided to clear out in the past hour, there will be a class-M Republic ship in the area of the Braccio system," said Cole. "I'm sure you're aware that it has already killed Four Eyes and Jacillios. It is the *Endless Night*, commanded by Captain Manfred Baltimore. That ship is our target."

"What approach do you suggest, sir?" asked Perez.

"We triangulate on it, and try to blind it," said Cole. "Take out its sensors, and blow away the shuttle bay."

"There won't be anyone down there," noted the Teroni.

"We're here to kill the ship and crew that killed Four Eyes," said Cole harshly. "I don't want anyone escaping on a shuttlecraft. It won't be protected by their shields, because the transmitter's wired into the bay, and they can't send out a distress signal through the shields."

"We can't match firepower with it," said Perez. "Even after we blind and partially disable it, its weapons will still work. Without sensors, they won't be able to target us at more than about fifty thousand miles, but if we just stay back and take target practice, their defenses will still protect them, sir."

"I know."

"Then I don't understand," said Perez.

"In the hold of the *Teddy R* are two dozen heat-seeking mines that are programmed to ignore this ship. If we can damage the *Endless Night* to the point where it has to get within fifty thousand miles of us for its weaponry to be effective, we'll post ourselves sixty thousand miles away and begin retreating while unloading the mines. As it pursues us, with its sensors gone, there's every likelihood that it'll collide with one of them."

"And if it doesn't?" asked Perez.

"Then we'll keep our distance and try to think of something else."

"You say you want to destroy it . . ." began Jacovic.

"That's right."

"What if they fly the equivalent of a white flag?"

Cole's face hardened. "We'll show them the same consideration they showed Four Eyes."

"Sir," said Jacovic, "I think you should consider demoting or replacing me before this action commences."

"Oh? Why?"

"I will not attack a ship or a crew that has surrendered."

"I'm not about to replace you," said Cole. "You're a fine commander and an ethical officer. That's why you were in command of the Fifth Teroni Fleet."

"And why I left it," Jacovic reminded him.

"This is personal," said Cole. "I won't ask you to do anything you can't do. Stick by your principles. If it becomes necessary, I'll handle the unethical behavior."

"Sir?" said Briggs.

"What is it?"

"We're about twenty seconds from returning to normal space."

"Thanks." Cole turned to the two images. "There will be no ship-to-ship communications until I break radio silence. If we can hear each other, you can bet the *Endless Night* can too. Let's get to work."

He nodded to Christine, who ended the transmission, then called down to Gunnery. "Val, are you awake down there?"

"We're ready. Just get close enough to the damned ship for us to get it in our sights."

"Start by killing the sensors, and if Perez or Jacovic haven't beat you to it, take out the shuttle bay."

"Right."

"Bull?"

"Yes, sir."

"Activate the mines and get ready to jettison them, one every three seconds, on my command."

"Yes, sir," said Pampas.

"Got 'em!" announced Briggs.

"Can you get a visual on them?" asked Cole.

The young lieutenant shook his head. "They're too far away, but they can't hide their neutrino activity."

"Where are they?"

"On the far side of Braccio V, sir."

Cole frowned. "That's a gas giant. There's nothing there."

"There's *something* there—the *Endless Night*," said Briggs.

"All right," said Cole at last. "They assumed that we were going to come to the Braccio system, and since the only inhabited planet is Braccio II, they figure that's where we'll go. The *Teddy R* can't land, but we'd go into orbit and send down a shuttle, and we'd all be sitting ducks." He paused. "Where's Jacovic?"

"I'm sure he's spotted the *Endless Night*, sir," said Briggs. "It's on the far side of the sun, heading toward Braccio VII, another gas giant."

"And Perez?"

"I've temporarily lost him, sir." Then: "Wait! There he is! He's at Braccio II."

"Shit! The *Endless Night* will blow him right out of the sky!"

"I don't think so, sir," said Briggs. "He's not in orbit, sir. He must have spotted the *Endless Night* too, because he let it get a good look at him, and now he's keeping the planet between them. I think he's trying to entice it there so you and Jacovic can attack it while it's concentrating on Perez and the *Red Sphinx*."

"Let's see if you're right. Pilot?"

"Yes?" said Wxakgini.

"If the *Endless Night* gets inside the orbit of Braccio III, go after it. If you spot Commander Jacovic going after it, make sure we approach it from a different direction."

"Understood."

"What now?" asked Christine.

"Now we wait and see if Perez can draw the *Endless Night* to Braccio II," said Cole, finally remembering that he was holding a cup of coffee in his hand. He took a sip, found that it was barely lukewarm, made a face, and tossed the cup and its contents into a trash atomizer.

"Do you want all the screens and shields activated, sir?" asked Domak.

Cole shook his head. "We haven't blown his sensors yet, and the first thing they'll spot is a ship with its defenses up. Let's wait until we're close enough for him to do us some damage if he decides to change targets."

It soon became clear that the *Endless Night* had no intention of changing targets. It made a beeline toward Braccio II, and it was clear from its angle of approach that it was going to come over the plane of the ecliptic and hopefully surprise the ship that was hiding on the far side of the planet.

It was within twenty thousand miles of Braccio II when Jacovic opened fire, killing two of its three sensors. Val eliminated the third a few seconds later, and now Perez brought his ship out of hiding, though he kept a healthy seventy thousand miles between the *Red Sphinx* and the *Endless Night*.

"They haven't sent any signals yet," said Val. "I'm going to take out the shuttle bay now and the transmitter now."

"Leave it to Jacovic. He's in a better position."

"Well, he'd better do it fast," she said. "There are always a few hundred Republic ships somewhere in the Frontier."

Even as the words left her mouth Jacovic blew the shuttle bay apart. The *Endless Night* came to a halt and turned slowly in space, trying to sniff out its enemies like a dog in the darkness.

"Okay, Val," said Cole. "*Now* fire on it."

"Why?" demanded the Valkyrie. "It won't do any good. We can't break through their shields, and Jacovic has already taken out the shuttle bay."

"Just do it!" ordered Cole. "I want them coming after us, not the others. We're the ones with the mines."

Val used the thumper, a Level 4 pulse cannon. They could see flashes of light as the energy pulses bounced off the *Endless Night*'s defenses, and suddenly the Republic ship began approaching the *Teddy R.*

"Bull," said Cole, "start releasing those mines. Every three seconds."

"Yes, sir," said Pampas.

"Pilot, keep us sixty thousand miles away from them."

"Yes," said Wxakgini.

"What now?" said Christine.

"Now we wait, and keep our fingers crossed."

"What if they don't hit any mines?" she asked.

"It's more a matter of the mines hitting them. They'll be attracted to heat and neutrino activity."

"But *if* they don't?"

"They can't go light speeds without sensors, so we'll have plenty of time to think of something else," replied Cole.

"It's passed the first three mines," announced Domak. "The first four."

"If they can read the heat, they'll follow it even after it passes them," said Cole.

"Five, six, seven," droned Domak.

And then, suddenly, there was a brilliant silent explosion, and the *Endless Night* hung dead in space.

"With Four Eyes's compliments," said Cole, turning away from the screen.

"What now, sir?" asked Christine.

"Wait half an hour for any other mines to be attracted to the conflagration, then tell Jacovic and Perez to finish it off," said Cole. "I'm going down to the mess hall to have a beer in Four Eyes's memory."

Twenty minutes later Christine's image appeared next to his table.

"What is it?" asked Cole.

"We require some ethical guidance, sir," she replied.

"What are you talking about?"

"Four ambulance ships from Braccio II have flown up to the *Endless Night*. Two returned to the planet empty, but our sensors have shown that the other two possess one casualty apiece. One is returning to the planet even as we speak."

"And the other?"

"It seems to be headed out of the system and toward the Republic, sir."

"Poor bastard must be pretty messed up," commented Cole. "They've got hospitals in the Republic that make the ones out here look like they were built and run by cavemen."

"We need to know what we are to do about them, sir," persisted Christine. "You specified no prisoners and no survivors. But if we shoot down either ambulance ship, we'll be killing not just members of the crew, but innocent medics who are here only to help them."

Cole sighed deeply. "We can't kill an ambulance ship. Let them go." He smiled ironically. "I've been spending too much time with Jacovic."

"Thank you, sir," said Christine. "I think even Val would be reluctant to shoot down an ambulance."

"Only because it can't shoot back," said Cole. "Oh, well, that's our good deed for the month."

He couldn't know it at the time, but it was an act of charity that would affect not only the ambulance ships, but would change the history of both the Inner Frontier and the Republic itself.

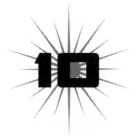

They made it back to Singapore Station without incident, and Cole gave each of the crews that had been in the battle a three-day shore leave.

He himself remained on the ship, and finally Sharon sought him out in his small, cramped office.

"Are you okay?" she asked as she entered.

He nodded his head. "I'm fine."

"You're sure?"

"I'm sure."

"You don't have to mourn alone," she said. "We all miss him."

"He knew the chance he was taking, leaving the ship and the station and going off with Jacillios," said Cole.

"I know why they killed him," said Sharon. "We're outlaws, and there's a price on our heads. But why did they—?" She broke off in midsentence. "This is the Republic, damn it! We used to be part of it. We're not even supposed to treat our enemies like that!"

"They were just trying to lure the *Teddy R* out of hiding," said Cole. "They succeeded."

"Would *you* lure a ship out of hiding that way?" she persisted.

"No, but—"

"But what?"

"But I'm not a member of the Republic anymore."

"It's hard to believe we all served in it," said Sharon.

"The *Endless Night* wasn't the Republic," Cole noted. "It was just one ship with a captain who should have been court-martialed."

"Even so," she replied, "it makes me feel dirty that we ever were a part of it."

He made no reply, and after a moment she walked over and sat down on his lap, putting her arms around his neck. "I miss him, damn it."

"So do I," said Cole.

"You don't show it," she said. "We're alone here. You don't have to keep up your stoic captainly demeanor."

"It's not a pretense or an act," said Cole. "It's the way I'm made. He was the best friend I ever had, but he's dead and he's avenged. I'll miss him for the rest of my life, but I've got a ship to run and a crew to take care of."

"I'm not worried about your crew," she said. "I'm worried about *you*. Everyone has to grieve, even you."

"I'll set aside time for it," answered Cole.

"How about right now?"

"Right now it's too fresh in my mind. I see a picture of what they've done to him, and I don't want to grieve, I want to kill." He sighed. "Those are not good thoughts for the captain of a ship that's outnumbered millions to one."

"Would you rather I left you alone here?" she asked.

"No, I'm happy to have you," said Cole. "I'm just not likely to be good company for the next few days."

"When's the last time you ate?"

He looked puzzled. "I don't know."

"Red shift? Yesterday's blue shift?"

He shrugged.

"Then I think we need to get some food into you. Can't have the captain starve himself to death."

He frowned for a minute, as if considering. "You know, I *am* hungry," he admitted.

"Idena and I found a lovely new restaurant on the second level of the station," she said. "Real beef, imported from Greenveldt. And a chocolate mousse that'll add two inches to your waistline." She got to her feet and pulled gently on his arm. "Come on. It'll be my treat."

He resisted for a few seconds, then got up. "What the hell. I'm not doing any good here. Lead the way."

They went to the airlift, descended to the shuttle bay, and stepped out into the docking arm. They were half a mile from the main body of the station. Cole considered walking the length of the enclosed arm, but suddenly a tram pulled up, they got on it, and half a minute later they were inside Singapore Station.

"Okay, where is this place you were talking about?" said Cole, looking around.

"Second level, like I said," she replied.

He followed her to an interior airlift, and a moment later they were being seated in a small bistro, the Home from Home, that did everything it could not to look like part of a shining metal space station. The chairs were an alien hardwood, as were the tables. The floor was covered with a self-cleaning carpet. The wallpaper came in five displays, each slowly superseding the previous one. There were actually ashtrays on the tables, though no one had smoked real tobacco in millennia. Most of the restaurants on the station had robot waiters, and a small handful had scantily clad women, but the Home from Home presented middle-aged waiters in crisp white jackets.

"How long has this joint been open?" asked Cole when a waiter had taken their drinks order.

"About three weeks," replied Sharon.

"They must have found those outfits in an antique shop."

"The place has a nice ambience, doesn't it?" said Sharon.

"It's okay."

The waiter returned with their drinks, they ordered, and then Sharon spoke of a new art gallery she had discovered while Cole pretended to listen politely. Finally the food arrived and they began eating.

"What do you think?" she asked.

"Not bad," said Cole.

"Not bad?" she repeated. "It's great!"

"I suppose so," he said. "We'll come back when I've got less on my mind."

"Forrice again?"

He shook his head. "Forrice is dead. We've still got a fleet to run. Which reminds me—where's Jacovic?"

"Somewhere on the station," she replied. "He'll probably come to Duke's Place later."

Cole nodded, then attacked his meal with more enthusiasm and became more talkative. When the meal was over they left the restaurant, took an airlift to the main level, and a moment later entered the Duke's casino. Cole made a beeline toward the Duke's table, where the Platinum Duke sat with David Copperfield and Val.

"Greetings," said the Duke. "I heard what happened, and I want you to know how sorry I am about Commander Forrice."

"We'll all miss him," said Cole. "I'm just sorry I couldn't blow up the whole fucking fleet for him." He paused, looking around the casino. "Is Jacovic here?"

"He hasn't stopped by to pay his respects yet," replied the Duke.

"I think I saw him at a Teroni restaurant as I was coming here," offered Copperfield.

"I'm going back to the ship," said Cole. "When any of you see him, tell him I'll be in my office and that I want to speak to him."

"You're not staying and sharing my liquor?" asked the Duke, and Cole could almost imagine a hurt expression on his platinum features.

"Not today," said Cole. "Or is it tonight?"

"It's always tonight out here," replied the Duke.

"Let's go," said Sharon, taking Cole's arm.

"You can stay if you want," said Cole. "I know I'm not being good company."

"No, I'll dance with the guy what brung me, to coin a phrase," she said.

He shrugged. "Okay."

They walked to the exit, and five minutes later they got off the tram and entered the *Teddy R*. Cole stopped by the mess hall, got a cup of coffee, wondered vaguely when he had become addicted to caffeine, and made his way to the bridge, where he found Christine and Domak. He made sure that everything was in order, then went to his office.

Sharon accompanied him to the door, then stopped.

"I've got some work to do," she said, "and you look like you'd rather be alone."

"Not really."

"Then call me back after Jacovic has come and gone," she said, turning and walking away.

Cole sat down behind his desk, sipped his coffee, and stared at the patterns of light that were shown on his small viewscreen. Ships came, ships went, hundreds of tiny brilliant lights in constant motion, producing an almost hypnotic effect. Cole relaxed and just watched the patterns. He lost all track of time and was brought back to the present by a knock at his door.

"Come in," he said.

The door irised, and Jacovic entered.

"David Copperfield said you wanted to see me, sir?" said the slender Teroni.

"Yeah," said Cole. "Have a seat."

Jacovic pulled a chair up to the desk and seated himself.

"You know," remarked Cole, "that's something Four Eyes could never do. You can't imagine how difficult it was to find anything he could sit on with those three legs of his."

"He was a good officer," said the Teroni. "I know how close you were to him."

"He's gone," said Cole. "And I need a new First Officer. You're the best I've got. I'd like you to turn over the *Silent Dart* to your second-in-command and come over to the *Teddy R.*"

"How will your crew respond to taking orders from a member of my race?" asked Jacovic.

"They had no problems taking orders from a Molarian," replied Cole.

"You were never at war with the Molarians," noted Jacovic. "The Republic has been battling the Teroni Federation for more than twenty years."

"We left the Republic three years ago," said Cole. "The Inner Frontier is no-man's-land. There are no Republics or Federations here. They'll follow your orders, because they've worked with you for a year, and they know you're an honorable and competent officer."

"Are you sure you wouldn't rather promote the Valkyrie?"

Cole shook his head. "I need a First Officer, not a loaded weapon, no matter how loyal and efficient she is."

"Then I accept, sir."

"Good," said Cole. "How soon can you move your gear here?"

"How soon do you need me?"

"A day or two," said Cole. "We've accepted no assignments, and we'll probably be here for another couple of weeks, but it's a good idea to get the crew used to the fact that you're the First Officer."

"All right," said Jacovic. "I'll transfer to the *Theodore Roosevelt* tomorrow." He paused. "Will the Valkyrie be upset that I have been promoted over her?"

"If she is, she can complain to me," said Cole. "I doubt it, though. As long as we aim her at the bad guys, she's content. You're here because I need a First Officer I can trust. She's here because I need a devastating weapon that I can control." He paused. "You served as Third Officer for a while when Val had her own ship, so you know your way around the *Teddy R*. Probably ninety percent of the crew is unchanged. You'll be in charge of red shift, starting the day after tomorrow. Any questions?"

"No, sir."

"Then that's it. I'll have Four Eyes's cabin reconfigured to suit your needs, unless you prefer another one?"

"I'm sure that will be fine, sir," said Jacovic. He saluted and left.

Cole went up to the bridge, where Christine was working at her computer console.

"You ever going to take a shore leave?" he asked her.

"Pretty soon, sir."

"That's what you said the last four times I asked you."

"There's nothing there that interests me, sir," she said.

"Maybe there are some great black-market computers," Cole suggested.

"I'm happy right here, sir."

"They've got art galleries, botanical gardens . . ."

She gave him a look.

"Okay, I know when I'm beaten," he said. "But you at least should take a little time off to relax."

"*This* is how I relax, sir. Really."

"You know we're going to have this conversation every day while we're docked here," said Cole.

"We always do," she said with a smile.

"All right," he said. "You win this time, but—"

Suddenly some code on the holograph floating above her console caught her eye.

"That's strange," she said.

"What is?"

"Just a minute, sir," she said, speaking to the machine in code that sounded as alien as any language he'd ever heard. Finally she turned to him with a puzzled frown on her face.

"What is it?" he asked.

"It's very odd, sir," said Christine. "There are six Republic ships in the Braccio system—but only one is in orbit around Braccio II, and that's the only inhabited planet in the system."

"When the hell did they show up?" demanded Cole.

"I just saw the notation on the screen, sir. It can't be more than a few minutes." She peered at the rows of code that suddenly appeared, asked a pair of questions in the same incomprehensible tongue, and waited until she had her answers.

"What's going on, Lieutenant?" said Cole.

"It doesn't make any sense, sir," she said. "One of the ships, the *Distant Drums*, sent a shuttle down to the surface, picked up two passengers, and returned to the ship." She frowned again. "I thought they only took *one* survivor back to Braccio."

"That's right—just one."

"Could his doctor be going with him?"

Cole shook his head. "With six ships they'll have a medical team on one of them."

"Then who could it be?"

"I've got a better question," said Cole. "Why does it take six ships to evacuate two people?"

"I don't know, sir."

He frowned. "Neither do I."

"It's very unusual, sir," said Christine.

"It's more than unusual," said Cole. "It's very *dangerous*. But for the life of me I can't figure out what they're doing there. One survivor made it back to the Republic. Either he or his medic or pilot surely told them that it was the *Teddy R* that killed the *Endless Night*, not some barrage from Braccio II. Hell, it was someone in Four Eyes's whorehouse who spotted him and informed the Republic he was there. They ought to be *thanking* them."

"Maybe they are."

"With six warships?" Cole shot back. Then: "Is Briggs on the ship?"

"I believe he's sleeping, sir."

"Lieutenant Domak, wake Mr. Briggs up and tell him to get his ass up here on the double."

"Yes, sir," said Domak, activating a new section of her computer.

"Keep watching the situation in the Braccio system, Christine," said Cole. "Let me know if it changes."

"The *Distant Drums* is already out of the system, sir," she said. "The other five aren't leaving, they're not going into orbit, and they're not landing."

"Something's very wrong here," said Cole.

"They're still holding their positions, sir."

Briggs approached the bridge just then, his hair unkempt, his tunic much the same.

"Sir?" he said, blinking his eyes rapidly.

"I'm afraid we need your services, Mr. Briggs," said Cole. "Lieutenant Domak, let Briggs take over your computer. No offense, but I need my two best operators, and he's one of them. Mr. Briggs, there are half a dozen Republic ships in the Braccio system. Christine is busy monitoring their movements; I want you to do the same with their messages. They'll almost certainly be scrambled and coded."

"Yes, sir," said Briggs, slipping into the chair as Domak vacated it.

"What can I do, sir?" asked Domak.

"Find another computer and help Briggs," said Cole. "He's monitoring the Navy ships' messages. You monitor everything else. There's a damned powerful computer in my office that I never use. Why don't you go there?"

She saluted and went off to find it.

"Still no movement, sir," said Christine after a few moments had passed.

"And if they're passing scrambled messages, or any messages at all," added Briggs, "they're doing it on a frequency that's beyond our capabilities."

"They're not," said Cole. "Until three or four years ago this *was* a Republic ship. We should be able to able to read anything a Navy ship sends."

"Then they're just going to stay out there between the fourth and fifth planets, send no messages, and make no threats," said Christine. "Why would they do that, sir?"

"I don't know, Christine."

"Me neither," added Briggs.

"*I* know," said a voice, and they all turned to see Domak's image, transmitted from Cole's office.

"Okay, what's going on?" asked Cole.

"The ship that landed was evacuating the Navy survivor."

"There were two passengers on it," insisted Christine.

"The other was the Molarian prostitute that informed the Navy that Commander Forrice was there. They wanted those two off the planet." Domak paused. "They know that the *Teddy R* was responsible for destroying the *Endless Night*. They don't know where we are, but they're convinced that someone on Braccio II must know. They've given them one Standard hour to reveal our location."

"I haven't heard any messages about it," said Briggs.

"You're monitoring the Republic ships. I heard a broadcast from the planet to a merchant ship that was returning home there. They told the pilot the situation. They warned him off, though they seem certain that everything can be worked out, that the Republic isn't going to kill two million inhabitants simply because they can't tell them where we are."

"Don't bet on it," said Cole grimly.

"But they're Republic ships, sir," protested Briggs. "They wouldn't—"

"They did to Four Eyes," said Cole.

"He had a price on his head. These are just civilians."

"Use your brain, Mr. Briggs," said Cole. "If it was just a threat, they didn't need six ships."

"But there are two million people down there—Men, Molarians, Lodinites, according to my records more than fifteen races, none of them at war with the Republic."

"This is the Frontier," said Cole. "Their status doesn't matter. If they'll kill men and Molarians, who serve in the Navy, they'll kill races who don't serve just as fast."

Jacovic came onto the bridge. "Colonel Blacksmith informed me of the situation, sir," he said. "I thought I should be here."

"Fine," said Cole. Then, raising his voice slightly, "Good thinking, Sharon."

"Is there anything I can do?" asked the Teroni.

Cole checked his timepiece. "There's nothing *any* of us can do except wait and see if they're bluffing."

Sharon's image popped into existence.

"Do you want me to send for anyone else?"

"Not unless we have any crew members from Braccio II."

"No," she said.

"Just as well," said Cole. "The bridge is crowded enough already."

"They could lie, I suppose," said Christine after a few minutes had passed. "The planetary government, I mean."

Cole shook his head. "Anyone who gives the ships any info is going to get hooked up to a Neverlie Machine, and the first time he lies it's going to burn out every brain cell he's got."

"I've never seen one on the *Teddy R*, sir," she said. "Maybe they don't have one."

"They have one," said Cole. "It's standard issue."

"Where is ours, sir?" she asked.

"I jettisoned it a few years ago."

"Before or after?"

"Before or after what?"

"Before or after we left the Republic?" she said.

"Before."

She smiled. "I should have known."

They all fell silent again. Finally Domak announced that the planetary government had sent out one last message, warning all space traffic away.

"Obviously they no longer think it's a bluff," said Cole.

"We'll know very soon," said Briggs. "There's ten minutes left."

"Sir?" said Christine.

"Yes?"

"The Republic ships are moving into firing range. There are three positioning themselves around the planet, and one each over the poles."

"Message coming through from the planetary government over all wavelengths, sir," said Briggs. "Do you want me to put it on ship's audio?"

"Why bother?" replied Cole. "We all know what they're saying. 'We don't know where the *Teddy R* is, we're telling the truth, and please don't kill us.'"

"They won't really do it," said Briggs. "Not two million people, when they know none of them had anything to do with us."

"I admire your optimism, Mr. Briggs," said Cole.

"They were trained in the Republic, sir, just like us," said Briggs. "No one ever told us to do anything like that."

"In case it's slipped your memory," said Cole, "I was court-martialed for refusing to kill twice that many people."

"Those were unique circumstances."

"All genocides occur under unique circumstances," said Cole. "But they still occur."

"Half a minute," said Christine. She uttered a command and the Braccio system appeared on a holoscreen two feet above her computer.

For a few seconds nothing happened. Then Braccio II seemed to burst into flame, and became a white-hot ball of destruction. The ships, which were not visible on the screen, couldn't have fired for more than two or three seconds, but the planet was still glowing an hour later.

"They did it!" said Briggs in shocked tones. "They really did it."

"What do you expect?" said Sharon's voice. "They're the Navy."

"They killed two million innocent beings, just like that!" continued Briggs.

"They couldn't find us, and they were determined to kill *somebody*," said Sharon.

"It's . . . it's . . ." Briggs was so furious he couldn't find the words.

"And the worst part of it is that no one's going to lift a finger," said Sharon. "We're the Inner Frontier. The goddamned Navy comes and goes where its wants and kills who it wants. And those bastards are going to get away with it, just like they always do."

Cole stared at the glowing ember that just moments ago had been a thriving world, his face an emotionless mask.

"No they're not," he said grimly. "Not this time."

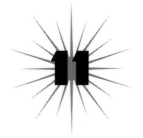

Cole decided it was time to have a conversation with the Platinum Duke. He half-expected the Duke would be in bed, but the Duke was up and trying half a dozen different types of hangover cures, each of them so noxious-looking that Cole felt they could scare a man off liquor for life.

"You've been out here a long time," said Cole. "You know most of your clientele."

"My regulars, yes."

"That's what I mean," replied Cole. "And you have no love for the Navy. I assume you've shared that sentiment with some of them?"

"Of course."

"I want a list of those who agree, or at least will listen with some sympathy."

The Duke's human eyes stared out at Cole from his platinum face. "You're really serious about this, aren't you? I mean, it's not going to be one or two attacks for payback and then out, is it?"

"No, it's not. This isn't the Republic I was brought up to honor, and it's not the Navy I was sworn to serve."

"It never was," said the Duke.

"Perhaps," agreed Cole. "But if we don't keep them out of the Frontier, eventually they'll destroy another dozen planetary populations looking for us, and two dozen more because we have the temerity to defend ourselves. Someone had to stand up and say 'Enough is enough.'"

"Nobody has yet."

"There hasn't been a Navy ship and crew taking up permanent residence here yet," Cole responded.

"I admire you, Wilson," said the Duke. "You remind me of all the reasons I want to see Susan Garcia dead. I wonder if she's still the Fleet Admiral."

"She was three and a half years ago," said Cole.

"You think she knows about Braccio II?"

Cole shook his head. "Not a chance. She's busy fighting a war. This is a sideshow."

"Damn!" said the Duke. "I wish I could blame her."

"You can."

"But you said—"

"I said she almost certainly doesn't know about Braccio," said Cole. "That doesn't mean that she hasn't set a tone that encourages such things."

"So she encourages slaughters, and then jails you for refusing to destroy a populated Republic world. Okay, I feel good about hating her again."

Cole smiled. "I'm glad I could bring a little sunshine into your day. But in all honesty, she's just another victim. They replaced four admirals over the years for not winning the war, and now it's her turn: she wins or she gets fired, though of course they'll come up with a more palatable word for it. She's under so much pressure to win this thing that I suspect there's nothing she won't do, and that kind of attitude filters down."

"You're too generous."

"Just realistic," he said. "The circumstances of her leadership don't make her any less my enemy." He paused. "I need a meeting place for all the members of my fleet."

"I've got a little theater I can let you use," said the Duke. "Six hundred seats."

"That'll do. I think we number about five hundred forty," said Cole. "I also need to talk finances with you."

"I was waiting for this," said the Duke ironically.

"You're the richest man I know," said Cole. "You're going to have to help finance us at the start."

"Only the start?"

"Only the start," repeated Cole. "Until I need every last ship, we'll still let you and David line up some mercenary work and take your commissions. Also, I'll give you salvage rights to any ship we destroy."

"I want something more," said the Duke.

"Name it."

"On any world that you free from either warlords or the Republic, I want Most Favored Nation trading status."

"You're not a nation; you're a space station."

"A space station with almost eighty thousand permanent residents, half a million transients, and more black marketeers than I think you realize. They are my partners, or they soon will be if they want any slice of these new markets. Do we have a deal?"

"As long as you don't strong-arm anybody or abuse the privilege, we have a deal."

The Duke extended his hand, and Cole took and shook it.

The word was passed that every member of Cole's fleet was to assemble at the theater at 1200 hours the next day.

"I'm as sorry as anyone about what happened, Wilson," said Sharon as they had dinner at the Home from Home that evening. "But you can't just go to war with the Republic. They've got something like three million ships."

"More," said Cole.

"And we've got sixty."

"Less."

"Well, then?"

"We'll talk about it tomorrow. Everyone will have a chance to voice an opinion then." A waiter brought their food to the table. "Now enjoy your meal."

They ate in silence for the next few minutes. Finally Sharon pushed her plate away.

"This is silly!" she declared. "You're talking about facing millions of ships, and you expect me to make small talk!"

He smiled. "I thought Val was the one who couldn't obey orders."

"Are you *ordering* me not to talk about it?"

"I'm asking you not to," said Cole. "Two million beings were incinerated. Tonight we'll mourn them. Tomorrow we'll talk about avenging them."

"It's crazy!"

"It's necessary," he said. "You don't think they're going to stop with Braccio II, do you?"

She looked surprised. "Why shouldn't they?"

"Because they didn't get what they wanted: our location."

"I hadn't thought about that," she admitted. "All right, Wilson. Tonight we mourn."

"Thanks."

They finished their meal, and Sharon returned to the ship while Cole took a few minutes to look at the theater where they would be meeting the next day. Then he, too, went back to the *Teddy R*. He felt restless, but he didn't want to socialize with any member of the crew, because he didn't want any questions about the upcoming meeting. He settled for going to his room, selected a mindless musical holo, and watched it until he fell into a dreamless sleep.

He awoke feeling fully rested, then realized he'd fallen asleep in his uniform. He took a Dryshower, changed outfits, went to the mess hall for some artificial fruit juice and a cup of coffee, sat in splendid isolation as his crew studiously avoided him—Sharon had evidently warned them off—and finally, half an hour before the meeting was to begin, he took a tram to the station and walked to the theater.

Fifty captains and crews filed in, along with the crew of the *Teddy R.* He had designated four seats in the first row for Jacovic, Christine, and Val, his First, Second, and Third Officers, and David Copperfield. The remainder of the first two rows was reserved for the captains of the other ships.

When they were all seated, Cole walked out onto the stage.

"I'm sure you all know that Commander Forrice and Ensign Jacillios were apprehended by the Navy of Braccio II and tortured. Both preferred death to revealing any information about the *Theodore Roosevelt.* They were our comrades, and we honor their sacrifice."

He paused for a moment, then continued. "Some of you may not know what happened yesterday. The Republic sent six military ships to the Braccio system. One of them evacuated just two people from Braccio II—a survivor of our conflict with the *Endless Night* and the citizen who informed the Navy of the presence of our two Molarians. Every other inhabitant of the planet was massacred."

There was some surprised buzzing. Most of them had heard of the destruction of Braccio II, but some, perhaps a fifth of them, had not.

"The Inner Frontier is supposed to be a no-man's-land, with no political loyalties to any empire, federation, or other political entity. The Republic has constantly ignored that fact. It could even be argued that many of the Navy's actions ultimately have a beneficial effect on the Republic; they recruit or impress crewmen for their vessels, they take materials that are needed within the Republic, they confiscate food that is vital to the worlds of the Republic.

"All that is on one hand. On the other is that the Navy has operated on the Inner Frontier without any military or moral restraint for longer than any of us has been alive. Thus far, no one has lifted a finger to oppose them, to remind them that they have no right to be here.

"That is about to change."

He surveyed his audience. They looked more curious than uneasy.

"I'll be honest with you. Commander Forrice was my closest friend, and a vital cog in the functioning of the *Theodore Roosevelt*. Even so, I would not be taking this action to avenge him. He was a military officer, he was aware that he was taking a chance traveling so far from his ship, and he paid the price—a terrible price.

"But yesterday two million innocent civilians were annihilated, not because they refused to reveal our location to the Navy, but simply because they didn't *know* our location. That arrogance and aggression cannot be allowed to stand without a response."

One of the newer captains stood up, and Cole gestured for him to speak.

"Are you seriously suggesting that we take on the Republic's Navy with a fleet of fifty ships?" he asked.

"No," said Cole. "I may be morally outraged, but I'm not suicidal. We will not venture one centimeter into the Republic. What they do within their domain is their business, not ours. But from this day forth, the Navy is no longer welcome on the Inner Frontier. We will make it clear to them that if they enter it without our permission, they will suffer the consequences. We will not allow another Braccio II."

Perez stood up. "How are we going to stop them? We can shoot down ten ships, but what if they come back with fifty, or three hundred? We can protect *some* planets from retaliation, but there are thousands of populated worlds. How do we protect them all?"

"We start by picking our spots," said Cole. "We don't attack every

Republic ship, not in the beginning. We attack those where we know we can win a total victory, and until we're stronger we take no credit for it. We let the Republic worry about who is destroying those ships that enter the Frontier."

"They'll just send the Eighth or the Eleventh Fleet," said another captain. "Neither is stationed that far away."

"Commander Jacovic," said Cole with the hint of a smile, "would you like to tell them why that won't happen?"

"The Republic is engaged in an all-out war against the Teroni Federation," replied Jacovic, standing up and facing the assemblage. "They are at almost equal strength. If the Republic moves either the Eighth or the Eleventh Fleet, they will lose galactic sectors containing upwards of three thousand worlds."

"And they're not going to open the door to the Teronis just to chase what they think are a couple of outlaw ships on the Frontier," said Cole.

"For a while," said Perez. "If we kill enough ships, they'll *have* to notice us."

"I agree," said Cole. "But we're not going to sit still and wait for that day. When the *Theodore Roosevelt* arrived on the Inner Frontier we were a fleet of one. Today we're a fleet of fifty-one. We'll keep recruiting more ships with grievances against the Republic—they should be easy enough to find—until the day that we're willing to let the Navy know exactly who they're up against. In the meantime, the Platinum Duke, who has no love for the Republic and even less for its Navy, has agreed to let us use Singapore Station as our headquarters."

"I don't think you can put together a thousand ships, even in five years' time," said another captain. "The Navy could send in a few thousand ships and never miss them."

"Then it's fortunate the Inner Frontier covers perhaps a fifth of the galaxy and that we know the territory better than they do," answered Cole. "Also, we'll have people on every world who are willing to act as spotters and let us know when and where the Navy shows up."

One very tall captain in the second row stood up. "We've already got a problem, and it's got nothing to do with the Republic," he announced.

"I was waiting for someone to mention it," said Cole grimly. "Go ahead."

"I'm happy to be a part of your mercenary fleet," said the man. "It's been very lucrative, and you've been an excellent commander. But I didn't know anyone on Braccio II, and I'm not willing to put my ship and crew at risk for them, especially with no prospect of reward." He stared at Cole. "I assume you're not planning on plundering the Republic."

"No."

"Perhaps just the nearer worlds?" the captain persisted.

"No," repeated Cole. "This isn't a democracy, and we're not taking a vote on my proposal. We're going to do exactly what I've said we're going to do. But I won't force any of you to join me against your will. I will give any captain, ship, or crew member exactly one Standard day to withdraw from our fleet without any objection. But if you're still a part of us at 1200 hours tomorrow, then you are placing yourself under my orders and my discipline. This means that you are committing to a campaign whose goal is to make the Inner Frontier off-limits to all ships in the Republic's Navy. I hope that's understood."

There was a general murmur of assent.

"One more thing," said Cole. "With the death of Commander Forrice, Commander Jacovic has been appointed First Officer of the *Theodore Roosevelt*. If I am killed or in any way incapacitated, he is in charge of the fleet and his orders must be obeyed. If anyone has a problem with that, I suggest you withdraw before tomorrow."

He paused to see if anyone was going to walk out right then and there—and sure enough, three captains and their crews did just that.

"They made an honest decision, and I don't want anyone here to hold it against them," he said when the last of them had left the theater. "Now, as for the immediate future: After tomorrow's deadline, we will disperse throughout the Frontier, recruiting spotters on each world, giving them secure channels to report the comings and goings of Navy ships. We'll pass the word that we're also recruiting ships and crews. I don't care what they've done in the past. If they'll pledge their allegiance and take our orders, they're welcome.

"Now," he continued, "once we start, we'll have to pick our spots very carefully. On any given day we're outnumbered on the Frontier, let alone in the Republic. There can be no survivors—at least none that are allowed to return to the Republic—until I say otherwise; it's too soon to let the enemy know who or what they're up against. When the time comes, we'll make sure a survivor or two gets back to tell them that they are no longer allowed here." He paused for a moment, ordering his thoughts. "Now understand, I am not ordering you to kill those who surrender or are too badly wounded to fight. They will be incarcerated in a prison and kept incommunicado until such time as we're prepared to let them return to their homes."

"I may know a world that can serve as a prison," offered one of the captains.

"Good," said Cole. "Talk to me about it when this meeting is over." He paused. "Now, sooner or later the Navy is going to find out where we are, so we're going to have to make Singapore Station impregnable, and give it ten times the defenses and firepower we supplied it with when we chased Csonti and his crew out of here a few months ago. Some of you are going to continue to accept commissions from the Duke and David Copperfield in order to pay for these improvements."

Cole looked around the room. "If there are no questions, that concludes this meeting."

"I've got one," said a crewman from the back of the room. "The Navy has been abusing the Inner Frontier since long before any of us were born. Just what did they do to Commander Forrice to elicit this kind of response?"

"It wasn't what they did to Forrice," replied Cole. "It was what they did to Braccio II."

"I'd still like to know."

"All right," said Cole. "I'll make the holo we received of Commander Forrice available to all of our ships, and you can draw your own conclusions."

And I hope that doesn't scare half of you off, he added mentally.

"Well?" said Cole as he reached the bridge the next morning. "What's the bad news?"

"We lost eight more ships, sir," said Rachel Marcos, who was at the main computer station.

"Can't say that I blame them," replied Cole. "They didn't know Four Eyes, they don't give a damn about the Republic, and there's no money in it for them."

"And we still have a fleet of forty ships," added Rachel.

"Yeah, when you're up against all those millions, I don't suppose there's a hell of a lot of difference between forty and fifty," said Cole wryly. "By the way, this is still red shift, isn't it?"

"Yes, sir."

"So where's Jacovic?"

"I believe he's at the station, sir."

"His first day on duty and he's already deserted his post," said Cole. "I've seen better beginnings."

"I'm back," said an alien voice, and they turned and saw Jacovic approaching them.

"You weren't supposed to be gone," said Cole.

"The ship is docked, and I saw the possibility of adding to our fleet," said Jacovic. "Two Teroni ships arrived last night. I took the liberty of visiting them, and they have pledged their support."

"Of course they have," said Cole. "They get to shoot down Navy ships."

"If I misunderstood you yesterday," began Jacovic, "I can tell them that—"

"You did fine," said Cole. "Executive officers are supposed to use their initiative. In fact, you might spend some of your time at Duke's Place and the non-human restaurants. There are bound to be other Teronis there. See if you can get them to convince their captains to join the cause. We're going to need all the help we can get."

"Yes, sir."

"And while I'm thinking of it, we've still got some Lodinites, Mollutei, and a couple of other races aboard the ship," said Cole. "Suggest to each of them that they spend some time on the station, recruiting members of their races and anyone else they know."

"I'll do that after I seek out Teronis on Singapore Station," promised Jacovic.

"Do it now," said Cole. Jacovic looked at him questioningly. "You're still on duty. This qualifies."

"Yes, sir."

He turned to Rachel. "Are you dating anyone at the station?"

"No, sir."

"As young and blonde and pretty as you are?" said Cole. "What a pity. You've taken one of my best recruiting tools away."

"Thank you," she said. "I think."

He looked over at Domak, a warrior-caste Polonoi with more natural body armor than some perfectly healthy men could carry, and decided that she wasn't seeing anyone socially—or, if she was, he was just as happy not meeting the object of her affections.

Suddenly the Platinum Duke's face appeared in front of Cole.

"How did your meeting go?" he asked.

"Don't pretend you don't know," said Cole. "I saw the holo camera blinking up in the balcony."

"Just in case you said anything momentous."

"Good. Shoot it over to the ship, and I'll have Christine send it out as a recruiting holo."

"No problem."

"I assume you watched it?"

"Of course," said the Duke. "You should have made me sound more heroic, donating Singapore Station to the cause."

"And simultaneously not losing more than five hundred drinkers and gamblers," said Cole with a smile.

"Well said," replied the Duke. "By the way, I haven't seen David Copperfield since your speech. I wonder where he's hiding?"

"Beats me," said Cole. "All I know is that he's not in a bulkhead. He used to hide there during battles, but then he found out that our sensor system could always pick him up. He's probably somewhere on the station."

"How did such a coward get to be the biggest fence on the Frontier?"

"He's a damned good businessman."

"But wasn't he terrified of the people he did business with?" asked the Duke.

"He always met them on his turf," replied Cole. Suddenly he smiled. "The first time I met him he had eight or nine hidden guns trained on me. That has to boost a coward's confidence."

"And he joined you solely because you called yourself Steerforth?"

"He joined me because I offered him protection and used the name of a character from *David Copperfield*. He stayed because he was able to earn a lot of commissions for us when we became mercenaries."

"Interesting little character, always dressing like something from Charles Dickens."

"Well, we can't all be things of metallic beauty like yourself," said Cole.

"Of course you can," said the Duke. "All it takes is a lot of time and even more money."

"Money's going to be in short supply for a while. We've got to turn Singapore Station into a fortress, remember?"

"It didn't take that much time or money the last time, when you had that little skirmish with Csonti."

"Probably because it *was* a little skirmish," replied Cole. "Csonti had fewer than thirty ships, and a number of them were not what one would call loyal. The Navy could come here with a hundred ships, each of which could do more damage that fifty Csontis."

"Point taken," said the Duke. "How do we go about it?"

"I'll send Mustapha Odom—that's our chief engineer—over later today. He's not much to look at, and even less to talk to, but he knows his stuff, and there's no one I'd trust more to make a place like this attack-proof. Probably I'll send Val over, too. Not much gets by her."

"We could just stand her on one of the docks armed with a thumper and a laser rifle, and that's all the defense we'd need," said the Duke.

"You won't need any for a few weeks, unless we screw up pretty badly," said Cole. "Then you'll wish you had five thousand of her."

"How soon do you expect to see conflict?"

"I don't know. No one fought those other five ships, and they're safely back in the Republic by now. I wish we could make them our target, but they may never even enter the Frontier again." He paused and ran a hand through his hair. "That isn't to say that there aren't a couple of hundred Navy ships here right now. We'll try to pick one that's all by itself, and destroy it so fast it hasn't got time to send out a message. We're not ready for the Republic to come looking for us yet."

"You're forgetting something, Wilson."

"Oh?"

The Duke nodded. "They know the *Theodore Roosevelt* is in the Inner Frontier, and they know you killed the *Endless Night*. Won't it be logical for them to assume you've killed any other ship that suddenly vanishes on the Frontier?"

"Perhaps. But if we do it right, if we don't leave any trace, if we prevent the ship from sending out an SOS, then I don't see what they can do about it short of sending in a couple of thousand ships they can't spare to do a really thorough search."

"That's a lot of ifs," noted the Duke.

"We're drawing a line in the dirt—well, in space—and telling the greatest military power in the history of the galaxy that they can't cross it," said Cole. "I don't know how you do it *except* with a lot of ifs."

"To say nothing of maybes."

"Yeah," said Cole grimly. "Let's not even think of *them*."

The next day the Duke showed Cole an unused building and offered to let him use it as his headquarters, a place that would be the nerve center of the operation, through which all orders and messages would pass. Cole thanked him politely, but turned it down.

"But *why?*" insisted the Duke. "Surely you realize the importance of keeping in touch with all your ships and all your spies and spotters."

"Of course," said Cole. "But I also realize the importance of being a moving target rather than a stationary one. Christine and Briggs can handle the operation from the *Teddy R.*"

"Then why have you got your engineer walking every inch of Singapore Station and its docks, making copious notes on our defenses or lack of them?"

"This is where all the ships will be coming for fuel and for supplies whenever it's possible. We can't keep it secret forever, so this is the place we have to spend most of our efforts protecting."

"I just wonder how much this is going to cost me," muttered the Duke.

"If it's too much, tell Mr. Odom you won't pay it and that he shouldn't install it."

"Have I mentioned what I think of your sense of humor?" asked the Duke.

"Not since yesterday."

"Well, it hasn't changed."

Suddenly Christine's image popped into existence. "Excuse me, sir, but we've got an urgent message coming in from Captain Velasquez."

"He's one of the ones who joined us after the Slocomb III opera-tion, right?" said Cole.

"That's right, sir."

"Okay, put him through."

Velasquez's image appeared. He was a middle-aged man, carrying several scars on his face and body from his experiences on the Inner Frontier.

"This is Marco Velasquez, Captain of the *Purple Streak*," he said.

"What can I do for you?" asked Cole.

"We've just spotted a lone Navy ship traveling from Mariano II toward the Stromboli system. Our sensors indicate that it has Level 4 thumpers and laser cannons."

"Can your ship stand up to that kind of firepower?" Cole asked him.

"Definitely not," answered Velasquez promptly. "But we have two other ships in the vicinity, and I think we can triangulate and take him out before he knows we're here."

"Did he do any damage in the Mariano system?" asked Cole.

"None that our instruments could find, sir."

"Stay out of his firing range, track him, and keep an eye on him, but take no action except on my direct order," said Cole.

"Yes, sir," said Velasquez.

"And report to me if he fires on anyone or forcibly takes anything that isn't his."

"Yes, sir."

Cole broke the communication.

"What was *that* about?" asked the Duke. "We've got three ships out there, and it's very likely this Navy ship is on some solo mission. Why not destroy him right now?"

"He doesn't seem to be on the warpath. We'll keep an eye on him.

If he starts taking food or other supplies at gunpoint, we'll move in on him, otherwise no. I want our first few actions to be against Navy ships that are in the actual act of harming, robbing, or intimidating citizens of the Inner Frontier."

"So you're just going to let this one go?" said the Duke.

"Don't worry," replied Cole. "We're not going to run out of targets."

"I just hope this doesn't bring us a million new ones."

"It won't," said Cole. "If they sent the fleet here, the whole Republic would be speaking Teroni by next month."

"How long before some of your pirate crews revert to form?"

"If we can give them some action and let them share some spoils, they'll stick around. If not, we'll go out and get more."

"You don't seem very concerned," noted the Duke.

"I've made my decision, and I'm comfortable with it," said Cole. "The crew of the *Teddy R* has been a lot of things we weren't trained to be—mutineers, pirates, even mercenaries. We're a military unit, and we still believe in all that crap military people are supposed to believe in. We joined up to help the helpless, to protect the weak, and to stand up to the bad guys. Somewhere along the way we made the same discovery about the Republic that Jacovic made about the Teroni Federation: The bad guys are *us*. We went to war against Csonti and Machtel and the others for money. Now we're going to war for the right reason, the same reason each of us enlisted in the first place. There's something very wrong going on, and we're going to put it right."

"I'm sure that brings you spiritual comfort," said the Duke, "but there are still a lot of them and very few of you."

"We've been aware of that from the day we left the Republic," replied Cole. "Maybe if we'd paid it a little less attention, Four Eyes would still be alive. Maybe two million inhabitants of Braccio II would be too."

"And maybe *you* wouldn't be."

Cole shrugged. "Maybe," he admitted. "Choices aren't always easy, and you don't always know right away if you've made the right one."

"Everything's a crapshoot," offered the Duke. "One Molarian whore comes into season last week and Forrice stays here, he and the other crewman live, the *Endless Night* lives, Braccio II lives, the next ship you're going to blow apart lives. All because she's not in season. Think about it."

"I try not to," answered Cole. "Think about it enough and you start to convince yourself that it's not the Republic's fault, that Four Eyes is really dead because of a fluke of timing right here on the station, that the villain isn't the *Endless Night* but Fate." Cole's face hardened. "But it wasn't Fate that tortured him to death, and it wasn't Fate that incinerated two million innocent people."

Suddenly the image of Marco Velasquez appeared again.

"What's up?" asked Cole.

"The Navy ship we've been tracking has gone into the Stromboli system and taken up orbit around the fourth planet. None of their weapons have been activated, none of their defenses are in operation, and they haven't communicated with the populace."

"They're just showing off their muscles and reminding everyone they're there," said Cole. "All right, Captain. Keep a watch on them and stay out of range of their weapons."

"What if they head back to the Republic?" asked Velasquez.

"They get safe passage," said Cole. "*This* time."

"Yes, sir."

The transmission ended, and Cole turned back to the Duke. "Thanks again for offering this building, but like I said, we'll run all the communications through the ship."

"I'll keep it empty anyway," said the Duke. "You can never tell when you might need it."

"That's up to you," said Cole. "I think I'd better be getting back to the *Teddy R.*"

"Whatever for?" replied the Duke. "What can you do there that you can't do here?"

"Sharon might blush if I told you," said Cole with a smile.

"She never struck me as the blushing type," said the Duke.

"Now that you mention it . . ." said Cole.

"Go ahead," said Sharon's disembodied voice. "Just keep talking about me as if I wasn't here."

"You *aren't* here," said Cole. "And isn't your spying supposed to end at the ship's hatch?"

"I'm not spying, I'm eavesdropping," she said.

"I assume you have some reason other that an incredibly misplaced jealousy?"

"You announced that we were at war, and then you failed to order an attack on the first enemy ship we spotted," said Sharon. "I was curious to know why."

"We'll catch one in *flagrante delicto* soon enough," said Cole. "That is, after all, what they *do* on the Inner Frontier."

"Are you coming back for lunch?"

"Yeah, I'm through here."

"I'm sorry to steal him away from you, Duke," said Sharon.

"Then don't," said the Duke. "Be my guests at the casino. I hired a new chef last night."

"Sure, why not?" said Sharon. "Ten minutes?"

"That'll be fine."

Sharon broke the connection, and then Cole and the Platinum Duke made their way through the corridors and levels of the station to Duke's Place, where they found Sharon already waiting for them.

They had gotten halfway through their meal when Cole received another transmission, this one from Vladimir Sokolov.

"What's up?"

"We've got one in our sights, sir," said Sokolov. "The *Bajia* out of New Brazil."

"Where are you?"

"I'm just outside the Rogentus system, sir, and the *Bajia*'s on Rogentus III."

"What's it doing there?"

"Appropriating farm produce that had been packaged for export."

"You're sure?" said Cole.

"Yes, sir," said Sokolov. "This has been confirmed by Mr. Moyer's ship, which is also in the area."

Cole looked across the table at Sharon and the Duke. "I told you it wouldn't take long."

"I didn't understand that, sir," said Sokolov.

"Sorry," said Cole. "I was speaking to someone else. Has the Navy ship got any visible defenses other than the standard screens?"

"No, sir."

"Okay. You and Moyer know its weakest points. Attack at will. Survivors are acceptable, provided they are apprehended and brought back to the station." He paused. "Escapees are unacceptable. Is that clear?"

"Yes, sir. Anything reasonable gets captured, anything else gets killed."

"That's right," said Cole. "No exceptions."

"Stay connected and I'll give you a report in just a minute," said Sokolov.

"Will do."

There was a moment of silence, and then Sokolov spoke again.

"We nailed him right where he sat on the ground, sir."

"Any survivors?"

"I sure as hell doubt it. Let me check . . . No, neither Moyer's sensors nor ours can spot any, sir."

"Stick around to make sure you're not missing anyone. If you do find any survivors, take them prisoner and then return to base."

Sokolov frowned. "To *base*, sir?"

"I'd rather not name the exact location on a subspace transmission that can be intercepted," said Cole. "Would calling it headquarters make it any easier?"

"Yes, sir," said Sokolov with a guilty smile as he broke the connection.

"Well, it's begun," said Cole to Sharon and the Platinum Duke as he broke the connection. "For better or worse, we are now at war with the Republic."

"So you've cost them one ship out of how many millions?" said the Duke. He uttered a sardonic chuckle. "How long do you suppose it'll be before they even notice?"

"Sooner than you think," replied Cole seriously.

Three days later Perez surprised another Republic ship while it was on the ground, gathering unwilling recruits. He blew it to pieces, then summoned four sister ships, which landed and hunted down the ten-man crew. There were no survivors.

The next morning the *Teddy R* got word that the crew of a Navy ship was causing all kinds of drunken havoc on Keepsake, a small world not far from Singapore Station. They arrived, sent two shuttles, the *Kermit* and the *Edith*, down to land at a Tradertown known as Moritat, found two taverns and a whorehouse in flames, and the street littered with the bodies of more than two dozen miners, gamblers, and adventurers. The survivors told him that a bunch of men and women from the ship had landed, gotten drunk and high on drugs, and when one of the taverns ran out of whatever it was that they wanted, they'd started shooting up the place. A few customers had tried to stop them, and a small-scale war had broken out. After killing a bunch of patrons, they had torched some of the buildings.

"Pass the word to all the locals to go back to their homes and stay there," said Cole to the few members of the populace that he found. "We'll take care of the problem."

No sooner had he spoken the words when one of the men grabbed his head, groaned once, and fell to the ground, blood pouring out his ears. Cole looked around and saw the sunlight flashing off the barrel of a screecher, a sonic pistol. He drew his own burner and fired a laser blast toward the man with the pistol. The man was in the process of pulling back behind a building, and Cole couldn't tell if he'd hit him. The locals had all run for cover, and half a dozen members of the shuttle's crew tried to form a protective circle around Cole, their weapons drawn, their eyes searching for signs of the enemy.

"Cut it out!" snapped Cole. "Flesh and bone's not going to protect me from whatever weaponry they've got. Just concentrate on spotting them."

"You're our Captain," said Jaxtaboxl. "It's our job to protect you."

"It's your job to obey my orders!" snapped Cole. "If you can't do it, go back into the shuttle."

An energy pulse whistled a foot above their heads, taking out a stand of trees a quarter-mile behind them.

"Back into the shuttle!" yelled Cole. "We're going to need body armor!"

He entered the shuttle and headed toward its tiny armory, only to find Sharon blocking his way.

"The Captain doesn't leave the ship in enemy territory," she announced. "You know that."

"I've *already* left the ship," he said. "I'm in the goddamned shuttle."

"We all know who should be in charge of hunting down the Navy crew," said Sharon. "You'd only slow her down."

He was going to object, but he realized that she was right. He turned to Val, who was so anxious to be unleashed that she was practically jumping out of her boots.

"All right," he said to her. "Grab some armor, take Bull and Domak with you, and don't take any foolish risks."

She grinned and walked past him, followed by her two teammates. "Armor slows me down," she said. "Don't worry—we'll find them."

"I never doubted it," said Cole. Then, as she left the shuttle, he added "And may God have mercy on their souls." He turned to

Jacovic. "Once she's cleared the immediate area, take a team over to the Navy ship. If they've left a skeleton crew, use whatever force is necessary to relieve them."

"Do you want the ship disabled or destroyed?" asked the Teroni.

"Neither. We ought to be able to make good use of a functioning Navy ship. Just don't let anyone else board it, especially the current owners. It's got to have some laser cannons. Keep them trained on all the approaches."

"It won't be much of a decoy without the appropriate recognition codes," noted Jacovic, "and we both know Val's going to kill anyone who might give them to us."

"Then we'll improvise," said Cole. "Besides, just about the only way we could get the codes is through torture, and we're supposed to be taking the high moral ground in this crusade."

"I merely made an observation," said Jacovic.

"Observation noted." They heard four agonized screams, and a triumphant curse from Val. "This seems like an appropriate time. I'm short three people on the *Kermit*, so choose a team from the *Edith* and get over there."

Jacovic left to gather his team, and Cole contacted Christine, who was at her computer console on the *Teddy R*'s bridge.

"Christine, check with Mr. Odom and see if we've got anything that can quench these fires before they spread."

There was a brief pause.

"Sir, he says yes. It's some kind of spray, and will work best if dispersed from one of the shuttles."

"Sounds good. Send Rachel and Jack-in-the-Box down to spray the fires, but not until I give the word."

"That's quite a blaze, sir," said Christine. "I'm watching it on one of the viewscreens. Are you sure you want them to wait?"

"Nothing would make me happier than having them go to work right now," said Cole, "but we can't put our people at risk like that."

"From the fires?" asked Christine, puzzled. "But they'll be in a shuttle."

"From the Republic. Wait until Val tracks down and"—he searched for the right word—"*neutralizes* the enemy. It shouldn't be too long."

Cole returned to the *Kermit* and had the small galley make him a sandwich. Sharon approached him.

"What do we do if Val doesn't find every member of the crew?" she asked. "Or at least, every member that didn't remain on the ship?"

"A lot of things can go wrong in any operation," said Cole. "But Val not finding and killing the enemy isn't one of them. I'm more concerned that they may have left a few crew members behind on the ship. It could be difficult for Jacovic to take it away from them."

"We'll hear from him if he's having any trouble," said Sharon.

"Probably."

"Seriously, Wilson, do you really think the Navy won't come looking for us after these last two days?"

"They won't even come looking for their two ships. Neither of them had a chance to send off an SOS—and there's something like eighteen billion stars in the Inner Frontier. You could spend a long time searching for a pair of ships that for whatever reason won't respond to your signals."

"What if this one *had* sent out an SOS signal and identified us?"

"Then we'd improvise." Cole grimaced. "Hell, we're improvising now."

"Don't you worry about it just a little?" she said. "Not what's happening today . . . but we're messing around with the *Republic*. We keep *saying* they can't spare a few thousand ships to come after us, to search the Frontier for our allies—but we don't *know* it."

"I don't know about you," said Cole, "but personally, if they send in a few thousand warships I'm going to be exceptionally sorry about it."

"Be serious!" she snapped.

"You saw what they did to Four Eyes and to Braccio," said Cole, his expression hardening. "*That* was serious. What you're talking about is fantasy. They can't spare the ships as long as the Teroni War is going on. You know it, I know it, even *they* know it." He sighed, then shook his head. "Look at that viewscreen," he said, indicating the bodies and the fires. "I can't believe we ever swore our allegiance to them, that we actually risked our lives for them."

Christine's image appeared. "Sir, Commander Jacovic reports that he is now in control of the Navy ship."

"Was there much opposition?" asked Cole.

"Two crew members were left behind to guard it," she said. "He offered them the opportunity to surrender, and they chose not to."

"Just as well," said Cole.

The transmission ended.

"Why did you say that?" asked Sharon. "We've got a brig. I know the prison planet's not ready yet, but we could have them transported down to an uninhabited planet and come back for them when the fighting's over."

"We're forty ships attacking the Republic—or at least that portion of the Navy that represents the Republic on the Inner Frontier," he said. "The odds are that the campaign will never be over unless we quit or lose—and I have no intention of quitting." He paused. "The Republic has prison planets; we don't. If those two were going to be stranded on some world with no shelter, no medicine, no radio, and no hope of ever leaving it, they were better off dying fast, right now."

Sharon looked dubious, but elected not to argue. Then Briggs's image appeared before them. "I just had to tell you the good news in person, sir," he said. "We just heard from Vladimir Sokolov. He nailed another one!"

"Where?"

"Out by the Quinellus Cluster. I don't know the details, but he evidently got much the best of it. He says there's fewer than ten hours of repairs required on his ship."

"There were no other Navy ships in the vicinity?" asked Cole.

"Not in the whole sector, as far as he could tell," replied Briggs.

"Well, I'm glad everyone else is having luck," said Cole. "I guess it's our turn right here on Keepsake."

It took twenty more minutes, and then he had his luck. Val, a triumphant smile on her face, returned to the *Kermit*, reporting that all the Navy personnel had been dispatched—and because she was Val she assured him that most of them had definitely not gone to a better place.

"Thanks," said Cole. "What was the grand total?"

"Eleven men, eight women, and three aliens," she said. "Bull's going to need some medical attention, but it's nothing serious."

"How about Domak?

"Nothing gets through that armor of hers."

"You're sure you haven't missed any of them?"

She merely stared at him.

"No, of course you didn't," said Cole. "Okay, get some rest. You did good."

"I'll have half a dozen victory drinks first," she said, heading for the exit. "There are still a few bars that haven't burned down."

Cole gave the order to spray the fires. It took half an hour to put them all out, after which the *Kermit* returned to the *Teddy R*. Cole went to his cramped office and asked Idena Mueller, who had replaced Christine at the communications console, to patch him through to Jacovic.

"Sir?" said the Teroni as Cole's face suddenly appeared before him.

"Mission accomplished," said Cole. "It's time to close up shop and go back to the station."

"We can be back on board the *Edith* in—"

"Mr. Chadwick can bring the *Edith* back to the *Teddy R*," Cole interrupted him. "We'll ride shotgun in case anyone thinks the Navy's still in command of the ship you're on. Dock it right next to us when we reach the station."

"Yes, sir."

The return to Singapore Station was without incident. Christine and Briggs were unable to pick up any subspace messages relating to the actions of the past two days.

"That's one advantage to being an ant attacking a dinosaur," remarked Cole after he was ensconced at the Duke's table in the back of the casino. "It takes the dinosaur a long time to know he's *being* attacked."

"Sooner or later the Republic's got to know," replied the Duke. "Or else why would you be doing all this?"

"All in good time," said Cole. "We've got to recruit more ships and more men."

"If they get mad, a thousand ships won't do you any more good than a dozen."

"They're already mad at the Teronis, and they're getting mad at the Canphor Empire, and they're not real fond of the Strek Unity," said Cole. "There's got to be a limit to how many they can be mad at all at once."

"Why?" asked the Duke. "I thought this whole campaign was precipitated by the fact that there's *no* limit to it."

"Well, the more they're mad at, the fewer ships they'll be able to spare for the Inner Frontier. We don't want to destroy the Republic.

Hell, we couldn't even if we wanted to. We just want them to understand that the Inner Frontier is off-limits."

"You can't always have what you want," said the Duke. "If you're successful, you'll just draw attention to yourself and invite a full-scale invasion; and if you're not successful, then think of the time, money, and lives you'll have wasted."

"If you feel that way, why are you giving us safe haven on the station?" said Cole.

"I have no more love for the Republic than you do, and I've got a lot less for Fleet Admiral Garcia," answered the Duke. "The fact that I'm a realist about the outcome doesn't mean I'm not an idealist about the *notion* of a rebellion."

"It's not a rebellion, and we're not rebels," said Cole. "We just want them to stop abusing their authority in a section of the galaxy where they *have* no authority."

"They have all the authority they need, Wilson," said the Duke. "Even out here—*especially* out here—might makes right."

"There are still millions of ants on Earth," noted Cole. "I'm told that no one's noticed a lot of dinosaurs there lately."

Cole declared a two-week moratorium on their undeclared war.

"As dense as the brass are, even *they* will figure out something's going on if they keep losing a ship or two every day" was his explanation.

The captured ship, which was named the *Shooting Star*, failed to yield any new secrets concerning the Republic or its weaponry, which wasn't all that surprising considering that the *Teddy R* had been a functioning ship in the Navy less than four years ago. Cole had Dan Moyer take command of it and select a crew. Slick, the Tolobite who, with his second-skin symbiote, could operate in the cold of space for hours at a time, gave the exterior a thorough inspection and made a few cosmetic repairs.

Cole didn't let the two weeks go to waste. By the end of the first week he'd recruited another twenty ships, mostly one- and two-man jobs, a few bigger ones, to his cause. Jacovic, Braxite, Jaxtaboxl, Domak, and the other aliens under his command sought out their own kind, and soon another twelve ships joined his small but growing fleet.

Braxite gathered a few other Molarians for a religious ritual that theoretically sent Forrice's soul on its way to the next level of existence—they had no word for Heaven—and Cole was allowed to attend. He had no idea what was being said—Braxite sat next to him and translated, but the concepts were as alien to him as the language—but it had a mildly cathartic effect on him. At least, he felt he would finally be able to sleep through an entire night without dreaming of his friend's final few agonized minutes of life.

From time to time sightings of lone Republic ships would be reported, but Cole stuck to his timetable: no military action for two weeks, do nothing to alert the Republic to the fact that anything unusual was transpiring on the Inner Frontier. The *Teddy R* remained docked at Singapore Station.

David Copperfield seemed increasingly uneasy. The little alien had no taste for conflict of any kind, and yet it was obvious that conflict was precisely what Cole's fleet was preparing for.

"You don't have to stay on the ship, David," said Cole one morning when Copperfield was awkwardly trying to find out when Cole planned to go hunting for Republic ships again. "You can stay on Singapore Station. No one will hold it against you."

"My place is at your side," replied Copperfield adamantly. "And since it's obvious that you're not going to remain in port, I will go into battle with you." He paused. "It is a far better thing I do than I have ever done."

"Do you really believe that?" asked Cole.

"Not for a minute," admitted the little alien. "But just once in my life I wanted to say it."

"There's another saying worth considering," said Cole. "He who opts to run away will live to fight another day."

"It's like hiding from the dentist," said Copperfield, making a face. "Eventually you have to see him."

"Yeah, I suppose that's one way of looking at it."

"As long as I can't talk you out of it, perhaps I can make a suggestion."

"Shoot," said Cole.

"You are going to war with the Republic. The Teroni Federation is already at war with the Republic. Why don't you join forces?"

"Because the enemy of my enemy is not necessarily my friend," replied Cole. "Besides, they've got over a million ships. I don't have much bargaining power if all I can bring them is another sixty or seventy. We'd just become a small unimportant unit in the Teroni Navy, and I don't believe in their cause any more than I believe in the Republic's. There are something like forty million dead on each side, and I'll bet half of the politicians and top brass don't remember or never knew just what it is they're fighting about."

Copperfield stared at him long and hard. "I had no idea you were this bitter, Steerforth."

"How would you like to be related to someone who lived on Braccio II?" responded Cole.

"The Navy has been pacifying worlds for a millennium."

"I realize that it's only a matter of degree, but there's still a difference between pacifying them and annihilating them." He paused, the muscles in his jaw tensing. "If you had vital information, information that could save thousands of lives, and you refused to give it to me, I would still never do to you what those bastards did to Four Eyes, and neither would my Teroni First Officer."

The little alien looked into Cole's eyes and decided it was time to change the subject.

"So how soon will we let the Navy know that we're the enemy?"

"They already know it. There's a ten-million-credit price on my head, remember?"

"I meant when will we let the Navy know that *we're* the ones who are attacking them?"

Cole shrugged. "I don't know. When we can withstand an attack by a couple of hundred ships, I suppose."

Copperfield relaxed visibly. "That might not be for a year or more."

"Anything's possible," said Cole noncommittally.

"Suddenly I feel better," said the little alien. "Come over to Duke's Place and I'll split a bottle of their best champagne with you."

"Yeah, why not?" said Cole. "I spend years cooped up in ships with claustrophobic rooms and seven-foot ceilings. Why the hell stay here when I don't have to?"

They took the tram to the station, and were on their way to Duke's Place when Rachel's image appeared alongside them.

"I'm sorry to bother you, sir," she said, "but you told me to keep you apprised of any Republic ships we could track within the boundaries of the Frontier."

"What have you got?" asked Cole.

"Twelve ships have recently shown up, six near the Quinellus Cluster, six more in the vicinity of Keepsake."

Cole nodded. "They're looking for their missing ships. They won't find the *Shooting Star*, of course, and my understanding is that Vladimir damned near vaporized the ship out by the cluster." He paused for a moment, considering the situation. "Keep tabs on them, Rachel; get Mr. Briggs or Lieutenant Domak to help if necessary, and alert Christine when she comes on duty. Inform Val, too. As long as they're just searching in space, fine—but if they land anywhere and become an indiscriminate punishment party, or they start taking captives for the kind of questioning they gave Four Eyes, I want to know about it instantly."

"Yes, sir," she said, saluting. Her image vanished a second later.

Cole turned to Copperfield. "You go ahead to Duke's. I've got something that I need to do."

"Are you going back to the ship?"

"Not just yet."

"I guess I'll see you later," said Copperfield as Cole began walking down a long metal corridor. Cole was back at the ship an hour later. Two robots accompanied him, carrying his purchases from the tram to the shuttle bay. He resisted the urge to either tip or thank them and went up to the bridge, where Rachel Marcos was still tracking the Republic ships.

"Anything going on?" he asked.

She shook her head. "No, sir."

"Keep me informed."

Sharon Blacksmith met him as he was going to his office. "I saw you bringing something aboard," she said. "What is it?"

"A little present for the Republic."

"Come on, Wilson," she said. "I'm the Chief of Security. If you don't tell me, I'll just open them up."

"If you tamper with them, they might explode."

"What the hell are they?" she demanded."

"They're mines."

"Like we used against the Republic? We've already got a bunch, don't we?"

"Yeah, but they're regulation Republic issue. I wanted some that are more than half a century old, and built by—what can I call them?—freelance bombmakers."

"Why?"

"The Republic's got a dozen ships looking for the *Shooting Star* and the one Vladimir took out in the Quinelllus Cluster. Hopefully they'll give up, turn around, and go home—but if they decide that something happened to those ships, that they're not merely lost or out of touch, they'll start questioning the locals, pretty much the way they questioned Four Eyes. Even if it's just one ship and we isolate it, we can't open fire on it. It'll almost certainly be in contact with ships that are out of range, and I'm not ready for the Republic to know what we're doing yet. So I'm going to pass these ancient mines out to some of our smaller ships, little one- and two-man jobs, and once we know that one of the Republic ships is causing trouble, we'll see to it that it hits one of these mines or vice versa. Then, when his comrades come along to learn what happened, all they'll find are the remains of a half-century-old mine, obviously left over from an earlier war . . . and no one will go home any the wiser." A tight little smile crossed his face. "That's the scenario, anyway."

"Who will you give them to?"

"I've got six of them," responded Cole. "I plan to give two apiece to Moyer, Bujandi, and one of Jacovic's Teronis."

"I'll contact them for you," she said.

"Good. The mines are so out-of-date that I'm going to have to show them how to activate the damned things."

The mines were placed aboard three small ships an hour later, and the ships promptly headed off, one toward Keepsake, two toward the Quinellus Cluster.

Cole checked with the personnel on the bridge every hour. The Navy ships had split up and were honeycombing the areas in question, but so far none of them had touched down. The situation was unchanged when he finally went to bed.

He was awakened three hours later by Christine, who informed him that a Republic ship had radioed Keepsake for landing coordinates.

"Which ship have we got over there?"

"Mr. Moyer's ship, sir."

"Patch me through to him."

"Yes, sir."

Moyer's face appeared over Cole's built-in dresser.

"Dan, one of the Republic ships is going to try to land on Keepsake. You know what to do?"

"Yes, sir," said Moyer. "You went over it with each of us."

"Okay. Good luck."

Cole broke the connection. "Give me a play-by-play," he said to Christine's image.

"Nothing yet, sir. The Republic ship—it's the *Johannesburg*—has been given its coordinates and is approaching Keepsake." Thirty seconds of silence followed. "Mr. Moyer just cut across the *Johannesburg*'s path. The *Johannesburg* has altered course and is in pursuit. Mr. Moyer is banking further away from the planet."

"That's the ballgame," said Cole. "He used the maneuver to hide the fact that he dumped the mines. They're coded not to go after him."

"No change yet, sir. *There!*" she yelled. "The *Johannesburg* is gone!"

"Okay," said Cole. "Now for Step Two. Patch me through to Slade McNeil, Slade McBain, whatever the hell his name is—the guy who owns the big casino on Moritat."

"Moritat, sir?"

"That's the Tradertown on Keepsake."

"Yes, sir."

A moment later the image of a burly gray-haired man with a bushy mustache replaced Christine's image.

"Good evening, Slade," said Cole. "You saw what happened?"

"It's afternoon here, Captain, and yes, we did. Lit up the sky. Beautiful sight."

"If the Republic asks about it, you don't know what happened, your instruments recorded the explosion."

"How can we not know?" said the burly man.

"Tell them that there was a battle between a pair of warlords about fifty or sixty years ago. One of them dumped a batch of mines, and when the war was over, the winner cleaned most of them up. Over the years you lost three or four ships to rogue mines that hadn't been deactivated. You thought you'd gotten them all, but evidently you were mistaken."

"That's pretty far-fetched," said the man. "Are you sure they'll buy it?"

"They will, when they find fragments of the mine. I'm going to log off now, but stay connected, and Officer Mboya will give you a scramble code to alert us if they *don't* buy it and start harassing you."

"Will do."

"Christine," said Cole, "take it from here."

"Yes, sir," she replied.

As Cole lay back on his bunk, he brought forth the image of Forrice in his mind, and smiled.

"You'd have been proud of us today," he murmured as he began drifting off. "Using those ancient mines was worthy of *your* devious mind. The Navy will reconstruct what happened, and in the end the only thing they'll do is warn their people away from Keepsake until they make sure there are no more uncollected mines floating in the vicinity. Yeah, you'd have been pleased with it."

And for the first time in days, Cole slept like a baby.

Cole spent the next three days on Singapore Station, most of it at Duke's Place, recruiting men and ships for his growing fleet. By the end of the third day he had seventy-four ships under his command, which was quite impressive until he remembered that only half of them could hold more than three men, and even less than that could withstand the pulse of even a Level 2 thumper.

"I wish I could convince myself I was doing our cause any good, getting all these little pleasure ships lined up," he confided to Sharon and David Copperfield as they sat at the Duke's table.

"Then arm them, the way you're going to be arming the station," offered David Copperfield.

"We're not made of money, David," said Cole. "Every credit we've got has to go into protecting the station."

Copperfield was silent for a long moment. Finally he looked up. "It is entirely possible that I have some funds I haven't mentioned to you, my dear Steerforth."

"It doesn't seem entirely unlikely," agreed Cole.

"I shall donate five hundred thousand Maria Theresa dollars and five hundred thousand Far London pounds to the rearming of your fleet. Will that be of some help?"

"Thank you, David. What brought forth this unexpected attack of generosity?"

"If we lose the war, what good will the money do me?"

"You're the only member of your race any of us has ever seen," said

Sharon. "You could simply say we were holding you captive and demanding ransom for your release."

Copperfield frowned. "You could have mentioned that before I offered the donation," he said petulantly.

"I won't hold you to it," said Cole, smiling.

"What are you grinning about?" demanded Sharon.

"He's grinning because he's read the immortal Charles, too, and he knows that David Copperfield would never renege on such a noble offer," said the little alien.

"It's your own fault for falling in love with Dickens," said Cole. "You could have chosen Dostoevski."

"No well-bred Englishman would read such a morbid Russian writer," said Copperfield with a sniff of contempt.

"Well, I thank you for your offer, and we'll put it to good use."

"Bloody well better," muttered Copperfield.

"You didn't get *that* from Dickens," said Cole.

"I *do* read other British writers, you know."

Suddenly there was a commotion from one of the tables. As he turned to see the cause of it, Cole saw Val's flaming red hair. A few seconds later the well-muscled body of a large man went flying through the air, landing with a bone-jarring *thud!* Val stayed in the area long enough to make sure he was still breathing, then walked over to the table, just as the Duke emerged from his office.

"What the hell's going on?" he demanded.

"You've got a cheater down there on the floor," said Val. She shook her head. "Can you imagine it, using a shiner against *me?*"

"You're sure?"

She reached into a pocket, withdrew a tiny mirror, and tossed it to him. "If you're not going to shoot him, at least bar him from ever coming in here again."

The Duke examined the mirror. "I've seen smaller."

"And duller. I caught the light glinting off this one."

"I should have hired you as my manager the first time I saw you, twelve, thirteen years ago."

"What fun is that?" she said. "I come here to drink and gamble. I can break heads anywhere."

"Honest and to the point," said Cole. "Enjoy the rest of the evening, but be back at the ship by 0700 hours."

"We're finally going to go hunt down some Navy ships?" she asked.

He shook his head. "We're going to go a little further afield to do our recruiting. Not everyone on the Frontier comes to Singapore Station."

"0700?" she repeated.

"That's right."

"Then I'd better cash in my chips and get over to the Gomorrah while I've still got time."

"Be gentle with them," said Cole. "They're only steel and titanium, you know."

She laughed and headed off to the cashier.

"I used to say that if I had fifty of her I could conquer the galaxy," remarked Cole as he watched her walk away. "Looks like I'm going to have to do it with just one. Probably lowers the odds to even money."

"Did you really mean that—about 0700 hours?" asked Sharon.

"Yeah. I had Christine pass the word to the crew. The station's well has pretty much run dry, at least for the time being. We'll try again in a couple of weeks, when there's a new batch of potential recruits." He turned to the Duke. "You want to have your computer send Christine a list of locations where we're likely to find people with a grudge against the Republic?"

"Try anywhere on the Frontier," said the Duke.

"You know what I'm looking for: men with ships, men with crews, and men who hate the Republic enough that they'll join us without demanding any pay."

"You could pay a few if you had to," noted the Duke.

"If I pay one man, I have to pay every man in our fleet, and *that* is beyond our ability to do. Besides, any man you recommended that I pay would just have to give you a kickback, and we're already spending most of our money on the station's defenses."

"Wilson, you cut me to the quick."

"Do I really?"

The Duke shrugged. "Well, you would if everything you said wasn't true." He laughed heartily. "I'll have the list to Christine before you take off."

"Thanks," said Cole. He turned to David. "You can stay here if you'd prefer."

"Desert my old school chum?" said Copperfield. "Not even when he's been amusing himself at my expense. Besides, you're just on a recruiting mission. It's not as if you expect to get into a pitched battle."

"True enough," replied Cole. "And speaking of your expense, you might transfer some money here so they can start arming the smaller ships while we're off finding more small ships for you to spend your money on."

"Do you enjoy teasing me, Steerforth?"

"If I didn't, I wouldn't keep doing it," answered Cole.

"Well, at least you're honest about it," said Copperfield with a deep sigh.

They remained at the Duke's for another half hour, then made their way back to the ship.

Cole was awakened at 0705 hours and informed that all personnel were aboard the ship except for Val.

"It's just a recruiting mission," he said. "We're not waiting for her."

He shaved, took a Dryshower, got dressed, and was heading to the mess hall for some coffee when he bumped into Val, who was looking a bit disheveled.

"You're late," he said.

"I'd explain why, but you look silly when you blush," she said, continuing on her way to her cabin.

"Yeah, probably I do," he said when she was out of earshot. "And probably I would."

He got his coffee, decided not to go up to the bridge, and gave the order to release from the dock and take off for Freeport, a commercial center some two hundred light-years away. Wxakgini announced that the quickest route would be through the McAllister Wormhole, with an ETA of six hours and two minutes, as opposed to seventeen days at top speed through normal space.

The trip was uneventful, and they emerged half a light-year from the Beyer system, of which Freeport was the third planet. They began approaching it, and as they passed the fifth planet Briggs announced that a small private ship was being pursued by two Navy ships. It had been hit by a charge from a thumper—a pulse cannon—and was following an erratic course, as if some of its stabilizing gyros had been damaged.

"Has it got any chance at all?" asked Cole, arriving on the bridge from his office.

Briggs shook his head. "It's losing oxygen. Even if they get it moving at speed again, they've barely got enough oxygen to get out of the system. I don't think they can even make the wormhole. They'll certainly never come out the other end."

"Who's in Gunnery?" asked Cole.

"I'm not sure, sir," said Briggs.

Christine Mboya checked her computer. "Mr. Pampas, sir."

"Wake Val up, and tell her to go join Bull down in Gunnery," said Cole.

"Yes, sir."

"Is Jacovic awake?

"No, sir. His shift ended before we entered the wormhole."

"Wake him and have him come to the bridge."

"Yes, sir."

"Malcolm," said Cole, "what kind of weaponry are these Navy ships carrying?"

Briggs had his computer analyze the ships. "Level 3 or Level 4 thumpers, and Level 5 burners."

"Okay, we can handle the lasers, and the Level 3 thumpers. If they both come after us with Level 4 thumpers at once, we're in deep shit—so let's hope they don't have them." He studied the holoscreen for a moment. "I'm going to let you handle the defenses, Malcolm. I know we can aim our own weapons from the bridge, but Val and Bull can adjust faster down in Gunnery."

"Should we give them a warning, try to call them off?" asked Christine.

"They're not going to listen, so why let them know we're inter-vening? Is Val down there yet?"

"Just this moment," said Christine.

"Patch me through." He waited the few seconds for Christine to make the connection. "Val, Bull, we're going to get as close to these two Navy ships as we can. I don't want you firing until you're sure you can disable them. They probably have superior weaponry, so I want to make sure our first shots do the trick."

"Got it," said Val.

He nodded to Christine to break the transmission as Jacovic reached the bridge.

"Pilot, I assume you've been paying attention. Plot an intercept course and get us as close to those two ships as you can."

"We may not make it before they kill the ship that's escaping them," said Wxakgini.

"Not to worry," said Cole. "The second they realize this is the *Teddy R*, they're going to forget all about that other ship."

He half-expected to hear Forrice's voice saying "Hard to disagree with *that*!" and then hooting with alien laughter, but there was no response except silence.

Suddenly Cole shouted, "Pilot, belay that order! Keep your distance!"

The ship almost lurched to a halt and hung dead in space.

"Val?" said Cole as Jacovic joined them on the bridge.

"Yeah?" she said. "What the hell is going on?"

"They haven't spotted us yet," said Cole. "That means all they're concerned with is that little ship that's trying to escape."

"So?"

"So they won't have their screens and shields up. If you and Bull can each man a weapon and make the first shot count . . ."

"Right," she said.

"Take your time and aim right, because you'll never get a second shot with their defenses down."

"Leave it to us," said Val.

"Malcolm," said Cole, "kill our defenses until Val and Bull take their first shots."

"Sir?"

"If either of those ships see a ship our size with screens up, even if they don't recognize that we're the *Teddy R*, they're going to raise their own defenses, just to be on the safe side."

"Defenses down, sir."

"What's keeping them?" asked Christine nervously.

"They're trying to lock on to a fast-moving target that is at the outer range of our cannons," replied Jacovic. "They know they only have one chance—and they have to fire simultaneously."

"Right," agreed Cole. "Wound or kill one ship before firing on the other and whatever we're shooting will just bounce off its shields."

Suddenly the viewscreen was filled with a burst of light, as one of the ships was blown into a million pieces. The other took a hit, veered crazily, and fired a wild shot at the *Teddy R*.

The energy bursts from the *Teddy R*'s pulse cannons bounced harmlessly off the Navy ship's shields, but at the same time the laser cannon was probing the surface of the ship—and finally it found a weak point, the spot where the initial hit had occurred. A brief adjustment, and the next pulse from the thumper went directly into the spot the laser had pinpointed, and that was the end of the second ship.

"Textbook," said Jacovic approvingly.

"Pilot, we'd better get that ship they were chasing before it runs out of air," said Cole.

Wxakgini was silent for a moment as he and the navigational computer he was tied into analyzed the ship's trajectory, plotted its course, and made arrangements to intercept it in another two minutes.

It took them one hundred seventeen seconds to catch up with the ship. They radioed ahead that they were friends, that indeed they were the ship that had killed his two pursuers, but it made no response or acknowledgment of their signal.

"Either it can't answer or it doesn't trust us," said Christine.

"Or it's out of oxygen already," added Briggs.

"Let's find out," said Cole.

The *Teddy R* drew alongside the ship, matched velocities with it, and sent Slick, the Tolobite with the sentient second skin, out to secure the ship. Once that was done, they opened both hatches and Cole and Jacovic entered the smaller ship.

"Jesus, he's a mess!" said Cole, staring at the only occupant, a young man who was fully conscious but sprawled on the floor of his ship.

"He's in urgent need of medical attention," concluded the Teroni, looking at the young man's blood-streaked face and garments, with fragments of bone sticking out through torn flesh. He alerted the *Teddy R*'s infirmary that they'd shortly be bringing in an emergency case.

"Can you stand?" asked Cole.

"I don't know," said the young man. He tried his limbs, then shook his head. "I think I've got some broken bones." He made a second effort and passed out.

"Come on, Jacovic," said Cole, stepping forward. "Give me a hand with him."

"Be careful, sir," said Briggs's voice. "I just checked his ship's registration, and it's a phony."

The two of them managed to get him through the hatch and into the *Teddy R*, where Luthor Chadwick and Braxite were waiting with an airsled.

"Do you think he'll make it, sir?" asked Rachel, who had just come onto the bridge to replace Christine.

"I hope so," said Cole. "Anyone who's an enemy of the Navy's is automatically a friend of ours." He paused thoughtfully. "Good-looking kid. I wonder who he is and where he comes from?"

He would find out before long.

They spent only a few hours on Freeport, since they were acutely aware of the fact that the Navy ships had almost certainly reported that they were in full flight after the young man's ship, and then had failed to report back or answer any signals that might have been sent to them. Cole wanted to leave the young man on Freeport, but he had a feeling they'd turn him over to the Republic the second a Navy ship showed up and started asked questions, so the *Teddy R* took him along in the infirmary. His ship was too badly damaged to save, so they sent it hurtling into the sun.

Cole decided to hit some of the larger Frontier worlds on the way back to port, and managed to recruit ships and crews on Binder X, Greenveldt, Ranchero, New Kenya, and Desdemona IV. There was a very modern hospital on New Kenya, but his patient asked to be taken to Singapore Station, and since his condition had stabilized Cole consented.

Cole was sitting in the mess hall, nursing a beer and trying to decide which world to try next, when Jacovic approached him.

"Hi," said Cole. "Have a seat."

The Teroni sat down opposite him. "I am afraid I have some bad news, sir."

"Forget the 'sir,'" said Cole. "I'm captain of a ship. You were Commander of the entire Fifth Teroni Fleet."

"That was then, this is now," replied Jacovic.

Cole sighed deeply. "Okay, so what's the bad news?"

"We have received word from the Platinum Duke that we've lost another twelve ships."

"Lost them?" repeated Cole, frowning.

"They have left our service in search of more profitable ventures."

"Well, I can't say that I blame them," answered Cole. "There sure as hell aren't any *less* profitable ventures. And," he added, "we *did* pick up another twenty-six ships since we left the station." He paused. "I think it's probably time to go back to Singapore Station and remind some of these people that they pledged to work with us, that the time when they could just pick up their gear and leave was over a few weeks ago."

"It wouldn't hurt to turn our young patient over to a hospital either," said Jacovic. "We're really not equipped to handle some of his injuries here."

"He's a tough kid. Never complains. If I had a son, I'd want one like that—only maybe a little bit more talkative."

"Has he got a name?"

"Ten or fifteen of them," replied Cole. "He doesn't answer to any of them, but that's how many passport disks and matching IDs he was carrying around with him."

"It makes him sound like a thief," noted Jacovic.

"Out here on the Frontier that's almost an honorable profession," said Cole. "At least when they take something they use some degree of subtlety. I never saw the Republic show such sensitivity for others." Cole paused thoughtfully. "I wonder what he needed ten passports for? I'd have thought two or three would be sufficient."

"We could ask."

Cole shook his head. "The poor kid's been through enough already. Best to get him to the hospital on the station. We can talk to him later. He's not going to get up and walk out anytime soon, not with those broken legs."

Wxakgini found a couple of favorable wormholes, and they docked at Singapore Station in another nine hours. Cole and Jacovic oversaw the unloading of their patient. Then, joined by David Copperfield, they went to Duke's Place, where Val was already ensconced at a card table and about half of the crew was either gambling or drinking or both.

"Welcome home," said the Platinum Duke. "I trust you had a successful trip?"

"We recruited some ships and shot down some other ships," said Cole. "We're satisfied with both."

"This calls for a bottle of my finest liquor," said the Duke. He gave a terse order to a robot, and a moment later it returned with four drinks on a silver tray.

"I do not imbibe," said Jacovic.

"No problem," said Cole. "If this is half as good as the Duke says, I'll have yours too."

"Take a taste, Wilson," urged the Duke. "Tell me what you think."

Cole took a sip. "Is this what I think it is?"

The Duke grinned. "Seven-hundred-year-old Scotch whiskey from Earth itself. I bring it out once a year."

"If there was enough of this around, I'm surprised they stayed sober long enough to develop space travel. Or even the wheel."

"I'm glad you approve."

"So do I," said Copperfield. "Smell the bouquet."

"I think you're supposed to smell wines, or maybe brandies," said Cole.

"That's how little you know," said Copperfield. The little alien, who couldn't metabolize a drop of it, held the glass up to his nose again. "Exquisite."

"I hear we had some defections," said Cole.

"They're gone, Wilson. Unless you want to go out after them, I think you're better off just forgetting them."

"They're not worth the effort to bring them back," agreed Cole. "If all they're after is money, I can't count on them when the chips are down."

"And they may be down sooner than we had anticipated," added Jacovic. "We *assume* that the Navy ships didn't recognize us and get off a message before we destroyed them, but we don't *know* it. And of course, we sent one of our shuttles down to Freeport to recruit help; someone could have told the Navy we were there at the time, and they may already have figured out that we are responsible for the loss of their ships."

"And if that's so," added Cole, "we could get visitors before too long."

"Then why are we wasting time talking?" demanded the Duke. "We should be fortifying the station's defenses!"

Cole chuckled. "They won't be here quite that fast."

"They'd better not be," muttered the Duke. Then: "Did you ever find out why the Navy was chasing that young man?"

Cole shook his head. "He seems to have been a thief, but that still doesn't explain anything."

"I'm not following you," said the Duke.

"He has *too* many identities, more than any thief needs. And if he's a thief, what did he steal? We didn't find anything in his ship. And also, if he'd stolen something of value, the Navy would have tried to get it back. You don't do that by blowing his ship apart at near light speeds."

"Ah!" said the Duke, his face lighting up. "A puzzle inside a riddle inside an enigma!"

"It'll remain one of life's little mysteries," said Cole. "At least until he's strong enough to tell me about it."

"*Will* he tell you, I wonder?"

"Why not?" replied Cole. "We saved his life."

"Gratitude is not one of the most common virtues out here on the Frontier," said the Duke.

"Well, there's no sense worrying about it or arguing it," said Cole. "We'll talk to him when he's well, and we'll find out." He paused. "Those were damned good forgeries, those passports."

Val walked over to the table just then.

"What are you guys drinking?" she asked.

"Awful stuff," said Cole. "You'd hate it."

She laughed. "It's *that* good? Pour me a glass."

"Have mine," said Jacovic.

She took it, downed the contents in a single swallow, and put the glass back on the table.

"Tastes nice and warm going down," she said. "What is it?"

"Scotch from old Earth," said the Duke. "Come to work for me and you can have the rest of the bottle."

"Not much of a trade," said Val. "I can finish the bottle in five minutes."

"That's sacrilegious!" exclaimed Copperfield.

"Control yourself, David," said Val, who seemed vastly amused by the little alien's outburst. "You'll have a stroke."

He glared at her but made no reply, and a moment later she headed back to the tables.

Cole stuck around another half hour, then decided it was time to return to the ship and get some sleep.

"Can I offer you one for the road?" asked the Duke.

"The road is only a quarter mile out on Dock H, but what the hell . . ."

The Duke poured him one last drink, and he took a small swallow.

"This is mighty fine stuff," said Cole. "It makes me think I should shoot a couple of Navy ships out of the sky just to get another drink."

Suddenly a hush fell on the room. Croupiers stopped their patter, gamblers stopped speaking, drinkers stopped drinking, and all eyes turned toward the front door, where the huge figure of the Octopus, unaccompanied by any of his bodyguards, had just entered. He looked around, spotted Cole, and began walking to his table.

He'd gotten two-thirds of the way there when he found Val blocking his path.

"That's as far as you go," she said, though her expression said she'd love for him to go one step farther.

"I don't want you," said the Octopus. "I just want to talk to your boss."

She shook her head. "No way."

He very gently, very carefully pulled out his burner and his screecher and handed them to her, butts first.

"You hold these until I'm done."

Whatever Val had expected, that wasn't it. She turned questioningly to Cole.

"It's okay," he said. "Let him pass."

She looked her disappointment, but stepped aside as the Octopus continued to make his way to the Duke's table.

"We meet again," said Cole when the huge bald man came to a stop in front of him.

"That we do, Wilson Cole."

"I assume from what you said that you've come here to talk to me?"

"That is correct," said the Octopus.

"Okay, I'm here," said Cole. "What's the problem?"

"I don't come with a problem, but with an offer."

Cole frowned. "What kind of offer?"

"Eleven days ago you saved a young man from an attack by two Navy ships."

"That's right," said Cole. "Jacovic and I dropped him off at the hospital as soon as we landed."

"And you have no idea as to his true identity?"

"None."

"That young man is my son," said the Octopus. "I've just been to see him."

"Well, now I know why the passports and IDs looked so good," said Cole. "I'm glad we could do you a service."

"A service?" the Octopus half-yelled. "The Republic killed my wife and two of my children. This boy is all I have left."

"Then I'm doubly glad we got to him."

"Captain Cole, I'm told you have vowed to drive the Navy out of the Inner Frontier. Is that correct?"

Cole nodded. "Yes, it is."

"It'll never work. You can't patrol the Frontier with only forty ships."

"I've got double that now."

"Forty, eighty, it's the same thing!" said the Octopus with a snort of contempt. He paused for just an instant. "How does a fleet of four hundred sound?"

"Impressive," said Cole cautiously.

"Good." He turned to the room at large and raised his voice. "Because Wilson Cole saved my son, I am putting myself and my entire fleet under his command." Suddenly he grinned, picked a glass off the table, and held it high above his head. "Now let's go kick some Republic ass!"

"So what was the kid doing with all those passports and IDs?" asked Cole.

He and the Octopus were sitting in the Duke's private office. Val stood just outside the door to make sure no one interrupted them, and if anyone had been considering it, the look on her face instantly dissuaded them.

"He was on a mission for me," said the Octopus, puffing on a smokeless cigar. "As good as those forgeries were, someone saw through one on Freeport. He'd never have made it if you hadn't intervened."

"We were happy to be able to take out a couple of the Navy's ships," said Cole. "The fact that we also saved your son was just an added bonus." He paused. "He sure as hell doesn't *look* like any kin of yours."

"The hands," said the Octopus, indicating the six hands growing out of his sides. "Obviously they don't breed on. I suppose that makes me a freak rather than a mutation." He shrugged. "Just as well for the boy. I put up with a lot of shit about these hands while I was growing up."

"What's his name?" asked Cole. "I can't keep on calling him 'the kid' forever."

"Jonah."

"That's not a name you hear very often."

"Well, since I'm the Octopus, it had to be a seafaring name. I toyed with Ahab, but he *lost* his battle with the whale. I figure Jonah fought his whale to a draw, which is fitting and proper. I want a son as powerful and competent as I am, but I acknowledge no one as my superior, not even my own flesh and blood."

"I thought you were taking orders from me," said Cole.

"That is my own choice. If you had insisted, you'd have another war on your hands."

"Good thing you volunteered, then," said Cole, sipping the drink he'd brought with him.

"It'll be a good fit," replied the Octopus. "You know the Navy and its machinations better than I do, and I know killing and slaughtering at least as well as you do."

"We're not in the killing and slaughtering business," said Cole, "at least not in the long run. We just want to convince the Navy that it's less expensive in terms of lives and vessels to stay out of the Frontier."

"Well, it'll be fun while it lasts."

"You sound like you think it's going to be over relatively soon," noted Cole.

"Probably."

"I don't anticipate an easy victory, not against the Navy."

"Neither do I," said the Octopus. "I figure we'll pick them off one and two at a time until we've got them really annoyed, and then one morning the sky is going to be black with Navy ships."

Cole shook his head. "Not while they're fighting against the Teroni Federation."

"Maybe they'll decide that five thousand ships can take a day or two off from the war."

"They won't," said Cole. "But even if they do, we know the Inner Frontier better than they do. We can lead them a merry chase for a month if we have to. And if they split up, we can also lead them into some pretty deadly traps."

"I'd bet you a couple of thousand Maria Theresa dollars or

Republic credits on whether or not they come in force, but I'd be betting against my own survival, so I think it's in my best interest to assume you're right." He took another puff of his cigar. "You damned well better be, or I'll haunt you from the grave."

"If I'm wrong," replied Cole, "you won't have far to look. I'll be in the next grave."

The Octopus chuckled and poured himself a drink. "I *like* you, Wilson Cole. I knew I would from the first second we met."

"I'm kind of fond of you too," said Cole. "Now that that's over with, tell me about Jonah. What was he doing that he needed all those passports?"

"I sent him into the Republic to learn the schedules of some of the major cruise and cargo lines that serve the Inner Frontier," said the Octopus. "There's half a dozen rewards out for me, so I couldn't go myself. I mean, I don't care what I rigged the passport disks to read, they'd take one look at me and know who I was. So I sent Jonah. His job was to hire on at one of the companies and stick around long enough to get its schedule for the coming year. I've got some people who you'd swear are half computer, and they schooled him well."

"I know the type," said Cole, thinking of Christine and Briggs.

"Anyway, as soon as he got what he needed he was to resign—poor health, family emergency, whatever reason he thought they'd buy. I didn't want him just vanishing, or they'd figure out why he was there and change their schedules."

"That explains *one* passport," said Cole. "What about all the others?"

"I didn't want to risk his hiring on at a second company on the same world, so his task was to hit seven or eight more worlds, spend a week or two on each after he hired on, hacked into the computer, and then resigned. If anyone got suspicious, I didn't want them tracing his movements, so he had a different ID for each world. Finally, when he had everything he needed—we didn't want to risk his transmitting it via subspace radio—he was to come back to my base." The Octopus grimaced. "Freeport was only his fourth world. Either the passport had a flaw, or their security is a hell of a lot better than the other worlds'. Anyway, whatever he stole is still in his ship. I trust you had the good sense to destroy it?"

"Of course," replied Cole. "We didn't have time to search the ship very thoroughly, and if there *was* anything of value in it we sure as hell didn't want the Republic to get their hands on it."

"Whatever there was is better lost," said the Octopus. "I'm out of the warlord and criminal trade, and into the revolution business."

"We're not revolting against anyone," said Cole.

"Who the hell do you think owns all the ships we're going to destroy?" demanded the Octopus.

"The Republic," answered Cole. "But we're not trying to overthrow their government. We're just trying to enforce our decree that the Inner Frontier is off-limits to them. Believe me, that'll be hard enough." He finished his drink. "I want to see your forger as soon as we can arrange it."

"What for?"

"I want him to make up a couple of passports and IDs for me."

"You're going into the Republic?" asked the Octopus.

Cole nodded. "Yes."

"What the hell for?"

"I've got to get into a Navy base and see how they schedule their patrols on the Frontier," answered Cole.

"You can't cancel them," said the Octopus. "They're committed to plundering the Frontier."

"No, I can't cancel them," agreed Cole. "But maybe I can change the schedule enough to send them to where three or four hundred ships are waiting for them."

"I *like* that idea!" said the Octopus, grinning.

"I thought you might."

Suddenly the grin vanished. "It won't work. You can't get away with it."

"Why not? It worked for Jonah. Well, on his first three worlds, anyway."

"Yeah, but he's a kid who was born on the Inner Frontier; they have no record of him. You're Wilson Cole, the most wanted man in the Republic. Every spaceport, every customs station, every immigration station has your photo, your fingerprints, your DNA, your bone structure, everything. My forger is as good as they come, but he can't control what the Republic's already got."

"There are ways around it," said Cole. "I entered the Republic twice during the time we were pirates."

"The fact that you did so probably means whatever ruse you tried won't work again. More to the point, even if you can land on a world, and avoid customs or fake your way through immigration, that's the easy part. You want to gain access to a Navy base during wartime, and to get into their heavily guarded computer system. How are you going to do that?"

"Just take me to your forger," said Cole.

The Octopus stared at him. "Okay, you thought of all that," he said at last. "And you still think you can get to the computer?"

"Yeah, I think so," said Cole.

"All by yourself?"

"No," answered Cole. "You're going to help me."

The Octopus ushered Cole into the small office two levels below Duke's Place.

"So he works right here on Singapore Station?" said Cole.

"Why not?" replied the Octopus. "You see any police around?"

"No," said Cole. "I also don't see a master forger."

"He'll be here. He knows I'm bringing you."

As if on cue, the door opened and a strange-looking alien entered the office. He was about five feet tall and so stocky he literally waddled, though Cole had a feeling he wasn't carrying an ounce of fat. His fingers were as long and thin as his body was short and stout. His mouth was clearly not shaped for human languages, and indeed he wore a T-pack—a translator mechanism—around his neck. His nostrils were two slits in the middle of his face, his ears were bell shaped and capable of independent motion—but his most outstanding features were his eyes: bright red, and fully two inches in diameter.

"Picasso, say hello to Wilson Cole."

"Your reputation precedes you, Captain Cole," said the alien, his translated voice coming out in a flat, emotionless, mechanical monotone.

"Yours doesn't extend much beyond this room," said Cole, "which I imagine is an advantage in your line of work."

"I have recognition and acclaim among those who require my services," said Picasso. "That will have to suffice. We cannot all be as famous as my namesake."

"I gave him his name," said the Octopus with a touch of pride. "No one except another member of his race can pronounce his real one."

"What can I do for you, Captain Cole?" asked Picasso.

"I need two passports and two IDs. My face is on wanted posters all the hell over the Republic, so when you run a holo, add a beard and mustache. I'll start growing them today."

"Forget that. It's too obvious. We'll begin by temporarily changing your eye color. I'll give you some pills that will take most of the color out of your skin and add more wrinkles than you can imagine to your face. The effect will vanish two days after you stop taking the pills. And since we're aging your skin by twenty or thirty years, we'll dye your hair gray as well."

"Are there any side effects from the pills?" asked Cole. "I'm going to need all my senses, and I may have to move fast."

"None at all," said Picasso. "I shall also need certain data."

"Shoot."

"To begin with, height, weight, age, scars, any previous broken bones that will show up on a scan."

"No problem," replied Cole. "What about dental records?"

"Yes, I was coming to that," said Picasso.

Cole spent the next fifteen minutes giving the alien what he wanted. He then allowed Picasso to take a skin scraping so that his DNA would agree with the reading on his passport.

"Name three worlds within the Republic that you have visited, either in your capacity as an officer or even as a tourist."

"Deluros VIII, Pollux IV, and Goldenrod."

"I'll have your passport show them as your three most recent ports of call," said Picasso.

"Just a minute," said Cole. "There's no naval base on Pollux. Change it to Spica VI."

"All right," said the alien, making a note.

"When will they be ready?" asked Cole.

"Two days," replied Picasso. "And I must take your holo for your ID before you leave—in a military uniform, of course, but preferably of a lower rank than captain or commander."

Cole shook his head. "I'll be back later for that."

"It will only take a few seconds."

"I know. I'll be back." He paused. "Are we done now?"

"Yes."

"I'll see you in a couple of hours."

Cole walked out the door, accompanied by the Octopus.

"Let me make an educated guess," said the Octopus. "You're going back to your ship."

"That's right."

"And you're going to get into your naval uniform."

"Wrong," said Cole.

"Wrong?" said the Octopus, surprised.

"I'm going to borrow someone else's uniform."

"Oh, of course," said the Octopus. "You don't want to be identified as a captain. It would be too easy for them to find out that you were a doppelgänger."

Cole smiled. "You're quick on the uptake."

"Well, I *am* a devious criminal kingpin," said the Octopus.

"The trick," continued Cole, "is to find one of the smaller ships. It would strain credulity for me to be the only survivor of a crew of thirty, and to be able to bring the ship back to port on my own."

"Strain it?" laughed the Octopus. "It would shatter it into a million pieces."

"I figure a six-man job, eight at the most. And we'll have to find some way to kill or capture the crew without harming the ship too badly."

"You can't capture them and then have them take you to their base, you know. Being the only survivor is one thing; being the only passenger is another."

"I don't really want to show up with five or six corpses," said Cole. "They'll spend all their time debriefing me. I'd much rather land with six or seven men in need of immediate medical attention."

"There are a *lot* of naval bases, even on the outskirts of the Republic," said the Octopus. "Are you sure you can find your way back to the right one?"

"I was an officer in that goddamned Navy for my entire adult life," said Cole. "And the Republic doesn't waste new ships on the Frontier. Whatever ship we capture, I'll be able to read its log and its directives, and if it's small enough I should even be able to pilot it alone."

"You could take one or two of your men with you, just to be on the safe side," suggested the Octopus.

"No," said Cole. "There would be more chance of making a mistake once we landed. There'd be three times the likelihood that one of us would be spotted, and of course there's a chance that we'd tell contradictory accounts during isolated debriefings." He shook his head. "No, there are just too many things that could go wrong."

"When you said earlier that I was going to help you, I assume you mean you want me to help you disable the ship and capture the crew?"

"Right." Suddenly Cole smiled. "I hope you weren't thinking I wanted you to come along. I don't think any amount of work by Picasso can get you in the front door of the Republic."

"It depends on where the door is. I'm not as notorious as you are— at least, not within the Republic."

"You just take care of the ship, and I'll handle the rest," said Cole. "I'd have the *Teddy R* take care of it ourselves, but there's every likelihood they'll get off an SOS or two, and I don't want them identifying us. That's the one thing that *could* get a few hundred ships out here in a hurry—the chance of capturing or killing the *Teddy R*. Let them report any other ship and it only enhances my story when I bring a crippled ship and a wounded crew back to port."

"Sounds good. But I've still got a question."

"Go ahead."

"Let's assume that everything goes the way you want, we disable the ship, we shoot up the crew but leave most of them alive, you enter the naval base unchallenged, you even get the information you need." The Octopus paused. "How are you going to get back out here?"

"I'll have to assess the situation when I'm ready to leave."

"I thought commanding officers were always supposed to have an exit strategy."

"I've got three or four," answered Cole. "I won't know which is the likeliest to succeed until after I'm there."

They reached the trams, and Cole took one out to the *Teddy R*. He decided that Luthor Chadwick was approximately his size, and sought out the young man, who was watching a holo in his cabin.

"Sir?" said Chadwick.

"I need a favor, Luthor," sand Cole.

"What can I do for you, sir?"

"You can loan me one of your old sergeant's uniforms from when you were stationed on Timos III."

"My sergeant's uniform?" repeated Chadwick, frowning.

"You've still got it, don't you?"

"Yes, sir. But . . ."

"I probably won't be returning it," said Cole as Chadwick went to a compartment and pulled it out. "Let me know how much I owe you."

"Nothing, sir," said Chadwick. "I was never going to wear it again."

"Then thanks," said Cole, taking the outfit from him. "Much appreciated."

Cole left the puzzled young man and went to his own cabin. He was about to change into the uniform to make sure it fit when Sharon Blacksmith entered the room.

"I take it we no longer believe in knocking," said Cole.

"All right, Wilson, cut the bullshit and tell me what's going on."

Cole sighed. "What the hell, I'm not going to be able to keep it from you much longer anyway. I'll soon be masquerading as a noncommissioned officer in the Republic's Navy."

"Where?"

"On a small ship that we will briefly incapacitate and use for our purposes."

"Who is 'we'?"

"Us. Our side in this conflict."

"You're going to pose as a member of the military and sneak into the Republic," she said accusingly.

"I'm not *sneaking* in," he corrected her. "I'm walking in bold as brass."

"Maybe you'd better tell me the whole thing," said Sharon.

He laid out his plan to her, half-surprised that she let him finish without yelling at him.

"Damn it, Wilson," she said when he was through, "how many times do you have to be reminded: the Captain doesn't leave his ship in enemy territory—and it doesn't get much more inimical than a Navy base."

"I have to go," he said. "There's no one else who knows what to look for, or what codes to use to access it. Four Eyes knew, but he's dead. Jacovic's never set foot in the Republic. Val was a pirate for the past dozen years before she joined us. Christine isn't cut out for this kind of work, and you know it. That takes care of my senior officers. Who do you recommend?"

"Send Malcolm or Luthor, or anyone else. We can't spare you."

"Rubbish. Jacovic has ten times the credentials I do. He was a Fleet Commander, for Christ's sake."

"This crew didn't leave their lives in the Republic behind and become outlaws for Jacovic," she replied. "We did it for *you*."

"I appreciate the sentiment, but there's no one else qualified to do this," insisted Cole. "I was a senior officer for fifteen years. I know the codes, I know the protocol, I know how to behave in the restricted areas, and once I gain access to the proper program I know how I want to change it. Look me in the eye and tell me that anyone on this or any other ship in our fleet has a better chance of success."

Sharon was silent for a long moment. Finally she spoke. "I've never asked before, but how old are you?"

"What's that got to do with anything?" he answered.

"*That* old?"

"I'm forty-one," he said begrudgingly.

"Don't you think you're getting a little long in the tooth for this kind of cloak-and-dagger shit?"

"The problem with twenty-two-year-old bodies," said Cole, "is that they come equipped with twenty-two-year-old brains. If any of them could do this, I'd let them."

"I don't believe that for a second, and neither do you." She stared at him. "But none of them *can* do it, can they?"

"No."

"Damn it," said Sharon. "Why couldn't I have fallen in love with Briggs or one of the others who never leave the ship except to drink and gamble?"

"Probably for the same reason I don't love someone as young and blonde and innocent as Rachel," said Cole with a smile. "We both have lousy taste."

"You just damned well better come back in one piece."

"Back is easy," he said. "One piece is a little harder." Suddenly he noticed tears rolling down her cheeks. "Hey, that was a joke."

"There's nothing funny about what you're doing, you stupid old man."

"Let's hope the Navy feels the same way."

He began taking off his tunic.

She laughed through her tears. "You really have to work on your timing, Wilson."

"I'm getting into Chadwick's uniform," he said. "I've got to pose for some holos in it for my passport disk and ID cube."

"Right now?"

He reached out and wiped a tear off her cheek.

"Oh, hell, I suppose it can wait another hour."

It was three days later when word came through. Cole, whose medication and dye job had added twenty-five years to his appearance, was having lunch with Sharon and David Copperfield in the mess hall when Rachel Marcos contacted him.

"Sir," she said, "the Octopus reports a sighting."

"Can you patch me through to him?"

"Yes, sir."

An instant later the image of the Octopus appeared before him.

"What've you got?" asked Cole.

"It looks like just what we've been waiting for," replied the Octopus. "A nine-man class-K ship, on a solo patrol. As far as we can tell there's not another Navy ship within a parsec."

"Sounds good," said Cole. "Where is it?"

"Out past New Bolivia. I don't know how long it will stay there, or where it's going next, so we'd better move fast."

"I'll have to check with our pilot to see how quickly we can get there."

"We're heading there even as I speak to you," said the Octopus. "Our pilot recommends the Bonetta Wormhole."

"I'll pass the word."

"If we get there first, I'm not going to wait for you," continued the Octopus. "I'm taking six ships with me, and calling in two from the general vicinity of New Ecuador, which is a light-year beyond New Bolivia. No sense letting this ship get away just because you're a few minutes late."

"Just remember: I want most of them alive, and I want the ship to be able to limp back to port."

"I know," said the Octopus. "Wormhole's coming up. It'll kill the transmission in another—"

The signal went dead as the wormhole swallowed up the Octopus's ship.

Cole took the airlift to the bridge and walked over to where Wxakgini hung suspended in his harness, attached to the navigational computer by long metallic tendrils that ran from the machine to his skull.

"Pilot, we've got to get to New Bolivia," announced Cole. "I'm told the Bonetta Wormhole is the quickest way."

"If it hasn't moved," replied Wxakgini. "It's very unstable. I'll have to check it out." There was a momentary silence. "It seems fine today. We'll use it."

"Transit time to New Bolivia?"

"Three hours and eleven minutes."

"Fine. Let's go."

"Sir," said Christina, "it will take an hour or more for all the crew to get back to the ship."

"We'll go without them. The Octopus is handling the shooting. All the *Teddy R* is doing is delivering me."

The ship took off for the wormhole, and Cole summoned Jacovic and Val to his office.

"I'm sure you're both aware of what's happening," he began.

"The freak spotted a Navy ship flying solo," said Val.

"Tactful as always," said Cole dryly. "We'll be entering a wormhole in a couple of minutes, and will emerge in or near the New Bolivia system in about three hours. The Octopus will already be there, along with seven or eight more ships. They should already have incapacitated the ship and done pretty much the same to the crew by the time we arrive."

Cole paused. "You both have some inkling of my plan. Jacovic, you're going to be in command of the *Teddy R* until such time as I return. Val, don't contradict him in front of the crew, even if he's wrong about something. And when he gives you an order, no arguing and no backtalk. You can get away with it with me because I've got a special relationship with the crew; most of them gave up everything they had back in the Republic to come to the Frontier with me. Jacovic is a newcomer, so don't tease him and don't hassle him; it will look like insubordination, not humor." He stared at her. "I mean it."

"I'm an officer aboard the *Teddy R*," said Val in hurt tones. "I know my duty."

This is a hell of time to show the first tender emotion I've ever seen from you, thought Cole. "All right," he said aloud. "Jacovic, you might as well start getting used to being the Captain. I'm turning over command to you as of this second."

The Teroni saluted. "I think I'll go to the bridge," he said. "I know we have eight other ships taking all the risk, but I want to make sure we can back them up if we have to." He paused. "Have you any objection to that, sir?"

"You're in charge," said Cole. "Who am I to challenge my captain's decisions?"

Jacovic left the office as Val surpressed a chuckle.

"What's so funny?" asked Cole.

"'Who am I to challenge my captain's decisions?'" she repeated with a smile. "As I understand it, that's exactly how you got to be Captain in the first place—by challenging your captain's decisions."

"This is what I was talking about, Val. I don't mind this kind of banter at all, but don't use it with Jacovic. He's a newcomer, and he's a member of a race that every one of us was trained to fight against. He's going to need all the support he can get."

"I know," she said.

"Fine. Now I've got to get Sharon down here."

"One last roll in the hay?" said Val. "I approve."

"You've got a single-track mind," said Cole. "She's got my pass-port, my ID, and my biography. And Val?"

"Yes?"

"I'm sorry if I hurt your feelings."

"That's what captains are for," she said, leaving the office.

Sharon arrived a few minutes later with his new identity.

He was Leslie Ainge, he was a sergeant, his home world was Roanoke II, and he was sixty-three years old. He was unmarried, he'd seen action in the Battle of Verona, he'd been decorated for bravery and busted for drunkenness. By the time he'd committed all the details to memory he felt that he could stand up under normal scrutiny, perhaps even a bit more.

He stayed in his office another hour, to give the bridge personnel time to get used to the fact that Jacovic was in command, then went down to the mess hall for a sandwich.

He pulled up an entertainment holo and watched it until Rachel contacted him and told him that they had emerged from the wormhole.

"What's the situation?" he asked.

"The . . . Mr. . . . the Octopus wants to speak to you."

"Fine. Put him through."

The Octopus's image suddenly appeared opposite Cole. "Are you ready to go to work?"

"That's what I'm here for," replied Cole. "How did it go?"

"Crew of nine. Three dead, six wounded, none fatally, but we bor-rowed some blood from the corpses and drenched the living with it. They look pretty awful."

"And the ship?"

"No way it will ever go light speeds again, but we can tow it to the Bassinger Wormhole, and that will let it off half a light-year from its base on Chambon V."

"How long will it take?" asked Cole.

"To get it to Chambon? Maybe two hours, using the wormhole."

"Will the wounded make it?"

"They're not that badly shot up," answered the Octopus. "And we can tranquilize them, or even put them out cold until you arrive."

Cole shook his head. "No. The medics would spot it in two seconds, and the last thing I need is to be pulled in for questioning. With a little luck I'll be out of debriefing before the patients are out of surgery, and I can lose myself on the base."

"One good thing," said the Octopus. "From what we can tell, there are close to thirty thousand men and aliens stationed at Chambon V. You just might sneak through. I was worried that with such a small ship and crew it might be the kind of minor-league outpost where everyone knows everyone else."

"Okay," said Cole. "I'm going to instruct my pilot to approach the ship. Just before we get there, find some way to knock out the survivors without killing them."

"We'll just lower their oxygen," said the Octopus. "They don't have that much as it is." A pause. "Why do you want them unconscious?"

"If they see me entering the ship, at least one of them's going to remember it long enough to mention it to the debriefers. Better to have them wake up after I've got the ship moving and have taken control; they're wounded, they're groggy, they're a bit oxygen-deprived; they'll see a guy in a Republic uniform, and then they should go back to worrying about their own injuries."

"And you're sure that'll work?" asked the Octopus dubiously.

"It has to," said Cole. "The only alternative is to kill them."

The *Teddy R* reached the wounded Navy ship a few minutes later, and Cole prepared to transfer to the ship.

"One last thing," he said.

"What is it?" asked the Octopus.

"We need a code word, a recognition signal," replied Cole. "Assuming I live through this, I'm almost certainly going to have to steal a Navy ship, or at least a ship registered in the Republic, and I don't want you blowing me out of the sky when I'm trying to get home."

"So pick a code word."

"Four Eyes," said Cole.

"Somehow I'm not surprised," said the Octopus. "Okay, by the time I get back to Singapore Station, every ship in our fleet will know it."

"Thanks," said Cole. "Here's hoping I don't need it."

And it was almost as if the cynical God of Overconfident Spacemen grinned and said: *Well, you can hope.*

Cole waited for Wxakgini to maneuver the *Teddy R* next to the Navy ship. When the hatch on the shuttle bay was opposite the main hatch of the wounded vessel, it extended until the two met, then bonded and slid back both doors. He stepped through, ordered the smaller ship's hatch to seal, and then the *Teddy R* slowly pulled away.

Cole looked around the ship. There were four cabins, and he assumed the wounded crewmen were in their bunks. He walked to the command section—it was too small to call it a bridge. The control panel showed that the ship was being towed toward the Bassinger Wormhole, and he spent the next few minutes acquainting himself with controls, though they differed only in minor respects from any other class-K ship he'd been on. He found that its name was the *Polar Star*, and it had been commissioned thirty-one years ago.

He checked the weaponry, and quickly contacted the Octopus.

"Problems already?" asked the huge man. "I'd have sworn they were all sleeping tranquilly."

"No, no problems," said Cole. "But I see that they never fired a shot. I think it'll make a better story when I get back to base if I say we killed a ship or two. I don't want to get court-martialed for recklessly endangering Republic property *or* for cowardice in the face of enemy fire."

"So jettison some ammunition."

"No, I'm going to fire it into space. When they examine the ship, I want them to know the weapons have been fired, and recently. I just wanted to alert you and the other ships so you don't think the wounded crew has overpowered me and started shooting."

"All right," said the Octopus. "Give me about thirty seconds, and then fire away. Damn, you think of everything!"

"Well, when God shorts me in the hands department, I have to compensate with a little brainpower," answered Cole.

The Octopus emitted a huge peal of laughter. "I knew I liked you, Wilson Cole! Now fire your cannons, because we're going to dump you in the wormhole in about five minutes, and you don't want to be firing weapons in there the way those holes twist back into themselves."

Cole fired each of his cannons three or four times.

"That should do it," he said.

"Then we're going to take our leave of you," said the Octopus. "Your trajectory will put you in the wormhole in about three and a half minutes, and the ship's not so badly damaged that you won't be able to make adjustments if you have to."

"Thanks."

"Good luck! We'll see you back at Singapore Station."

Cole looked at the viewscreen. He'd never seen a wormhole. Theoretically no one had, though he had his suspicions about Wxakgini and other members of the Bdxeni race. But as he approached it, suddenly everything seemed to shimmer, and just as he entered it it looked like the entire universe was losing its structural integrity. Then he was inside it, everything seemed normal again, and the brighter stars were visible as if through a translucent veil of darkness.

He instructed the navigational computer to alert him just before they left the wormhole and entered normal space again, then went back to the cabins to check on the wounded crew.

They were pretty badly shot up, and he knew no one was going to grill him over tranquilizing them. He looked at them again and sighed. They were all so *young*. This one could be Rachel, that one could be Chadwick, this other could be Morales, the kid he'd lost during a pirate operation. Didn't they have even a single mature officer who knew his way around, who wouldn't blunder into a trap like the one the Octopus had laid for the *Polar Star*? But of course they didn't, or he wouldn't be standing here, in possession of a Navy ship and staring at the wounded bodies that used to run it.

He found the cargo area where the three dead crewmen were stashed, borrowed some blood from a sergeant to splash on his face and uniform, memorized the corpse's ID, and then jettisoned him into the wormhole. Maybe he could pass muster with his phony passport and ID and maybe he couldn't—but he'd never get through if they started counting bodies and realized the ship had left with a crew of nine and returned with ten.

He went back to the command area, inserted his Leslie Ainge ID on the duty roster and deleted the jettisoned crewman, then called up what the data banks had on the base at Chambon V. It was big, bigger than he'd thought, and security was tight—but he was going to be escorted to precisely where he wanted to be, well inside the security perimeter. He managed to find a holo of the base, but it was an architect's vision, not a finished product. He was sure the streets and buildings and walkways were exactly as depicted, but nothing was identified. He could pick out the enlisted men's barracks, and a large mess hall, and of course the landing fields and parade grounds, but there were another fifteen large buildings that seemed almost interchangeable. Since he couldn't know which structure he wanted, he concentrated on learning escape routes.

Finally the *Polar Star* was spit out of the wormhole and entered normal space, and within less than a minute it was surrounded by half a dozen Navy ships.

Suddenly the image of a naval officer popped up in front of him.

"What the hell happened here?" it demanded.

"We were ambushed on the Frontier," said Cole.

Dumb! he thought. *I should be bandaged and covered with blood. Now they've got an extra half hour to study my face and see if my voiceprint matches anyone in their files—like Wilson Cole. I can't believe it; I'm out of the wormhole thirty seconds and I've already blundered.*

"Was it the *Theodore Roosevelt?*" asked the officer.

"I think so, yes."

"Where is the rest of the crew?"

"We took a lot of casualties, sir." *Did I call him "sir" before? I don't think so. Did he notice?* "Six wounded and in their bunks, two others dead."

"How about yourself? Any wounds?"

"Something cracked into my head," said Cole. "I'm pretty groggy. I'll be all—"

Cole fell to the floor.

Okay, now you can't study my face. It serves another purpose, too. If I'm unconscious, you have to tow the ship and I don't have to guide it to the right spot at the landing field.

He could hear the voices from the nearest ship.

"For three years he wasn't worth the effort to hunt him down. I think now maybe he is."

"What the hell does he want? He kept clear of us all this time, and suddenly it's like he's taunting us."

"That son of a bitch isn't going to get away with this! He may think he's safe out there on the Frontier, but we'll hunt him down like the goddamned mutineer that he is."

Cole spent the next few minutes listening to all the hideous things the Republic was going to do to the captain of the *Teddy R* when they finally caught up with him. Then they touched down, and he and the six survivors were rushed to the base hospital and taken to a series of linked emergency rooms.

Cole pretended to return to consciousness and soon found himself alone in a room with an aging medic who immediately began examining him.

"I'm not wounded," said Cole. "I just got my head banged up against a bulkhead when one of the pulse blasts hit."

"I'll be the judge of that, Sergeant," said the doctor, hooking him up to a number of machines.

"I want to get back to my quarters. A good night's sleep and I'm sure I'll be fine."

"Pulse, normal. Blood pressure, normal. Heart, normal. Lungs, normal. No abrasions to the face or the skull. Coordination seems unhindered."

The doctor checked another dozen readings. Then, just as Cole was sure he was about to be dismissed, the medic frowned. "That's curious," he said.

"What is?"

"Your retina. It doesn't match any we have on record."

"I was just transferred here the day before we took off," said Cole, glad that the pulse machine was already disconnected.

"It's got to be in the computer somewhere," said the doctor. "What was your name again?"

"I'll give you my ID," said Cole. It gave him an excuse to get off the examining table and onto his feet as he reached into a pocket and pulled out his false identification.

The doctor held it up for the machine to scan.

"There's no record of you, Sergeant Ainge," he said, frowning. "I'd better call Security and let them figure this out."

"Here," said Cole. "This will explain everything."

He reached out to hand his passport to the medic, faked a spell of dizziness, and let it fall to the floor as the doctor reached out for it. The doctor leaned over to pick it up off the floor, and Cole brought the edge of his hand down hard on the back of the older man's neck. The doctor collapsed without a sound.

Cole knew he couldn't escape attention in his blood-spattered uniform. He made sure the doctor was still breathing, then removed his uniform, got into it, and let himself out into a corridor. It was empty for the moment, since the emergency teams were working on the six wounded crew members, and he walked in the opposite direction from which he had entered.

He knew he only had a few minutes before someone checked on him or the doctor awoke. It didn't make sense that there would be just one location for the information he wanted, not the way these bases were wired from end to end and attached to a master computer. He left the medical building, walked at a normal pace to the next building, saluted a pair of officers who passed him going the other direction, decided he had time to go another forty yards to the next building—if and when they began looking for him they'd of course start with the nearest building—and soon entered a complex, multileveled structure.

He walked through the lobby, saluted everyone he saw, acted as if he had every right to be there, and took an airlift up three levels. He stepped out, headed down an angular corridor, looked into the windows of each office he passed, and finally came to an empty one.

He tested the door, found that it was unlocked, entered, closed it behind him—he wanted to lock it, but didn't know the voice codes—and activated the computer.

It was password-protected. Christina had given him a crash course on getting around the protection, and he was sure she could have done it in seconds, but it took him long, agonizing minutes before he breached the computer's security. After that, it was easy enough to find the information he needed and begin changing it, because it was the same system the Republic had been using when the *Teddy R* was still a part of it rather than its number one enemy.

After a few minutes he hid his electronic footprints as Christina had taught him, deactivated the machine, walked back out into the corridor, and began making his way to the exit. It was going better than he'd anticipated. All he had to do was get to one of the hangars, commandeer a small one-man or two-man job, and take off before anyone knew what was happening.

He heard a commotion at the medical building and knew they'd found the medic he'd knocked out. He headed in the opposite direction, resisting the urge to break into a run and remembering to salute all the officers he passed. He knew that a base as large as this would have more than one hangar, and finally he turned a corner and saw one.

There were no Security personnel standing guard, which he found surprising and a little disconcerting. Still, the noise from the medical building was starting to spread and get a little closer, which meant they were looking for him, and *that* meant that he didn't have time to pick and choose. It would have to be this hangar, and whatever ship was inside it.

He walked to the entrance, took one look back to make sure no one was following him, and entered the building.

Suddenly a shrill siren went off. All the doors closed, locks slid into place, windows were covered by titanium panels, and a mechanical voice spoke out: "There is a virus infecting these premises. It is human, male, five feet nine inches tall, one hundred sixty-two pounds, unarmed. Assistance is called for."

"*Shit!*" muttered Cole. "We didn't have systems like this five years ago!"

He knew he had a minute at most. He looked around, saw that the closest ship was a four-man vessel, raced over to it, climbed into it, activated the power, and checked for weaponry. He found it had only a Level 1 pulse cannon, which wasn't appreciably more powerful than a pulse pistol, though it has a far greater range.

He knew the door would be reinforced, so he swiveled the ship on its base, aimed the cannon at a wall that he hoped was not composed of anything with a tight molecular bonding, fired the weapon and gunned the accelerator at the same time, and hoped the wall had vanished in the quarter-second it was going to take him to reach it.

Cole half-expected to crash into the wall, but it was gone a microsecond before he reached it. He skimmed a few hundred feet above the planet's surface until he was well clear of the base, then shot up toward the stratosphere. He couldn't believe that he hadn't been shot down yet, but evidently no one had expected him either to be in the hangar or to fly out of it. The first few laser beams just barely missed him as he made it out of the stratosphere and could finally accelerate to light speeds without burning up from the friction of the atmosphere.

He knew that they'd expect him to head for the Inner Frontier, and he also knew he didn't have the speed to evade them, the defenses to survive their attack, or the firepower to hold them at bay. He aimed the ship deeper into the Republic, had the navigational computer produce a holo of the sector he was in, and looked for a likely place to land and acquire a less recognizable ship.

Serena II was the closest inhabited planet, but it was a thinly populated farming world. The next two oxygen planets were mining worlds. He needed something bigger, something where he could ditch this ship and obtain a new one—and where he could hide if he had to. He hit upon Piccoli III, a world with ninety-eight percent Standard gravity, a normal oxygen content, and a commercial center housing some three hundred thousand men and a few thousand aliens of various species, and laid in a course for it.

He was sure that the Navy was in hot pursuit, but at light speeds his instruments couldn't spot them and his viewscreens couldn't display them. He found the proper wormhole, entered it, and moments later emerged in the Piccoli system. He immediately headed to Piccoli III, and soon entered the atmosphere.

"Computer," he said, "where's the eject mechanism?"

"*I am not equipped with an eject mechanism.*"

"Wonderful," muttered Cole. "Is there a parachute on this damned ship?"

"*No.*"

"You have to have *some* safety feature," said Cole. "What is the crew supposed to do if you're disabled or shot down in a battle?"

"*I possess four suits for deep-space usage, and four jet packs for use in atmospheres.*"

"Where are the jet packs?"

The ship directed him to the proper storage area. He removed one and put it on, then found a laser pistol in the small armory and bonded it to his right thigh.

"Can your sensors find an area that has no human habitation within ten miles of it?"

"*There is a mountain range at 37 degrees 18 minutes 4 seconds north and—*"

"That'll do," said Cole. "Enter the atmosphere, head toward it, and let me know when you're within sixty seconds of reaching it."

The ship was silent for almost three minutes. Then: "*I am now within sixty seconds of the mountain range.*"

"Open the hatch."

The hatch opened.

"I want you to crash into the mountains," said Cole.

"*I cannot comply with that order. I am compelled to protect my own existence.*"

"That's a Priority R1 order."

"I will crash in 42 seconds."

Cole leaped out of the hatch. He was at about fifteen thousand feet, and he activated the jet pack. He stayed in the area long enough to see the ship crash into the side of a mountain, then headed in a southerly direction. He had no idea where the cities were, but he was sure that he'd come to some long before the jet pack's power ran out. He decided to cruise at a height of two hundred feet. He wasn't worried about being spotted by radar or sonar; he wanted to be close to the ground so if anyone started firing at him he'd have a chance to land safely before he was shot down.

It seemed to him that he'd been cruising half the day, though it had probably been no more an hour or so, when a city came into view. It wasn't much of a city, it couldn't have a population of more than forty thousand, but he knew that he had to land soon. The Navy would surely have traced him to Piccoli III and would have found the ship's wreckage by now. It might take them a while to realize there was no corpse, but in an hour or two they'd know, and then they'd come looking for him—and he didn't want to be this easy a target when that happened.

He spotted a farm that was growing large mutated tomatoes about a mile off to his right, and he banked and headed there. He saw a laborer walking through the field—the tomatoes were too delicate for a machine to harvest them—and he landed a few feet away, only to discover that the worker was a robot.

It stopped and stared at him, as if waiting for a command.

"Who's in charge here?" asked Cole, removing the jet pack.

"You must be more explicit, sir," replied the robot. "Are you referring to the farm, the city, the planet, the sector, or the Republic?"

"The farm."

"The McDade Corporation, headquartered on Far London, sir."

"Let me try it a different way," said Cole. "Who gives you your orders?"

"Dozhin, sir."

"Dozhin," repeated Cole. "Man or alien?"

"He is not a Man, sir."

"And is he on the premises?"

"Yes."

"Then, to coin a phrase I've always wanted to use, take me to your leader."

"I do not understand your directive, sir," replied the robot. "I am alone. No one is leading me."

"Take me to Dozhin."

"Follow me, sir."

The robot set off at a fast walk, and Cole fell into step behind it. When they had gone almost half a mile they came to a small domed structure, about twenty feet on a side.

"In there, sir," said the robot, stepping aside.

"Why don't you go in first and tell him he has a visitor?" suggested Cole, stashing the jet pack under a bush.

"Robots are not permitted in Dozhin's personal quarters, sir," answered the robot.

"Okay, I'll take it from here," said Cole. "And thanks for your help . . . have you got a name?"

"I do not know, sir. Dozhin calls me HT23. Most humans call me Boy or Robot."

"Well, then, thank you, HT23."

"You are welcome, sir. May I return to my work now?"

"Yes."

The robot turned and headed back to the fields, and Cole

approached the door to the structure. It sensed his presence, a holo camera came out of a wall, and Cole knew it was transmitting his image to the occupant of the little domed building.

"Come in," said a sibilant alien voice.

"Thank you," said Cole, entering the place. He found himself facing a tall, very slender, red-brown being, humanoid but never to be mistaken for human. Its eyes were horizontal slits, its nose so long it almost seemed prehensile, its mouth absolutely circular. Its skin was covered with a rust-colored fuzz that looked less like hair the closer Cole got to it. "My name is Leslie Ainge," he said. "My vehicle broke down, and I need some directions—or better still, transportation to the spaceport if you can provide it."

"I can provide it," said Dozhin. "But not to Leslie Ainge, who doesn't exist, at least not on Piccoli III."

"I can show you my ID and passport."

"I'm sure you can," answered the alien, "and I'm equally sure that they'll pass muster on all but two or three worlds out here, Captain Cole."

Suddenly Dozhin found himself looking down the barrel of Cole's burner.

"Put it away, Captain Cole," said Dozhin. "I have no animosity toward you and no love of the Republic."

"What makes you think I'm Cole?"

"I know from message transmissions that the Navy matched someone's DNA to the notorious Wilson Cole, and that he escaped from the Chambon system three hours ago. I know no ship has landed at our spaceport today. And I know you are a stranger to Piccoli III. What other conclusion can be drawn?" He stared at Cole. "Will you lower your weapon now, please?"

Cole bonded the laser pistol to his right thigh again. "All right," he said. "What now?"

"Now I offer you sanctuary for as long as you want it," said Dozhin. "I am here because the Republic decimated Cicero VII, which, though a human colony, was also my home world, since it is the world I was born on."

"I remember hearing about it back when I was serving in the Republic," said Cole. "They say it was pretty bad. You're lucky to be alive."

"I lost my parents, my wife, my children, and my home," replied Dozhin. "I could have done without such luck."

"I'm sorry to hear it," said Cole.

"I was sorry to experience it. That is why I will offer sanctuary to any enemy of the Republic."

"But you're working on a Republic world."

"My specialty is agriculture. They destroyed my fields. If I am to work, it must be on worlds where things still grow. They have provided me with this domicile. I am happy to share it with you."

"I appreciate the offer, but I can't stay on Piccoli. The ship I used to get here is no longer operative. I need to find a ship that can get me back to my own vessel, or at least to the Inner Frontier."

"That may be difficult," said Dozhin. "I know the Navy followed you to Piccoli III. Whatever you did with your ship to make them think you are dead, they will soon discover that there is no corpse—or if you thoughtfully provided them with one, it will not match your DNA. They will doubtless send teams down to the planet to search for you, and more importantly, they will be patrolling from orbit and will doubtless be under orders to shoot down any ship whose pilot, crew, or cargo is in any way questionable."

"And knowing the Navy, the mere act of leaving the planet makes a ship questionable," said Cole.

"So it is possible that I may take you to a ship, or a ship owner, or a ship renter," concluded Dozhin, "but it is every bit as likely that the Navy is already in position to shoot that ship down."

"I can't spend the rest of my life here," said Cole. "I'll take my chances once I find a ship."

"I don't think you realize the gravity of your situation," said Dozhin. "The rest of your life could very well be measured in hours, or even minutes, if you try to leave the planet in the face of the Navy's opposition."

"It's a chance I'll have to take. I've got to get back to my ship. I have vital information. I didn't have a chance to transmit it when I acquired it, and I don't dare try to send it from here. They'd intercept it, learn the scramble codes, and send the *Teddy R* and the rest of my fleet a phony message that would lead them into a trap."

"Did you say a fleet?" asked the alien.

"Yes."

"How many ships do you have under your command?"

Cole shrugged. "A little over four hundred."

"Four hundred?" repeated Dozhin. "That is very interesting."

Cole stared at him expectantly.

"I know a man—a human—who might be able to help. He might not. There's a huge reward on your head. He may decide to turn you in for it instead. But if he doesn't, he *might* be able to help."

"You don't sound too sure of him," said Cole.

"I am not. But you have very limited choices. You can take the chance of stealing a ship without being shot down, you can take the chance of hiding here and hoping the building-to-building search never reaches this farm—or you can take the chance of meeting a man who, if he is so inclined, is in a position to help you. What is your decision?"

"What do you think it is?" said Cole wryly. "Let's go meet your friend."

"He is not my friend," replied Dozhin. "I do not like him." He paused thoughtfully. "In fact, I don't think anyone on Piccoli III does."

Great, thought Cole. *I'll say this much for my luck: It's consistent.*

Dozhin accompanied Cole into the small city. It was typical of the kind of municipality that had evolved on colony worlds, which is to say, there seemed to be almost no city planning at all. Originally there'd been some houses—usually geodesic domes—and eventually a general store, then a bank, then a bigger more modern store, then a vehicle shop, a farm supply shop, and before long everything you would expect in such a city: restaurants, hotels, entertainments, specialty stores— but none of them in any order. The original domes still stood, and businesses had been built wherever there was an inviting piece of terrain. Roads zigged and zagged, tall buildings mingled with single-level dwellings, and though Cole knew there had to be a small spaceport he couldn't spot it.

"What's the name of this place?" he asked as they approached the city.

"Piccoli III," said Dozhin.

"I mean the town."

"Bloom."

"I don't see any flowers in bloom," said Cole.

"Bloom was the name of the first settler," explained Dozhin. "Actually, legend has it that it was Bloomenstein, but when he started painting his name on the feed and grain store he opened, he used such big letters that he realized he couldn't fit them all on the sign, and rather than make another one, he simply changed his name to Bloom."

"Sounds more like the way people change names on the Inner Frontier."

"Eventually he moved there."

"And what's the name of the man we're going to meet?" asked Cole.

"Lafferty."

"Has he got a first name?"

"Probably," said Dozhin. "Unless it has atrophied from lack of use."

"Where is he located?"

"There is a very small bookstore about a quarter mile from here."

"Did you say a *book* store?"

"Books, tapes, disks, cubes, holos. Very few books, actually, but collectors come from all over the sector and beyond just to buy them."

"I think I'll get along just fine with him," said Cole.

"No you won't," said Dozhin. "Nobody does."

"*I* will."

They walked the rest of the way in silence and arrived at a tiny shop, barely twenty feet on a side. The place was empty, and Cole began examining the stock while Dozhin simply took a position just inside the door. There were perhaps thirty books in a heavily protected case, while the rest of the place was given over to more common entertainments.

He was still looking at the case when a voice said, "May I help you?"

"I'm looking for a first edition of *Pride and Prejudice*," replied Cole.

"You and ten thousand others," said a wiry, grizzled man with a thick shock of white hair. "How many planets are you willing to spend on it?"

"Then how about the original limited edition of *Seven Pillars of Wisdom?*"

"Why don't you just ask for something easy, like a kingdom of your own?"

"All right," said Cole. "I'll ask for something easy: passage to the Inner Frontier so I can return to my ship."

The old man's eyes opened wide as he studied Cole carefully. "Was the namesake of your ship an author too?"

"Among other things."

"I've heard a lot about you, Wilson Cole."

"And I've heard very little about you, Mr. Lafferty."

"What makes you think I can help you?" said Lafferty.

"Dozhin isn't a what, he's a who," replied Cole.

"I am not enamored of word games," said the old man. "What makes you think I would be interested in helping a convicted mutineer?"

"Because neither of us has any love for the Republic."

"I despise its treatment of aliens," said Lafferty. "Suppose you tell me why I should help a man who mutinied against an alien captain of his ship?"

"We were stationed in the Cassius Cluster . . ." began Cole.

"Never heard of it," interrupted Lafferty.

"You have that in common with most of the Republic," said Cole. "It only had a handful of inhabited planets, and only two with major populations. Each of those two was a major fuel dump. We were under orders not to let the Teronis get their hands on either of them." The muscles in Cole's jaw tightened as he recalled the situation. "We were the only Republic ship in the whole damned star cluster, and suddenly the Fifth Teroni Fleet showed up, all of them armed to the teeth. My captain, a Polonoi named Podok, took our orders to mean that under no circumstances could we let the Teronis appropriate the fuel. There was no way we could stand against more than two hundred Teroni class-M warships, so she turned our weaponry on one of the planets.

We blew up the fuel dump, but we also killed almost three million inhabitants. It was her intention to do the same to the other planet, which housed almost five million men. I took over command and told Commander Jacovic, who was leading the fleet, that he could have the fuel if he promised not to harm the populace and to give us safe passage out of the cluster. He did, and that was that."

"You should have gotten a medal, not a court-martial," commented Lafferty after a moment.

"I thought so too," said Cole wryly. "But Podok went to the press, and they ran with the story about a human mutinying against an alien who had come up through the ranks, and at that point it became obvious that if I'd been found innocent, let alone been commended, there'd have been riots all the hell over the Republic. I was never going to get a fair trial, so my crew broke me out of jail and we headed off to the Inner Frontier."

"That does put a new light on it," said Lafferty.

"So will you help me?" asked Cole.

"That depends."

"On what?"

"I need a quid pro quo," said Lafferty.

"I don't follow you."

"We'll help you if you help us."

"Who is 'us'?" asked Cole.

Lafferty turned to the alien. "Dozhin, you can stay here and listen, or go outside and pretend you don't know what's going on. Either way, if what I'm about to say gets out, you won't live an hour."

"I will stay," said Dozhin.

"Do you want to lock up the store first?" asked Cole.

"Everyone saw you come in. Why draw attention by pretending you didn't?"

"Whatever you say," said Cole, who was deciding that the old man was a pretty sharp customer.

"All right, Mr. Cole," said Lafferty. "You and I have one thing in common: Neither of us has any use for the Republic. I don't know what you're doing here, but I can hazard a guess. You represent a warship . . ."

"I represent more than four hundred ships," interjected Cole.

"Better and better. I speak for cells that have sprung up on dozens of worlds. Our goal is to overthrow the Republic."

"Forget it," said Cole. "You have a few dozen cells, they have a few million ships."

"You have to start somewhere," said Lafferty. "In fact, now that I know the facts, I think a case can be made that you fired the first shot by *not* firing a shot."

"I'm not a revolutionary," said Cole. "I'm a mutineer with a price on his head."

"So was Robin Hood."

"Robin Hood was a fairy tale. I've got four hundred ships, of which no more than twenty qualify as warships, and maybe two thousand men that I will not sacrifice on a principle or for a noble cause. Our job is to survive, not to make a bold statement on the way to the grave."

"We've got to get rid of the Republic," insisted Lafferty. "It had its uses, and even its noble causes, when it was created, but it's become increasingly repressive and corrupt."

"You don't want to get rid of it," said Cole firmly. "The Navy is the only thing standing between you and the Teroni Fleet."

"What makes you think one is any worse than the other?"

"The Republic's not going to demand retribution for all the men you killed and the ships you destroyed. I wouldn't bet on the Teronis doing the same—and they've been stockpiling losses for a quarter of a century."

"All right," said Lafferty. "You say you don't want to overthrow the Republic. You're not a thief, so what the hell are you doing, sneaking into the Republic?"

"I'm not trying to overthrow it," said Cole, "but I damned well aim to keep it out of the Inner Frontier. It has no authority there, it has no business there, and its presence will no longer be tolerated there."

"Ah!" said Lafferty with a smile. "I think we can do business after all."

Cole looked at him expectantly. "Well?" he said at last.

"I can probably put another four to five hundred ships at your disposal, as well as a constant stream of information not only from observation posts within the Republic, but also from certain covert agents—I cannot reveal their names—who are actually in the Navy."

"And just how many quarts of blood do you want in exchange?" asked Cole suspiciously.

"None at all," replied Lafferty.

"Right," said Cole. "You're doing it out of the goodness of your heart."

"No. I'm doing it because if you won't attack the Navy *here*, the next best thing is to attack it *there*."

"The Republic's at war. Maybe you ought to give a little thought to who your *real* enemy is."

"Don't preach to me," said Lafferty. "I just heard your story, and as far as I can see, *your* real enemies were the captain of a Republic warship and the free press."

Cole was about to offer a heated reply, but suddenly he stopped and shrugged. "All right, you old bastard, you have a point. We'll each choose our own enemies and stop arguing about it."

The old man grinned and reached out a gnarled hand, which Cole shook.

"I'll take you to the spaceport," said Lafferty. "You can borrow my ship and pilot."

"Sounds good," he said.

Lafferty led him and Dozhin to a large vehicle. "Climb in. Dozhin's my driver when he's not nagging robot farmhands."

It took them only about ten minutes to reach the small spaceport. Lafferty's ship had been pulled out of the hangar, and seemed ready to go.

"So where's your pilot?" asked Cole.

"He must be in the bar," said Lafferty. "Come on. I'll introduce him to you. He's a fellow conspirator."

"How many are you?"

"A few hundred in this sector. I have no other hard information on other sectors or their leaders, and that way the Republic can't torture it out of me, but I suspect there are upwards of ten thousand."

"The Republic doesn't torture its enemies," said Cole. "You're not going to convince me it tortures its citizens."

"I'm not even going to try," said Lafferty. "Just don't get caught, and you can feel smug and superior to your heart's content."

"I do not drink human stimulants," said Dozhin as they neared the bar.

"So go to the alien bar around the corner."

"I am here on business," said Dozhin, holding out his hand.

"I thought we were supposed to be on the same fucking side," muttered Lafferty, reaching into a pocket and pulling out a handful of Maria Theresa dollars. "Here you are, you scheming little bastard. And I'll want change."

Dozhin took the money, made a production of counting it, and headed around the corner.

"Just out of curiosity, how many ships have you killed so far?" asked Lafferty as they walked.

"A few," said Cole. "Not many."

"That's due to change."

"I agree."

"For a while, anyway," added Lafferty.

"The Navy will never launch a full-scale attack in the Frontier," said Cole. "They can't pull that many ships away from the Teroni war."

"You're convinced of that, are you?"

"Yes."

"That conviction will hold right up to the day that you're doing more damage to the Navy than the Teronis are, and not one second longer."

"They're not going to put enough ships into the Frontier for us to do them that much damage," said Cole.

"Yes they will, once they know you're shooting them down," said Lafferty. "If I didn't think so, I wouldn't give you the help and spend the money on the fuel that you're going to cost me for the next two days." He reached the entrance to the bar. "Here we are."

A young man stood alone at the bar, and Lafferty and Cole immediately approached him.

"Harold," said Lafferty to the young man, "say hello to the Republic's most-wanted felon."

The man stared at Cole and finally shook his head. "I don't get the joke."

"This is Wilson Cole."

The man shook his head. "I know what Cole looks like. I've seen his face on enough posters and holocasts." He stared again. "This guy's close, but it isn't him."

"I'll have to compliment my makeup artist," said Cole with a smile.

"You're *really* him?" said Harold excitedly.

"I'm really him."

"Are you here to lead us against the Republic?" asked the young man eagerly.

"My battle with the Republic is limited to the Inner Frontier," Cole answered.

"Well, once you wipe them out there, why not come and do the same thing here?"

"Have you ever seen the base on Chambon V?" asked Cole.

"Yes."

"Pretty impressive, isn't it?"

"If it wasn't, we'd have taken it out already," said Harold.

"Well, let me tell you something," said Cole. "The Republic's got more than three hundred bases spread around the galaxy, and most of them are between three and ten times the size of that one. You're not about to overthrow the Republic or beat the Navy into surrendering."

"But most of the Navy's busy fighting the Teroni Federation," said Lafferty. "Even you pointed that out."

"If there was a serious internal threat, the Republic would end the war so fast it'd make your head spin. They'd give away a third of their territory, including all the outlying worlds like this one, and the war would be over five minutes later. And I suspect you wouldn't be any happier under the Teroni Federation than you are under the Republic."

Harold turned to Lafferty. "Are you *sure* this is the guy the Navy's been trying to kill for the past few years?"

"I'm just being a realist," said Cole. "And if I can talk you out of any suicidal military missions, so much the better."

"The man makes sense," said Lafferty. "We have to soften the Navy up while we're building strength. That's what he's going to do."

"I thought he was talking about the Inner Frontier," said Harold.

"He is," said Lafferty. "We have to start somewhere. And they're weaker on the Frontier than anywhere else."

"If he's not recruiting help, and he sure as hell sounds like he isn't, what's he doing in the Republic?"

"Stealing vital military information," said Lafferty. "Now I'm loaning him my ship to get him back to the Frontier."

"You'll never see it again," said Harold.

"I admire your trust and confidence," said Cole dryly.

"You were one of my heroes," said Harold. "But damn it, you sure don't sound like any hero."

"The Navy had their hands on him and he escaped," said Lafferty. "He's still alive, isn't he? That's heroic enough."

Dozhin entered the bar at that moment. "Are you ready to leave yet?"

"Dozhin, can you pilot a ship?" asked Cole.

"Yes," said the alien, surprised. "That's how I *got* to Piccoli III."

Cole turned to Lafferty. "He's the one I want to fly me back to Singapore Station."

"But Harold's my pilot."

"He's not *mine*," said Cole.

"What the hell," said Lafferty with a shrug. "You want him, you've got him."

"You've only had that ship a year or two," said Harold. "Are you sure you want to trust it with an alien?"

"Shut up," said Cole.

"What?"

"As bad as the Republic's treated you, they've been ten times as hard on the alien races. If someday, decades or centuries from now, you actually mount an army and navy and go to war with them, you're going to need every alien you can find, and they're not going to support your cause if you've neglected them or treated them with the same contempt the Republic shows." He stared coldly at the baker. "Until you learn that, you're not worth fighting for."

"What the hell brought that on?" asked Harold, suddenly all innocence.

"The best officer I ever knew was a Molarian," said Cole. "The Republic tortured him to death a few weeks ago. You'd better prove to me and to the Republic's aliens that you wouldn't do the same thing before you can expect any help from us." He turned to Lafferty. "Let's go."

Cole was in a black mood as he passed through customs. Neither his passport nor his ID roused any suspicions on the part of the Navy inspectors who had to pass on anyone leaving the planet. The mood remained as he entered the ship. Dozhin sensed it and kept silent, even after the ship got its flight plan approved and took off.

There are some decent men and women in the Navy, Cole thought as he sat silently staring at the viewscreen of the endless waste of space. *And of course there are some assholes among the general population, even among those who are committed to fighting the abuses of the Republic.* He sighed deeply. *But are fools like that what Four Eyes died for, what I threw away my career for, what we're about to risk our lives for?*

And because he never lied to himself, he acknowledged that that was precisely who he was fighting for. There were decent people too, literally billions of them, but Cole knew that every time his side took a casualty, they'd be taking it for Harold and people like him, as well as all the nameless people who simply tried to get from one day to the next without causing grief to those they loved.

And since there were so many of those nameless people, he knew they'd accept those casualties and those deaths, and pretend they were taking them solely for the decent and downtrodden members of all the Republic's races. It was a good story, and it made a good rallying point.

Only the Captain of the *Theodore Roosevelt*, he thought grimly, would know better.

"So far, so good," said Cole as they neared the edge of the Republic.

"I keep expecting warships to stop us and question us," admitted Dozhin.

Cole shook his head. "We passed the Navy's inspection. My guess is that the Republic is less concerned with who *leaves* than with who *enters*."

"I hadn't thought of it that way," admitted Dozhin. He paused hesitantly for a moment. "May I ask you a question?"

"Go ahead."

"I've never seen any military action. What was it like to take a warship into battle?"

"Very uncertain," answered Cole. "The *Theodore Roosevelt* is almost a century old. It should have been decommissioned seventy years ago, but the Republic keeps fighting wars and it needs all the ships it can get, even cannon fodder like mine."

"But I've heard all about your exploits," protested Dozhin. "You have won four Medals of Courage."

"Three of them were aboard a pair of other ships," said Cole. "I was removed from command of them for insubordination."

"Insubordination?"

"I never believed in blindly following stupid orders when the enemy is shooting at me," said Cole. "As for the fourth medal, I won it for actions performed on the ground, not on the *Teddy R*."

"What is the *Teddy R*?" asked Dozhin.

"A diminutive of the *Theodore Roosevelt*. Got any more questions?"

"I'm sorry. Do they bother you?"

"No, they keep me alert. I haven't had any sleep in . . . oh, it must be close to two days now. My species needs it every day."

"Why don't you go to sleep now?" suggested Dozhin. "You've already programmed the navigational computer, and we're on course for this station—Sing-something—that you mentioned."

"You know, I think I'll take you up on that. We'll hit the Nesterenko Wormhole in about two hours, and once we do, we're in the hole for three hours and then it's maybe two more to Singapore Station."

The ship was too small to have private cabins, but a bulkhead opened out to reveal a bunk, and Cole lay down on it. He was asleep in less than a minute.

He was awakened when Dozhin gently shook him by the shoulder.

"Are we there already?" he asked, swinging his feet to the floor.

"No."

"Then why did you wake me?"

"Three Navy ships are tracking us. One of them just ordered us to halt and prepare for inspection. I have a feeling they think we're smuggling some contraband material."

"Why? We're legitimate. We filed a flight plan, we're unarmed, we—"

"I believe Mr. Lafferty has occasionally smuggled in arms from the Frontier aboard this ship," said Dozhin.

"It's a hell of a time to tell me," muttered Cole. He walked over to the main computer. "All right, where are they?"

Dozhin gave a brief command, and the computer cast a holo showing the ships' position. One was directly behind them, the other two were triangulating from the sides.

"What's the ETA for the Nesterenko Wormhole?" asked Cole.

"Seventeen minutes and thirty-six seconds," answered the computer.

Cole grimaced. "We can't keep ahead of them that long, not in this ship."

"Shall we perform evasive maneuvers?" suggested Dozhin.

Cole shook his head. "If it looks like we're even thinking of losing them, they'll blow us apart."

"Then what do we do?" asked the alien.

"We obey their orders and let them board us. They can't know who I am, so hopefully they're just looking for weapons or drugs, and when they don't find either, they'll let us continue on our way."

"Harold would stand and fight," noted Dozhin.

"For a few seconds," agreed Cole. "Then he would fall down and bleed all over the nice clean floor." He looked at the alien. "Bravery without intelligence is probably even less of a survival trait than cowardice without intelligence. Harold did not strike me as a man who uses his brain." He took one more look at the viewscreen. "Computer, signal the nearest ship that we are coming to a stop and have no objection to being boarded. Then wipe all record of our destination from your memory."

"*Working . . . done,*" announced the computer.

"It is just as well we're not armed," noted Dozhin. "Otherwise we would have to jettison our weapons."

"If those ships are after smugglers, the first thing they're going to notice is anything you jettison," said Cole. "Just relax, let them satisfy themselves that we're not carrying any contraband, and we'll be on our way."

"They will be here in less than two minutes," said Dozhin.

Suddenly Cole tensed. "*Shit!*"

"What is it?" asked the alien, startled.

"We're in trouble," said Cole. "I was sleepy. I didn't think it through."

"Think *what* through?"

"Just as they don't care who's leaving, they don't care what kind of contraband we're taking *out* of the Republic," said Cole. "They only care about what's coming *in*, so they're not after drugs or guns at all."

"They couldn't know Wilson Cole is on the ship," said Dozhin.

"I agree," said Cole. He frowned. "Then what *do* they think they're going to find?"

"I don't know."

"Well, we've no time to search for it," said Cole. "And maybe they're just flexing their muscles." He checked the computer. "They'll reach us in another ninety seconds."

"What are we to do?" said Dozhin, panic creeping into his voice.

Cole looked around the ship. There was nothing he could use as a weapon, not against men armed with pulse guns, laser and sonic pistols, and probably wearing body armor. He uttered a quick command to the navigational computer, which blinked an acknowledgment, then turned to the main computer.

"Computer," said Cole, "disable the radio's transmitting mechanism for the next ten minutes."

"*Working . . . done*," replied the computer.

"Now we can't even signal for help!" complained Dozhin.

"Three Navy ships are bearing down on us. Who do you think is going to help us?"

"Then what—?"

"Shut up and listen," said Cole. "I haven't got time to argue. When the nearest ship reaches us, it's going to dock next to us, bond the area around the hatch doors, and then open theirs and demand that we open ours."

"How will you know?" asked Dozhin bitterly. "You disabled the radio."

"Only for transmitting, not for receiving," replied Cole. "Now, these are two class-H ships and one class-J. The class-H carries a crew of three; the class-J, seven to ten. Right at the moment they're pretty much equidistant from us. I'm going to maneuver the ship to make sure one of the class-H ships reaches us first."

"Then what?"

"Then, when I give the word, race through the hatch as if your life depended on it, which it will."

"That's *it?*" demanded Dozhin. "That's your entire plan?"

"That's the first step," said Cole. "What do you want on two minutes' notice?"

"Something more than that!"

"Fine," said Cole. "I'm open to suggestions. But make them fast; we've only got about twenty seconds left."

"None of this was supposed to happen!" whined Dozhin. "I was just supposed to take you to Singapore Station and come back."

"Follow my orders and you've got a chance of doing just that," said Cole as the ship suddenly shuddered. "We have company," he noted. "They should be bonded to us in another ten seconds. Get over there, just to the side of the hatch."

The alien moved where Cole directed him as the hatch slid open. A moment later two soldiers entered the small ship.

"Name?" said one of them.

"Leslie Ainge," said Cole.

"Home world?"

"Roanoke II."

"Business in the Inner Frontier?"

"My son works on a mining world. I'm going there to visit him."

"And the alien?"

"His name is Dozhin. He's my personal servant."

"Let me see your ID."

Cole pulled it out and handed it over.

"We'll run this through our computer. If it checks out, you're free to continue."

"What's the problem?" asked Cole.

"A wanted criminal escaped from Chambon V. We have reason to believe he landed on Piccoli III. We're checking all outgoing flights from there."

"Well, we're certainly not hiding him here," said Cole.

"Perhaps," said the soldier. He turned to his companion. "Check the bulkheads."

The other soldier began examining each bulkhead. Cole made a production of getting out of his way, which put him just a step from the hatch. He faked a seizure of coughing until he was sure the first soldier's eyes were on him. Then he stared into a far corner of the ship. "What the hell is *that*?" he murmured.

The soldier turned to see what he was looking at.

"*Now!*" shouted Cole.

Dozhin dove through the hatch and Cole followed half a second later. He knew the structures of all Navy ships, and he hit the Close control as he hurled himself at the one remaining soldier, who was caught by surprise. A blow to the chin, a kick to the groin, and a chop to the neck, and the soldier was unconscious before he could draw his weapons.

"Do you know how to break the bonding?" asked Dozhin.

"You don't get to be a Commander in the Navy unless you know every ship they've got inside out," said Cole. "They didn't change codes in the fifteen years I served. Let's hope they haven't changed 'em in the last few years." He uttered a code, and the ship slid away.

"What now?" asked Dozhin.

"Now we send some brave men to their graves," said Cole with no sense of triumph. "With the transmitter disabled, the men aboard Lafferty's ship won't be able to report what happened. The other two ships don't know anything's wrong, and will assume their companions still control this one. I can't assume that we can outrun them to the wormhole—one of them's a class-J, and it can almost certainly catch us—so the alternative is to fire on them before they know who's in charge of this ship."

"And the two on our ship?"

"The ship's working, and the transmitter will be functional in another seven minutes. They can make their way back to their base."

"What about this one?" asked Dozhin, indicating the unconscious man at his feet.

"Collect his weapons and bring them to me, and then tie him up," ordered Cole. "I'm not going to shoot him or jettison him while he's asleep. We'll just have to play it by ear." He paused. "And now to business. Computer, do either of our two companion ships have their shields up?

"*No.*"

"Aim your pulse canon at the bridge of the farther ship."

"*Done.*"

"On my command, fire and then immediately aim at the bridge of the closer ship and fire again. *Fire!*"

A pulse of energy shot out and hit the farther of the two ships. Before the nearer one could raise its defenses, the ship fired again, and less than three seconds after the battle began it was over.

"Remarkable," said Dozhin.

"Fish in a barrel," said Cole with no show of emotion. "Now let's head for the Nesterenko Hole, because the transmitter on Lafferty's ship is going to become operative in a few minutes, and the last thing we need is another confrontation."

"Why not just shoot the ship? It's clear that Lafferty's never going to possess it again."

"Because it's too much like murder," answered Cole. "Maybe we weren't at serious risk, but at least the two ships we killed had weaponry. There's no way in the world the two men stuck in Lafferty's ship can harm us if we just head for the wormhole right now."

Dozhin shot him a look that said he wasn't behaving like a storied military hero, but he kept his silence, and Cole had the computer lay in a course for the Nesterenko Wormhole. They entered it a few minutes later.

"Well, that's that," said Dozhin.

"That was the easy part," replied Cole.

"I do not understand the human sense of humor."

"There's nothing funny about it. We'll be out of the wormhole in another three hours."

"And we'll be safe in the Inner Frontier."

Cole just stared at him. "We will be a lone Republic ship in an area that has sworn to destroy any Republic ship that shows up. I've got a code word, and I'll try to signal any approaching ships with it—but given what we are, there's every possibility that they'll shoot first."

Suddenly Dozhin's stomach began to hurt.

"Computer, what the hell's the name of this ship anyway?" muttered Cole, his eyes scanning the various control panels.

"*I am the* Raging Tiger," answered the computer.

"What's a tiger?" asked Doshin.

"*A large predatory feline carnivore native to Earth. Date of extinction: 2109 A.D.*"

"Well," said the alien with a shrug, "that explains why I never heard of it."

"Computer," said Cole, "give me an ETA for Singapore Station."

"*Eighty-three minutes.*"

He stared at the screen. "You'd think we could see it by now."

"*According to my data banks, it is only seven miles long. You will not see it until we are within two minutes of it.*"

"I see something else, though," said Cole, checking the viewscreen, where five ships had just appeared. "I want to send a message on every possible wavelength—and I want it on visual, too."

"*Ready.*"

"This is Wilson Cole. I have captured the Republic ship known as the *Raging Tiger*. My code word is Four Eyes. May I have an escort to Singapore Station, please?"

"This is Miguel Flores, Captain of the *Golden Dawn*," came a reply. "I'm not aware of any code word. Also, I've met Captain Cole, and you're not him."

"What the hell are you talking about? The code is Four Eyes."

"Nobody gave me any code word," said Flores.

"Let me guess. You just joined this week."

"That's right."

"Before you do something rash," said Cole, "contact the *Theodore Roosevelt*. They will confirm my current appearance and my code word."

"They'd better," said Flores. A minute later his image was back. "All right, Captain Cole. You've got an escort."

His image vanished.

"What if they'd shot first?" asked Dozhin.

"You'd be past worrying about it by now," answered Cole.

"Is that all you've got to say?" demanded the alien.

"What do you want me to say?" responded Cole. "I'm the one who declared open season on Republic ships once they enter the Frontier. I can hardly get mad at anyone for carrying out my orders."

"I have come to the conclusion that you are not a military hero after all," said Dozhin after some consideration.

"That's what I've been telling you all along."

"What you are," continued Dozhin, "is a madman with a death wish!"

"If you say so."

"Hah! You don't deny it?"

"Would it do any good?" said Cole. "Your mind's made up. But don't forget that this madman kept you alive when Lafferty's ship was stopped, and again just now."

"Dumb luck."

"The intelligent don't depend on luck," said Cole. "And the dumb don't understand how it works."

The alien glared at him but remained silent, and in a little over an hour and a quarter the *Raging Tiger* docked at Singapore Station. Cole emerged from the ship to be confronted by half a dozen armed men.

"I'm not carrying any weapons," he said.

"I assume you won't mind if we don't take your word for it," said Flores. He nodded to a companion, who came over and thoroughly frisked both Cole and Dozhin.

"This is silly," said Cole. "You've already confirmed my identity."

"Probably," said Flores. "The only thing I know for sure is that I've confirmed that a man who resembles the Wilson Cole I know is in possession of the proper code. You will be treated with the utmost respect, but I need positive identification."

"You're either the most thorough officer I've met in years, or else you're a fanatic who could be more trouble than he's worth," said Cole. "I hope it's the former. Now please escort me to either the *Theodore Roosevelt* or to Duke's Place. There will be people at either who can vouch for me."

"Duke's Place," responded Flores. "I don't want you near the *Roosevelt* until we know for sure that you're Wilson Cole."

Cole posed no objection, and he and Dozhin were taken to the casino. As soon as they entered, Cole spotted Val at one of the tables.

"Do you see that tall redheaded woman?" he asked Flores.

"The one they call the Valkyrie, yes."

"Do you know that she's Third Officer aboard the *Theodore Roosevelt?*"

Flores nodded his head.

"Call her over."

Flores turned to two of his men. "The giant redhead. Bring her over here."

"Ask her politely," added Cole. "She doesn't like to be ordered."

"We have *these*," said one of the men, holding up his burner.

"Threaten her with that and she'll take it away and shove it right up your ass," said Cole. "Just ask her politely."

"Do as he says," ordered Flores.

"Good decision," said Cole. "They wouldn't be much use to you after they got her mad."

Flores chuckled, and a moment later the two men accompanied Val across the room to stand in front of Cole.

"Welcome back, Cole," she said. "Sharon was worried sick about you, but I figured you're such a devious bastard you'd find a way to survive." She looked down at Dozhin. "What's this?"

"I am a who, not a what," said the alien with dignity. "My name is Dozhin, and I am Wilson Cole's most loyal friend." Cole stared at him. "Within limitations," he added lamely.

"I'll just bet," said Val. She looked at Cole. "Do you need me for anything, now that I've convinced them you're not Admiral Garcia, or can I go back to enjoying myself?"

"You are free to go," said Flores.

"I didn't ask you, Shorty."

"Go place your bets," said Cole.

"She called me Shorty," said Flores as Val returned to the gaming tables. "I am six feet three inches tall."

"Everything is relative," said Cole.

The Octopus entered the casino just then, saw Cole, and walked over to him. "I just got here," said the Octopus. "How did it go?"

"It went okay," answered Cole. "I'll fill you in later."

The Octopus jerked a thumb in Flores's direction. "He giving you any problems?"

"No, no problems."

"Damned well better not be," growled the Octopus, heading off for the Duke's table.

Flores turned to Cole. "I'm sorry if I have embarrassed or inconvenienced you," he said uncomfortably. "I was just doing my duty."

"Actually, you're to be commended for your thoroughness," replied Cole, trying to put him at his ease.

"Thank you for your understanding." Flores saluted and left.

"I suppose we'd better find you a ship to go home in," Cole said to Dozhin.

"Don't be in such a hurry," replied Dozhin, staring at the colorful gaming tables and the even more colorful characters standing at them. "This is a fabulous place, this station. I just may stay here."

"You're welcome to," said Cole. "But this fabulous place figures to be under a serious attack by the Republic in the not-too-distant future."

"You're better protected here than I was on the farm."

"True, but why would the Navy attack a Republic farm?"

"Why do they do anything they do?" responded Dozhin. "I need to weigh my decision carefully—and I can't do that until I have seen more of Singapore Station."

"So go look," said Cole.

"I intend to."

"The bottom three levels were specially built to accommodate aliens, though since you seem comfortable in Galactic Standard gravity and atmosphere you can stay on the human levels if you want."

"I'll look around and then I'll decide."

"Fine," said Cole. "Have a good time."

"There is one problem," said Dozhin hesitantly.

"Only one?"

"I do not have any money."

"Not even Republic credits?"

"Nothing."

"I hope you don't expect me to believe that you managed that farm for free," said Cole.

"My money is in a box under my bed."

"What the hell, I wouldn't trust a Republic bank either."

"But I have no currency of any kind with me."

Cole reached into his pocket and pulled out a ten-dollar Maria Theresa note. "Here," he said, handing it to Dozhin. "Don't spend it all at once, and when you run through it, go over to that big table in the corner. Walk up to a man with a platinum mask and tell him that I said he should give you a job."

"I don't *want* a job."

"Suit yourself. I hope you and the ten dollars have a long and happy life together." Cole began walking toward the Duke's table.

"But I want to fight against the Republic."

"If I come to a situation where I can use you, you'll get your chance. In the meantime, if you feel that strongly, you could donate half your earnings to the cause."

"What cause?" demanded Dozhin, looking around. "I don't see anyone rushing to join a cause."

"Good. If you can't spot them, maybe the Navy can't either. Now go enjoy yourself before I take my money back."

That statement galvanized the alien into action, and he was out of the casino and heading for an airlift to the lower levels almost before anyone noticed he was gone. All eyes turned to Cole as he made his way to the Duke's table, which was currently occupied by the Platinum Duke, David Copperfield, and the Octopus.

"Have a drink," said the Octopus. "You had us worried when we heard about the commotion on Chambon V."

"Which reminds me," said Cole, pulling a small cube out of his pocket. "Here's an early birthday present."

"What is it?"

"Your copy of the Inner Frontier patrol routes for all the ships at the Chambon V base."

"For how long?"

"Two months."

"That'll help," said the Octopus.

"More than you think," said Cole.

"Oh?"

"I changed some of their routes. I don't think I left any footprints, so they shouldn't know what I did and shouldn't change it back."

The Octopus grinned. "There's going to be good hunting this month!"

"And we've now got two Republic ships to use as decoys," added David Copperfield.

"Right," said Cole. "I forgot all about the first one."

"Getting shot at and chased around the Republic will do that to your memory," said the Octopus.

"I bear glad tidings from the Republic, too," said Cole.

"Please tell me Susan Garcia is dead of a painful, disfiguring disease," said the Duke.

"She's alive and well, and probably thinks pretty much the same of you as you think of her—on those rare occasions that she can be bothered to think of you at all."

"All right," said the Duke. "What secondary good news do you bring?"

"Once I figure out how to contact them again, I've got another four hundred to five hundred ships on our side."

"Five hundred ships?" repeated the Octopus. "Where are they?"

"In the Republic."

"That makes it official," said the Duke.

"What are you talking about?" asked Cole.

"When it was just you and few ships out here, ships with no allegiances, you were an illegal rabble. But with ships from the Republic —now you're officially a rebellion."

"Semantics," said Cole.

"But *meaningful* semantics," said the Duke. "This will make it much easier to raise money and recruit more young men and women to your side."

"I don't have a side."

"Then to your banner."

"So now it's only two-million-to-one odds against us instead of five-million-to-one," said Copperfield.

"It'll be a less than that," said Cole. "Those four hundred ships aren't from all across the Republic. They're just from Piccoli III and its vicinity. I'll bet we could pick up a few hundred ships near every Navy base in the Republic."

"Wouldn't those near the bases tend to be the most patriotic?" asked Copperfield.

"The nearest ones will have had the most interaction with the Navy," said Cole. "These days, that's not always a pleasant experience."

They spoke a few minutes more. Then the Octopus went off to his ship to study the cube, and Cole and David Copperfield headed toward the *Teddy R.*

"Tell me the truth, Steerforth," said the little alien. "What are our chances?"

"A little better than they were last week," said Cole.

"That's all?"

"David, against something like the Republic, that's a giant step forward."

"Yes, I suppose it is," admitted Copperfield. "When you consider the odds, don't you ever feel overwhelmed?"

"I don't think of the odds," said Cole.

"What *do* you think of?"

Cole paused for just a moment. "I think of Four Eyes," he said. "And a thousand others who met the same fate."

"You couldn't have saved him."

"No," said Cole. "No, I couldn't have. But maybe we can save the next thousand. At least, we've got to try."

Cole was sitting at the Platinum Duke's table with David Copperfield, nursing a beer, when the Octopus and his son walked over.

"Mind if we join you?" said the Octopus.

"Be my guest," said Cole. "Or, more accurately, be the Duke's guest."

The two men pulled up chairs and seated themselves.

"How are you doing, kid?" Cole asked Jonah.

"Better," replied the young man. "I'll be in therapy for a while to get rid of the limp, but I'm doing okay."

"I keep telling him: A prosthetic leg wouldn't limp and would never feel pain, but he's just stubborn," said the Octopus.

"I can get an endless supply of artificial arms and legs," said Jonah. "If I let them cut off the ones I was born with, I can never change my mind and get them back."

"Kid's got a point," said Cole. "Besides, I see you never had your extra hands removed."

"Why should I?" said the Octopus. "If I did, I'd just have to go find something else that makes me stand out in a crowd."

"May I assume that when you're all through pretending you're annoyed with each other you're going to get to the point of this visit?" said Cole.

"You cut me to the quick," said the Octopus. He flexed all eight of his hands. "And that's a lot of quicks to cut. Can't we just be here on a friendly visit?"

"This being a casino, I'd give plenty of ten-to-one against it," said Cole.

"Well, since you put it that way . . ." said the Octopus. He turned to his son. "Go ahead. It's your idea."

"There's a place, out beyond the Hayakawa system," began Jonah, "where you can cross from the Frontier to the Republic and still be seven light-years from the nearest Republic world."

"Good for you, kid," said Cole. "You've got a head on your shoulders."

"You figured it out already?" asked Jonah, surprised.

"The strategy, yes. The location, no. I've never heard of the Hayakawa system."

"It's halfway between here and the Pericles Cluster."

"You're sure about the seven light-years?"

Jonah nodded. "While I was laid up in the hospital, I did all the research. Seven-point-one-two light-years, actually."

Cole nodded. "It ought to work."

"What are you talking about?" demanded David Copperfield.

"We're sitting on two Navy ships," explained Cole. "The *Shooting Star*, which we captured on Keepsake, and the *Raging Tiger*, which I just returned in. We'll use one of them as bait—probably the *Shooting Star*, since it's the far bigger ship. We'll send out a distress call and be waiting for the rescue force with as many ships as we can put together. And we'll have a few men aboard the *Shooting Star* itself, ready to fire on the rescuers the second they appear." Cole took a sip of his beer. "Now, the second they realize they've fallen into a trap, the ships are going to call for backup, and the trick is to attack them in such an isolated spot that the cavalry can't reach us before the battle's over." He turned to Jonah. "The closest planet is seven light-years. Where's the closest wormhole?"

"They keep moving—they're very unstable in that section of the Frontier—but two days ago the closest one was almost a light-year away."

"Okay," said Cole. "Even stripped down at top speed, no force from the Republic is going to arrive in time."

"Then you approve?" asked Jonah eagerly.

"Tentatively. I want to have my pilot check the wormholes, and it wouldn't hurt to send a couple of ships out there to scout the area out, make sure there are no populated planets waiting to become the next Braccio II when the Republic decides to send a punishment party a week or two after the battle."

"I hadn't thought of that," admitted Jonah.

"No one should have to," replied Cole. "*My* Navy would never do that—but I guess this isn't my Navy any longer. The next thing to do is check the schedules I brought back and find out when there will be a Navy patrol in that area."

"Why?"

"Because our argument and our battle is against Navy ships inside the boundaries of the Frontier. I don't want Navy ships from the interior of the Republic responding to a distress call. The Navy ships we destroy, assuming that we *can* destroy them, are those that remain on the Frontier."

"The Navy is the Navy," thundered the Octopus. "I say kill 'em all."

"We're probably biting off more than we can chew, just trying to kick them out of the Inner Frontier," said Cole. "There's no sense declaring war on all their millions of ships."

"All right, all right," muttered the Octopus.

"I'll send a couple of ships out there to check things out, make sure the wormhole is where my pilot says it is, and set Slick to work on the *Shooting Star*."

The Octopus frowned. "Who is Slick, and what work is there to do? My understanding is that it's suffered no damage on Keepsake and is in fine working order."

"Slick is a Tolobite . . ." began Cole.

"What the hell is a Tolobite?"

"He's a humanoid crew member," answered Cole. "But more to the point, he's a symbiote."

"With what?"

"A very smooth, shiny second skin called a Gorib. I don't think it's intelligent, though Slick seems happy enough with it. The Gorib protects him from the cold of space and provides him with hours of oxygen, so whenever we're in space and we have work to do on the exterior of the ship, Slick and his symbiote go out and do it."

"You wouldn't happen to have another Tolobite you'd like to loan me, would you?" asked the Octopus.

"They're pretty rare. I'd never heard of them before I joined the *Teddy R.* If you were to ask me to name my most valuable crew member, depending on the situation it'd either be Val or Slick. Anyway, we don't know for sure that the Navy isn't aware of the fact that we've captured the *Shooting Star*, so I want Slick to give it new registration IDs on its exterior. I'll have Malcolm Briggs dig into its computer and change the ID to match."

"Will the Navy come if they don't have a record of the ship?" asked Jonah.

"They'll have a record of it," said Cole. "There's a man on Piccoli III named Lafferty who will give us the name and ID of a ship that'll be in the Navy's computer."

"Will that work?" persisted Jonah. "I mean, the Navy is certainly going to respond to the signal before setting out on a rescue mission. What happens when they get a reply from the real ship saying they're okay?"

"That's would be a problem if the ship could send and receive messages," said Cole. "But Lafferty's got as many ships at his disposal as we have. If they can't destroy a Navy ship so quickly that it can't get off a signal, they can at least jam all its communications."

"You hope."

"I hope," agreed Cole. "If it was easy, someone would have kicked the Navy out of the Inner Frontier a long time ago."

They spoke for another few minutes, and then Cole, accompanied by David Copperfield, returned to the *Teddy R*. He told Briggs to transfer everything he could find on the Hayakawa system to his personal computer, as well as the navigational computers in Vladimir Sokolov's and Braxite's ships.

"How big a fleet do you expect to answer the SOS?" asked Copperfield.

"There are too many variables to even guess," said Cole. "How many ships can reach the *Shooting Star*—or whatever we wind up calling it—in time to rescue the crew from whatever we say the problem is? Loss of control is one thing; loss of oxygen is another. Will they suspect a trap, and if so, will they come in force, or will they even come at all? And what we tell them will make a difference, too. Did the controls merely fail, or did it survive an attack from the *Teddy R*, which is still the most wanted ship in the galaxy?"

"Well, of course you'll hint the *Teddy R* is in the area," said Copperfield. "That will draw the greatest response."

"We may not be thrilled with that," replied Cole. "A lot of them might be class-M warships. The only class-M on our side is the *Teddy R*, and we haven't been re-outfitted in a quarter of a century. We were the biggest, toughest ship on the Frontier when we were fighting pirates or warlords, but we're pretty much overmatched against the Navy."

"You make me wonder why you're doing this at all," said Copperfield sullenly.

"Because someone's got to."

"We could go back to being mercenaries."

Cole shook his head. "If we ignore the Navy, there'll be another Braccio II every year. How many young men and women have they ripped from their homes and impressed into the service? How many farms have they bankrupted by taking a year's harvest and not paying for it? How many mining worlds have been abandoned because you can't make a profit when the Navy is confiscating half of what you produce? They say they're entitled to it because they're protecting us from our enemies, and since I was on the front line against those enemies for years I never questioned it. But now that I'm on the Frontier it's clear that someone has to protect us from our protectors."

"You never used to feel this way," said Copperfield.

"David, I've spent three and a half years *avoiding* the Navy. I had intimations of what they were doing, but I didn't *know*. Well, now I do, and if you turn your back on something like this, then you're not any better than the perpetrators." He grimaced. "I should have known sooner. I mean, hell, I know almost all the top brass in the fleet, from Admiral Garcia on down, and the most honorable officer I ever met was Jacovic, who was fighting for the other side."

"You're going to be hell to live with until we get this operation up and running, aren't you?" said Sharon's disembodied voice.

"Probably," acknowledged Cole.

"Well, if it'll make you feel any better, Mr. Briggs has already transferred what we have on the Hayakawa system to Vladimir and Braxite."

"It's a start," said Cole. "I'd better contact Lafferty and tell him what we're going to need."

"If he can deliver," she replied. "A lot of people make promises when they want to impress the famous Wilson Cole, but that doesn't mean they can keep them."

"There's an ugly little creature named Dozhin wandering the station who will vouch for him."

"Can you trust the ugly little creature?"

"He didn't have to leave Piccoli with me," said Cole. "No one would have forced him."

"All right," said Sharon. "I hope you're right."

"Well, at least you're worrying about the right thing."

"Why is that?" asked Copperfield. "I'd be more worried about the size and strength of the rescue ships."

"Tell him, Sharon."

Her image finally popped into existence.

"Because, David," she said, "the one thing we have to take on faith is Lafferty's word that he's killed or disabled the ship we're going to impersonate. If he lies, or if he's simply mistaken, we're going to be in serious trouble."

"Why?" asked Copperfield. "If they know it's a trap, they won't come."

"David, if they know it's a trap and they think it's been set by the gentleman standing next to you, they'll come in such numbers that they'll blot out the stars for hundreds of miles around."

"I hadn't thought of that," admitted the little alien.

"Don't worry, David," said Cole. "Lafferty will kill the ship, and this thing will run like clockwork." *I hope.*

"Sir," said Christine from her station at the main computer console, "a report just came in from Mr. Moyer. He and three of the Octopus's ships just took out a lone Navy six-man ship, just beyond the Kronos system. He wants to know if you have any instructions."

"I'm not clear what he means," said Cole. "He's already killed the ship."

"He thinks it's salvageable, and wants to know if you'd like it towed back so we can repair it and have yet another decoy ship."

Cole shook his head. "We've already got two decoys. Even the Navy isn't dumb enough to fall for the same trick three times." He paused. "Did the ship get off any messages before he killed it?"

"He says he doesn't think so."

"Tell him to make sure no Republic battleships are headed his way. If not, and the ship has any laser or pulse cannons above Level 2, have him bring them back. We can always install them in some of our ships."

"Yes, sir," said Christine, breaking the connection.

Cole waited until Christine had time to contact Moyer, then had her patch through a transmission to Lafferty on Piccoli III.

The old man stared at his image. "You look younger," he said at last.

"The wrinkles are wearing off, and my hair's its normal color," said Cole.

"Where's my ship?"

"Probably on Chambon V," said Cole. He related what had happened when the Navy had boarded it.

"Shit!" exclaimed Lafferty. "By now they know it was registered in my name!"

"So you'll just tell them that the notorious Wilson Cole stole it at gunpoint. Hell, I stole a much better-protected one from Chambon. They won't have any trouble believing it."

"Okay, that makes sense," agreed Lafferty.

"Now I need a favor."

"Another favor, you mean."

"Fine. Another favor."

"What is it?"

"I want you to get me the registration of a Navy ship, and any computer codes unique to it—and then either destroy it or at least put it out of action for a week, without letting it send any messages. Can you do that?"

"Some revolutionary I'd be if I couldn't!" snorted Lafferty. "How soon do you need it?"

"The sooner the better. I've got to rig a ship to impersonate it, and I can't do that until you give me the information I need."

"Give me two days."

"Fine."

"And have dock space ready for five hundred ships," continued Lafferty. "Once we do this, I think we're ready to take our place at your side."

"Are you sure?" asked Cole. "You're a lot safer where you are."

"We've been talking about rebellion for years. We've committed all these men and ships. Now we've got a leader who's known throughout the Republic. If we don't do it now, we never will."

"Then we're happy to have you," said Cole. "You know the coordinates of Singapore Station?"

"Someone in our fleet will," said Lafferty. "You'll be hearing from me soon, and then we'll be off to join you."

The transmission ended.

"Well, David," said Cole, "we just doubled our size again."

"We're almost a thousand ships now," said Copperfield. "I'm starting to think that this just might work."

"We don't need a thousand ships to attack a rescue party."

"I mean this whole thing—kicking them out of the Inner Frontier for good." The little alien looked at Cole. "Don't you agree?"

"Anything's possible," said Cole.

Lafferty got his Navy ship in thirteen hours, and sent all the information to Cole. It was the *Hungry Raptor*, it held eight men—Cole didn't ask what had become of them—and within a day Slick had managed to change the *Shooting Star* into the *Hungry Raptor*, bonding glowing letters and registration numbers to the nose and sides of the ship. At the same time, Malcolm Briggs removed all trace of the ship's original registration, and all transmissions would now carry the *Hungry Raptor*'s registration and codes.

By the time the ship was ready, Lafferty's ships had arrived at Singapore Station. Cole joined him on one of the dock arms, walking up and down the row of ships, seeing exactly what he was adding to his fleet.

"Nine Level 4 thumpers," he said, impressed, when the inspection was done. "That's better than I anticipated."

"Got better than that," said Lafferty.

"Oh?"

"Got a Level 5 laser cannon."

"I didn't see it," said Cole.

"Haven't had a chance to install it yet," said Lafferty. "It was on the *Raptor* until yesterday. It's in one of the cargo holds."

"I want it installed in the new *Hungry Raptor*," said Cole. "I'll send a crew by to pick it up, and alert my engineer. I'd like to get this show on the road sometime tomorrow."

"Sounds good to me."

"I'll need five of your ships with the Level 4 pulse cannons," said Cole.

"What about the rest of them?"

"I can't hide a thousand ships," said Cole. "This is supposed to be an ambush. The Navy will see all those ships and hightail it back to the Republic. We're going to take a dozen ships and hide them as best we can, but the *real* damage will be done by the mock *Hungry Raptor*. Even with their shields up, the kind of ships the Navy will send on a rescue mission aren't going to be able to stand up to a Level 5 burner."

"I repeat: What about the rest of my ships?" said Lafferty. "We've left our homes and made a commitment. We're not here to watch from the sidelines."

"We should be back in three days, tops. Then we'll start dividing up the Frontier into maybe ten sections, and put a hundred ships in charge of each. Their jobs will be to recruit still more ships to our cause, and to attack any Navy ship that's, well, attackable. In the meantime, let 'em relax on the station. It'll be a while before they get to unwind here again."

Lafferty nodded. "Send your men to my ship, and I'll give them the Level 5 burner."

"Fine," said Cole. "I'm glad you decided to join us. We're going to need all the help we can get."

He left Lafferty by his ship, contacted Jacovic and told him to select a crew and send them over to Lafferty's ship with whatever they'd need to move a Level 5 laser cannon, then headed to Duke's Place.

"I hear we've got company," noted the Platinum Duke as Cole reached his table and sat down.

"Not company," said Cole. "Allies."

"When do you leave?"

"Tomorrow."

"Just as well," said the Duke, his human lips smiling through his platinum mask. "Your redheaded friend's on a winning streak. I'm out almost forty thousand Far London pounds."

"Let her keep playing," said Cole. "She'll lose it back."

"Do you know anyone who can stop her from playing when she feels like it?" responded the Duke.

"Not offhand."

"Well, if we're going to have close to a thousand ships docked here with all this time on their hands, that translates into a few thousand men. Maybe they can help me make up for what the Valkyrie wins."

"If Mr. Odom ever finishes his goddamned survey, maybe we'll put most of them to work shoring up your defenses."

"But in the meantime, you don't mind if I send a few trams down to their ships to ferry them back to the casino?"

"They're grown men. If they want to play at your tables, it's not my job to warn them off."

"Well, I certainly hope there are some grown aliens among them," replied the Duke. "I mean, hell, half my casino consists of alien games like *jabob* and *stort*."

"There'll be aliens," said Cole. "They've got even less reason to love the Republic than the men do."

Cole spent a few more minutes visiting with the Duke and having an Antarean brandy, then made his way back to the new *Hungry Raptor* to see what kind of progress they were making mounting the cannon.

"Installing it is the easy part," explained Mustapha Odom when Cole queried him about it. "Disguising it will take some skill. A ship this size shouldn't have anything bigger than a Level 2 thumper or burner. If the rescue ships spot a Level 5, they're either going to open fire immediately or turn tail and run."

"I'll trust to your expertise," said Cole. "After all, that's why we're paying you so much money."

"You're not paying me at all."

"We would if we had any money."

Cole returned to the *Teddy R* and went directly to the bridge, where Rachel Marcos and Domak were at their stations.

"Rachel, have Vladimir Sokolov or Braxite reported back yet?"

"Yes, sir," she replied.

"And?"

"Mr. Sokolov says that there are no colony planets within eight light-years."

"That ought to be far enough to be safe from reprisals," said Cole. "Still, you never know . . ." He paused for a moment. "What about Braxite?"

"He says that if the rescue force isn't already on patrol in the area, it will almost certainly be dispatched from New Patagonia."

"Okay, so we know what direction they're likely to come from. Send Sokolov and Braxite each a message not to return to base, that we'll be heading out to the Hayakawa system tomorrow and I want them to stick around."

He left the bridge, went to the airlift, and was in his cabin a minute later.

Everything seemed to be going smoothly. His advance scouts knew the area. His new allies had given him a powerful weapon. His computer expert and his Tolobite had thoroughly disguised the *Shooting Star*. All that was left was the one decision he could no longer put off making.

Who would pilot the mock *Hungry Raptor* and man the weapon against an unknown number of oncoming Navy ships?

The obvious choice was Val, but he couldn't be sure she wouldn't jump the gun and start firing too soon. The best pilot he had—except for Wxakgini, who was literally connected to the ship and couldn't be moved—was either Vladimir Sokolov or Dan Moyer, but that made them too valuable to remove from their own ships.

As he felt sleep overwhelming him, he knew that there was really only one person he trusted to handle the job.

"Goddammit, Wilson!" shouted Sharon when he told her his decision as they had breakfast in the mess hall. "I thought we've had this all out before. The Captain never leaves his ship in enemy territory!"

"It's not enemy territory," Cole said calmly. "It's the Inner Frontier."

"Don't give me that bullshit!" she snapped. "It's enemy territory the second the Navy shows up!"

"I was in the service for fifteen years before the mutiny. There's no ship and no weapon that I can't handle. I'm the best qualified for the job."

"Sure," she said sarcastically. "You're a *much* better shot than Val."

"No," he said. "But I'm a much calmer, more rational one."

"What about Bull Pampas? He's been a gunnery officer since before you ever set foot on the *Teddy R*, and you've never seen him lose his temper. Are you a better, calmer shot than him?"

"No, but he's no pilot, and there's every likelihood that the *Hungry Raptor* will have to do some serious evasive maneuvering."

"Why do you keep doing this?" demanded Sharon. "You know better! You're a middle-aged man! You've got people like Val and Bull to take the risks. You have thousands of men and women and aliens who will follow you to the gates of hell, so what more do you have to prove?"

"Knock it off, Sharon," he said irritably. "I made a decision. It stands."

"Well, it's a dumb decision."

"It could be," said Cole. "I'm not perfect."

"You really won't send Val or Bull?"

"I really won't."

"Then let *me* do it," said Sharon.

He stared at her as if she'd lost her mind.

"Don't you understand?" she said. "We can't afford to lose you."

"I don't believe in suicide missions," said Cole. "I'm taking every possible precaution, and I have no intention of dying."

"Neither did Forrice," she said bitterly.

"That's it," he said, genuinely angry now. "The subject is closed."

Cole got to his feet, walked to the airlift, and was on the bridge a moment later.

"Are all twelve ships ready?" he asked Jacovic.

"Armed and ready," replied the Teroni. "Also, I had Mr. Briggs lay in a course to Hayakawa on your ship's navigational computer, so all you have to do is release from the dock and it will do the rest."

"All the wormholes are programmed in?"

"Yes."

"Christine, is Bull down in Gunnery?"

"Yes, sir," she answered.

"Put me through to him." He waited for the connection. "Bull, did you test the laser cannon?"

"Yes, sir," said Bull Pampas. "Accurate to one hundred and forty thousand miles, probably farther."

"How long is it good for?"

"Forty-eight ten-second bursts on its own power, and Mr. Odom has wired it to the ship's nuclear pile for auxiliary power."

"Sounds good," said Cole. "Thanks."

"It's a honey of a weapon," said Pampas enthusiastically. "Is there any chance we can transfer it to the *Teddy R* after this engagement?"

"That's not a bad idea," said Cole. "We're sure as hell never going to get away using the *Hungry Raptor* again."

He signaled Christine to break the connection.

"Okay, Mr. Jacovic," he said. "You're in command of the *Teddy R* and the other eleven ships. You know how to position them once you reach the Hayakawa system. Just remember: No one breaks radio silence until the shooting starts."

"I understand, sir," said the Teroni.

"All right," said Cole. "I'll see you there."

He turned, walked to the airlift, took it down to the shuttle bay, walked out the hatch, and had a tram take him to the *Hungry Raptor*.

He entered the ship, walked directly to the Level 5 cannon, made sure he understood the mechanism and felt comfortable with it, and then sat down in the Captain's chair.

"Computer, activate."

"*Activated.*"

"Disengage from the dock."

"*Working . . . disengaged.*"

"You're programmed to take me to a preselected spot in the Hayakawa system," said Cole. "Accelerate, and speak to me only if you encounter difficulties in transit."

The *Hungry Raptor* soon reached light speeds and headed for the first of the two wormholes Wxakgini had selected for it and the twelve other ships. Since there was nothing to do until he arrived at his destination, Cole decided to take a nap and instructed the computer to wake him when they reached the outskirts of the Hayakawa system.

He ordered his chair to turn into a bed, and he was asleep within a minute. It seemed to him that he'd just closed his eyes when the computer awakened him to tell him that they were thirty million miles out from Hayakawa IX, the outermost planet.

Hayakawa IX was a ringed gas giant with eleven moons, and seven of the ships would be hiding in the rings and behind the moons. There was a cloud of comets, similar to Sol's Oort Cloud, a couple of hundred million miles behind him, and he knew that the *Teddy R* and three other ships would be there. He had no idea where the Octopus's ship was hiding, but he had to admit it was well concealed, because his instruments couldn't detect it.

Cole waited an hour, just in case there were any laggards in the second wormhole. Then he turned the nose of his ship toward New Patagonia, though the planet was invisible against the brightness of its type G-7 star. Then he killed the engine, activated the emergency life-support system, made sure the laser cannon was receiving power from the nuclear pile, and send out an SOS on the broadest possible wave-length. He decided not to add a verbal request for help; after his adventure on Chambon V, it was possible, even likely, that the Navy had sent his voiceprint to every ship functioning in or near the Inner Frontier.

Then there was nothing to do but wait. Half an hour passed, then a full hour, then a second hour. Just as he was wondering if he should send another SOS, he received a reply.

"Attention, *Hungry Raptor*. We read you loud and clear. Can you feed us your coordinates, all three dimensions?" Pause. "*Hungry Raptor*, do you read us?"

Cole elected not to speak, because he didn't want the receiving ship to identify his voiceprint, so he had the computer acknowledge receipt of the message.

"Are you disabled, *Hungry Raptor*?"

Cole made no response.

"Repeat, please," said the unknown voice on the radio.

Cole remained silent, but left his transmitter on so the Navy could trace the signal to its source—his ship.

"*Hungry Raptor*, if you can answer, please do so. If not, we'll have to assume that you may have fallen to a military attack. If so, rest assured that we will be coming to you in force, and that we will arrive with the ability protect you, destroy your enemies, and evacuate your sick or wounded to a hospital on New Patagonia."

Cole had the computer signal that the message was received, and croaked an unintelligible word to prove he was still alive while disguising his voice. He checked the cannon once more, wished he had some coffee with him, and then sat back and waited. It occurred to him, not for the first time, that war was composed of endless waiting separated by brief periods of incredible violence. He was bored now, but he knew that once the shooting started he'd wish he was back in this position, sitting comfortably in his chair and not facing enemy fire.

How did it come to this? he wondered, staring at empty space on his viewscreen. *I was more than just a good officer; I was a loyal one. I never intended to go up against the Navy. Hell, I was the Navy. I feel like the same man I always was, but I've been a mutineer and a pirate, and here I am, preparing to ambush and destroy Navy ships and their crews. And far from feeling guilty about it, I feel justified. A shrink could have a field day with me.*

After fifteen minutes had passed he received another transmission.

"Our instruments have found you, *Hungry Raptor.* We see no sign of any enemy ships. We should be able to board you and evacuate you within three minutes."

He looked at the viewscreen. There were no ships.

He checked the cannon's computer to see where the ships were. The computer was dead.

Oh, shit! Of course the viewscreen and the cannon can't find you! The ship's power is off.

He didn't dare activate it. The Navy ships would instantly know what he'd done and approach much more cautiously.

He considered his options. There weren't many. With the power off, the viewscreen acted much like a porthole, which meant that he wouldn't see the ships until they were within two or three miles. It also meant that he couldn't do anything to arouse their suspicions, because with no power he had no defensive shields. He had a weapon that could disable or destroy them at one hundred thousand miles, and he couldn't use it until they were a mile away, and since he had to aim the cannon by sight, a quarter mile would be even better.

He was glad Jacovic was in charge of the *Teddy R*. If it had been Val, they'd have been firing already; but the Teroni was an old hand at warfare. He might not know *why* the *Hungry Raptor* was hanging dead in space, but he'd know that Cole had to have a reason, and he'd wait until Cole made the first move.

The only thing that worried him was the Octopus. He still didn't know where the warlord's ship was, and now that the Navy had arrived no one dared contact him to tell him to wait until Cole precipitated the action. Cole finally concluded that the man didn't get to be the commander of three hundred and sixty ships by being stupid, and that he'd know enough to wait, especially when he saw that all the other ships were holding their fire.

"We're almost there, *Hungry Raptor*," said a new transmission. "We've made visual contact. If you are capable, please acknowledge that you're receiving this signal."

Cole waited silently, staring at the viewscreen.

Suddenly he was able to see the ships. There were six of them, all class-L, one of them an ambulance. He chose the nearest ship and manually aimed the laser cannon at it.

He was pretty sure they didn't have their shields up, but without his instruments he couldn't tell. Two of the ships suddenly veered off out of his field of vision, one to each side. It was an absolutely standard approach, in case of a trap. They would keep their weapons trained on him while the ambulance ship made physical contact, bonded the hatches, and began the evacuation.

Now they were within half a mile. For an instant he thought he could see Hayakawa's sun glint off something, and he thought: *Damn it, Octopus! Just sit still for twenty more seconds!*

He wished he could turn the cannon on one of the ships at his side, because they'd be firing sooner than the ones approaching him, but without instruments he couldn't see to either side, and while he could pivot the weapon he'd be firing blind—and he knew he had time for just one shot, two if he was very lucky.

The ships came still closer. At a quarter mile he was ready to fire. Then he decided that since the ruse was working, why not wait until they were at point-blank range? If he could only fire once, he didn't want to miss.

The lead ship closed to within two hundred yards, then one hundred, then fifty—

—and then Cole fired the laser cannon, and instantly activated the ship's systems. He felt a jarring *thud!* just as the shields dropped into place and knew he'd taken a hit. His instruments told him that air was escaping, and he quickly climbed into a space suit.

When he looked into his viewscreen again, he saw two Navy ships—the one he'd hit and one other—hanging dead in space. His instruments found ships approaching from the rings and moons of Hayakawa IX, as well as the comet cloud. They were clearly setting up an englobement maneuver, but none of them were firing, and Cole realized that from that distance they were afraid of hitting him.

He frowned. Then who had killed the other ship, and what was stopping the ships on his sides from trying to pierce his shields?

"Are you just going to sit there?" said a familiar voice on his subspace radio. "Or do you think you can use that damned weapon?"

"Octopus!" said Cole. "Where the hell are you?"

"Right behind you. Who the hell do you think's been protecting your ass?"

"How come they didn't spot you?"

The Octopus laughed. "I'm not on my ship. I set a couple of Level 3 thumpers up on a stray meteor and gave it a push when you came out of the wormhole. I've been your rear guard ever since."

"A *meteor?*" repeated Cole.

"A very small, very dead one."

Cole lined up the ship that had wounded the *Hungry Raptor* and fired the laser cannon. It literally sliced the Navy ship in half.

"I got the one on the other side," said the Octopus. "Just two to go."

And a minute later, when the *Teddy R* was close enough to lock onto a single ship and fire its pulse cannon, there was nothing left but the ambulance ship.

"What are your orders?" asked Jacovic. "The ambulance ship is unarmed."

"Cole, this is Val," said the redhead. "You know what happened the last time you let an ambulance ship go."

"It makes no difference," said the Octopus, who had been monitoring their transmissions.

"What do you mean?" asked Cole.

"The ship the *Theodore Roosevelt* just killed got off a pair of scrambled signals before it was destroyed. The ambulance ship's been sending nonstop. My ship hasn't been able to break the code yet, but I think it's a safe bet that New Patagonia knows what happened, and they can probably guess who was responsible for it."

"All right," said Cole. "We'll let it live."

"Watch it, Cole!" shouted Val.

Suddenly there was a bone-jarring collision, and Cole realized that the ambulance ship had rammed the *Hungry Raptor* amidship. He was hurled into a bulkhead, and then to the top of the ship as the gravitational controls failed.

"Cole, are you all right?" said the Octopus.

"I didn't have any oxygen before the ship rammed me. Now I don't have any gravity either. Nothing's broken, but the *Teddy R* had better send a shuttle over to get me off this thing."

"What about one for the cannon?" asked Jacovic.

"The firing mechanism's busted, but it could be a long time before another Level 5 falls into our hands," said Cole. "Yeah, send another shuttle. We'll take it along and repair it when we get a chance."

"I will send the *Kermit* and the *Edith* immediately," said Jacovic. "ETA should be three to four minutes. Have you enough oxygen?"

What would you do differently if I said no? Cole wanted to ask, but he simply answered in the affirmative.

"Gutsy guys, those medics," commented the Octopus.

"We'll load them onto the *Kermit* when it arrives," said Cole.

"Only if you want to bury them," said the Octopus. "Their ship split wide open on impact. They couldn't have had time to get into their space suits."

"Maybe they were wearing them before the crash," said Cole.

"You're giving them credit for being warriors, not medics," said the Octopus. "My instruments say nothing's alive there, but you can take a closer look."

"We have to," said Cole. "We can't leave them stranded in a powerless ship."

"They'd have been happy to do the same to you. Those were *doctors* that rammed you."

"It was a suicide attack," said Cole. "They saw what we did to the others, they figured there was no way we'd let them walk away, and they decided to take an enemy with them."

"Whatever it was, it was damned stupid," said the Octopus. "You're alive and they're dead."

The *Kermit* arrived then, piloted by Idena Mueller, and Cole transferred to it, then confirmed that there were no survivors on the ambulance ship.

"You'd better get back here quick," said Val's voice as Idena turned the shuttle toward the *Teddy R.*

"What's the problem?" asked Cole.

"I don't think we have to wait to translate those messages the Octopus says were sent."

"Oh?"

"We just heard from the Duke. A force of three hundred Navy ships is approaching Singapore Station." She paused. "He says he's pretty sure they are not going there to carouse and gamble."

The twelve ships were traversing the final wormhole, and Cole was speaking to his senior staff. He hadn't wanted to do it on the bridge, which was too public, and his staff wouldn't fit in his cramped office, so he had commandeered the mess hall, tossed everyone out, and locked the doors when the meeting began. In the room with him were Jacovic, Christine Mboya, Val, Sharon Blacksmith, and Mustapha Odom.

"Well, Mr. Odom," Cole was saying, "you were designing the defenses before this little encounter. How much is actually done?"

"Maybe a third of it," replied Odom. "Most of the weaponry was supplied by black marketers who ply their trade there, and they view it as a business expense."

"But only a third is done," repeated Cole. "Where is the station most vulnerable?"

"That depends on the nature of the ships that are docked at any given time," said Odom.

"Explain, please."

"If they're heavily armed ships like the *Teddy R* and that of the Octopus, then the most vulnerable place is the lowest of the three alien levels of Singapore Station."

"The bottom of the station," clarified Cole.

"Top and bottom are meaningless in space," said Odom.

"Skip the nitpicking," said Cole. "You know what I mean."

"To continue," said the engineer, "if the docks aren't currently home to heavily armed vessels, then of course *they* are the most vulnerable area."

"I know we've installed some powerful thumpers and burners around the station," said Cole. "What about defenses—shields and screens and the like?"

"Impractical," replied Odom. "The station is seven miles long. The longest ship in the Navy is a quarter of a mile, and the power drain for its shields is enormous."

"How many Level 4 and Level 5 cannons has the station got in place?"

"There were quite a few left over from your battle with Csonti last year," said Odom. "Given them, and what we just added, I'd say eighty, maybe eighty-five."

"That many?" said Cole, surprised.

"That number is misleading," continued Odom. "The station was not built at once, but was pieced together from literally hundreds of small stations. The exterior is not a consistent line, and the cannons are positioned in such a way that they cannot be brought into play against an attack on certain portions of the station."

"Thank you, Mr. Odom. Christine, have we got any communication channels that the Navy doesn't know about?"

"I doubt it, sir," she replied. "After all, this *is* a Navy ship."

"Any scramble codes that the Duke can read that the Navy can't break?"

"I don't think so, sir. We've never felt the need to carry on secret communications with the Platinum Duke or with Singapore Station, so we've never programmed his computers with our codes."

"So we're out of luck?" said Val.

"Not necessarily," said Cole.

"But if they can read all our transmissions . . ."

"We'll just have to feed them some transmissions we *want* them to read."

"If you mislead them, you'll also mislead the Duke," said Val.

"Which is more important?" asked Cole. "Misleading the Navy, or not misleading the Duke?"

"Okay," acknowledged Val. "Good point."

Cole turned to Jacovic. "We've got a thousand ships defending the station. Or at least that's what we have before the Navy gets there. I've commanded a fleet once, a year ago, and the enemy broke and ran. You did it for years. Once we get there and appraise the situation, I'm going to depend heavily on your expertise."

"Knowing how to use them is one thing," said Jacovic. "Having them act like a cohesive unit when they have never practiced together is another. They will not know how to organize into offensive and defensive formations, they will not know—"

"I'm sure you could write a book on all the things they don't know," interrupted Cole. "We'll just have to improvise, but I still want you right next to me when I start issuing orders to what's left of them."

"How much damage do you think the Navy can do before we get there?" asked Sharon.

"I don't know," said Cole. "It won't be a surprise attack; the Duke knew they were on their way. And hopefully someone will take charge of the ships that we left behind."

"Lafferty, perhaps?" suggested Jacovic.

Cole shook his head. "I don't think he's military, just political. We can't worry about *who* will take command against the first assault; we'll just assume *someone* will."

"I think we can expect pretty heavy casualties in the initial attack," said Jacovic.

"Probably," agreed Cole. "But we do outnumber them a little

better than three-to-one, and the Duke had time to put crews on those cannons. We won't be the only side to take some serious losses."

"An awful lot of our ships don't exactly classify as warships," noted Sharon.

"They're ships, they're armed, and this is a war," said Cole. "That makes them warships." He turned to the Valkyrie. "Val, if we can possibly get close enough for you to make the transfer safely, I want you on the station."

"I'm supposed to be on the ship with you," she said.

"Bull can handle Gunnery, and I'll have Jack-in-the-Box to help him. But sooner or later—probably sooner—the Navy's going to land some men on the station and try to disrupt whatever we're doing. That's where you can be the most use to us."

Suddenly a smile spread across her face. "Yeah, I wouldn't mind that at all."

"Somehow I'm not surprised," said Cole dryly. "If we can land a shuttle close enough on one of the dock arms we will. But it might work better and attract less attention if you just climbed into a space suit and used a jet pack. We'll decide when we see the situation." He frowned. "And speaking of seeing the situation, just how much longer before we get there?"

Christine activated her communicator. "Mr. Wxakgini, what is our ETA?"

"We emerged from the wormhole twelve minutes ago. Our ETA is seven minutes and fourteen seconds."

"All right, meeting's over," said Cole. "Get back to your stations. Jacovic, stay close to me once we get there. Val, get a suit and pack handy in case that's the way we decided to get you there." He opened the doors. "Let's go."

Odom returned to his engine room, Sharon to her monitoring station in Security, Val to the shuttle bay to pick up a space suit, and the others to the bridge, where Christine replaced Rachel at the main computer console.

"Can you pull any images up on your screen yet, Mr. Briggs?" asked Cole.

"Not yet, sir," responded Briggs. "There's a lot of shooting going on, and the station's taken some hits, but I won't have any clear images for another minute or two."

"Christine, try to contact the Duke and see what the situation is."

"No response, sir," she said. "I think they may have taken out his transmitter."

Cole shook his head. "I doubt it. He's got transmitters all over the damned station. He's probably just deactivated them. The ships won't take their orders from him, and he doesn't want the Navy to hear what he's saying to his own men, so he's probably using a bunch of two-way communicators."

Val returned to the bridge, carrying a suit and a pack. "How's it going?" she asked.

"Ask *him*," said Cole, indicating Briggs.

"It's hard to tell," replied Briggs. "Both sides are still firing. The ships are all clustered so close to the station that I can't tell which are out of commission and which are still fighting."

"We'd better start coordinating our plans," said Cole. "Christine, put me through to the Octopus and the rest of the ships in our party."

"Are you sure you want to break radio silence, sir?" she asked.

"If our instruments can see them, theirs can see us," replied Cole. "And if some of them want to break away from attacking the station and come after us, so much the better."

"You are connected, sir."

"This is Cole," he said. "I trust you can all see what's happening at the station. I'm going to turn you over to Commander Jacovic, who will explain our strategy to you."

"Thank you, Captain," said Jacovic. "There is no sense splitting up and getting into a bunch of what you know as dogfights. We have a thousand other ships to do that. Between our twelve ships we have enough Level 4 pulse and laser cannons to pierce through the defenses of any ship below dreadnaught level, and there are no dreadnaughts in this conflict. As we select each target, we will transmit its location and image to you, and then we will attack it in unison. We haven't worked as a unit, so there is no sense attempting any complex maneuvers. We will have our greatest success massing our firepower against one major target at a time."

Cole studied Briggs's computer screen. "There's a class-M ship, name the *Jolly Roger*, registration number 38259 and the rest is illegible. He's our first target."

The twelve ships homed in on the *Jolly Roger*, and it soon became apparent why it had been chosen. It was at the outskirts of the battle, obviously hanging back to spot and shoot down any of Cole's and Lafferty's ships that broke formation and tried to flee. But that meant it wasn't surrounded by other Navy ships, and was relatively easy to approach.

Vladimir Sokolov's ship was the first to reach it, followed by the Octopus. By the time the *Teddy R* got there, the *Jolly Roger* had taken four major hits from pulse cannons. Its side was caved in and it was losing air.

"He's dead, sir," said Dan Moyer's voice. "What's our next target."

"Finish this one off," said Cole. "It only takes one man with a space suit to work a laser cannon when you leave it for dead and don't defend against it as you fly by."

Jacovic nodded his agreement. "You heard your captain," he said.

Moyer fired two more energy pulses into the ship, and finally it exploded in a brief flare of light. Cole immediately picked their next target.

Val walked over to Cole. "There's no way the shuttle can leave the ship and dock safely. I think it's time for me to climb into the suit and jet over to the station."

"There's too much action and stray fire," said Cole. "Wait until both sides are thinned out a bit."

"If they land first, I don't want to run into any reception committees."

"If I tell you to wait, you're just going to come up to me every minute or two and ask if you can leave yet, right?"

"Probably," she said.

"All right, leave," said Cole.

"I'm on my way!" she yelled over her shoulder as she raced to the airlift.

"Get me Gunnery," said Cole.

Bull Pampas's image popped into view.

"Bull, your redheaded sparring partner is about to don a space suit and use a jet pack to get to the station. Forget whatever Jacovic has targeted; we have eleven ships to take care of business. I want you to ride shotgun for Val. Any ship that even looks like it might be getting her in their sites, start firing until they drop or you're out of power."

"Yes, sir."

Cole turned to a viewscreen. For a moment all he could see was ships firing at each other. Then a tiny figure shot into the picture, making a beeline toward a hatch at the top level of the station.

"That's her!" said Briggs.

"I know. Bull damned well better be protecting her ass."

A small Navy ship approached her, and was suddenly bombarded with energy pulses. It took five, six, seven consecutive hits before it simply disintegrated.

"Mr. Lafferty's signaling us, sir," announced Christine.

"Put him through."

Lafferty's image appeared. "Welcome back. I take it we have you to thank for all this?"

"We didn't want you to feel neglected," said Cole. "What's the situation?"

"I've lost about a hundred ships, you've lost maybe seventy."

"What about the Republic?"

"Maybe forty."

"Have any of them made it into the station yet?"

"Not to my knowledge."

"We'll have Val there in another minute," said Cole. "If any of your people sees a boarding party getting through, have them contact her and tell her where the breach occurred."

"I don't know any Val."

"That's right, you don't," said Cole, surprised that *any*one didn't know the legendary Valkyrie. "Then signal us and we'll pass it on to her. How's your ammunition holding out?"

"No problem. My guess is that the Navy will run out first."

"Try picking out a ship and have twelve or thirteen ships attack it in unison," said Cole. "I don't think you've got the ships to win any dogfights."

"I've got five hundred cantankerous individuals," said Lafferty. "This is a hell of a time to teach them to work as a unit."

"They can work as a unit or die as cantankerous individuals," said Cole.

"Perfect."

"What are you talking about?"

"I just captured that comment," said Lafferty. "I'm going to transmit it to all my men."

"Whatever works," said Cole. Suddenly the *Teddy R* shuddered. "Got to sign off. We're under attack."

"Our shields are up, sir," said Briggs.

"Mr. Odom, any damage to the engines?"

"None," said Odom.

"Do we still have our structural integrity?"

"So far so good," said Odom.

The ship shuddered twice more.

Cole looked up at the viewscreen. All he could see were Navy ships, closing in on him from all directions.

"I think," said Sharon's voice, "that they've figured out who we are."

As if to emphasize her point, the *Teddy R* shuddered from three more pulse blasts.

"Mr. Odom, how are our shields holding up?"

"So far so good," said Odom. The ship shuddered again. "But I won't vouch for them if we take another dozen full-force blasts from Level 4 cannons."

"At the rate they're coming," said Cole, "that gives us about forty-five seconds to think of something."

Two more explosions followed in quick succession.

"Make that forty," he muttered.

Cole stared at the viewscreen. He counted fifteen Navy ships, and he realized he was probably missing some.

He thought of ordering Wxakgini to back away, but he knew there were ships behind him too. He then considered asking Jacovic if he had any suggestions, but he knew the Teroni would have offered them if he had.

"Bull?"

"Sir?" said Pampas.

"Jettison every mine we have left."

There was a brief pause.

"Done, sir."

"After the first one takes out a ship, at least they'll approach us a little more cautiously," he said to Jacovic.

"Look at *that!*" exclaimed Briggs, pointing to a viewscreen. "No mine did that!"

They all looked, and saw a ship being torn to pieces by a pair of energy pulses. Suddenly a second Navy ship exploded, and then a third.

"What's going on?" said Cole. "I don't see any of our ships firing at them."

"It's coming from the station," said Christine.

"That's got to be Val," said Cole as another ship was destroyed.

"Why her?" asked Briggs.

"Because she hasn't missed yet."

Three more ships exploded, and suddenly they ignored the *Teddy R* and concentrated their fire on the station.

"Pilot!" said Cole. "Get us the hell out of here before they start firing at us again!"

Wxakgini, who was in constant rapport with the navigational computer, instantly withdrew to a distance of five hundred miles.

"Something's wrong," said Cole, staring at the screen. "I thought the Navy only had three hundred ships."

"That's correct, sir," said Briggs.

"We've only got a thousand, counting all the ships that the Octopus and Lafferty bring to the table."

"Yes, sir."

"Well, damn it, either I'm going blind or I see about three thousand ships out there!"

"I just had my computer do a count, sir," said Christine. "There are three thousand six hundred and twenty-seven ships engaged in the battle."

"Put me through to Lafferty," said Cole.

She nodded that the connection had been made.

"Lafferty, there's too damned many ships out there," said Cole. "Are they ours or the Navy's?"

"Ours," replied Lafferty. "You don't think the Navy can spare three thousand ships just to wipe out a space station, do you?"

"Then who the hell *are* they?"

"They're all the men and aliens who live here and work here and dock their ships here," said Lafferty. "This is their home. It's under attack, and they're fighting to defend it." His image displayed a grin. "I think the Navy bit off a little more than it can chew."

"Well, I'll be damned," said Cole.

"Probably," said Lafferty. "But we're going to send the Navy ahead of us to warm up some seats by the fire."

The transmission ended, and Cole turned to Jacovic. "The Navy blew it this time. If you're going to send out a punishment party, you'd better punish the people you're mad at, and not just the first people you come across."

"Still, our side is too disorganized to take any orders or apply any reasonable tactics," noted the Teroni.

"And they're probably too mad, too," said Cole. "I think we'll stay where we are, and withdraw perhaps twenty of our ships and another twenty of the Octopus's to encircle the battlefield, if that's the word for it and I suspect it's not. Let's cut off all escape routes for the Navy."

Jacovic nodded his agreement. "I'll pass the word." He walked over to Christine and began listing the ships and pilots he wanted pulled.

"Incoming message," said Briggs.

"On yours, not Christina's?"

"She's moving them here while she's sending out Jacovic's orders."

"Okay, let's have it."

"Hey, Cole!" yelled Val, her red hair disheveled, grinning like a wild woman. "I got ten of 'em! Does that get me a bottle of that Scotch you were drinking?"

"That's up to the Duke," said Cole. "But I'll buy you a bottle if you get ten more."

"You're on!"

"How much damage have they done to the station?"

"These walls have pretty tight molecular bonding," she replied. "I think they've only been breached in three places, and we've got repair crews working on the damage. The biggest problem I've got now is there are so many of *our* ships out there I can't get any clear shots at the enemy."

"It's better than *not* having anyone on our side," said Cole.

"They're really pissed off," she continued. "I've seen you mad at the

Navy before, but not like this. It's as if they all decided at once that you can't ignore these bastards anymore, you've got to get into your ships and kill 'em."

"I just wish more than a handful of them had decent weaponry," said Cole.

"It's not stopping them from trying," she said. "I tried to give them a battle cry—'Kill for Cole!'—but they seem to like 'Save Singapore' better."

"No reason why they shouldn't," said Cole. "Singapore's what they're fighting for."

There was an explosion and the transmission went dead.

"What happened?" demanded Cole.

"The station took a major hit right where she was standing," said Briggs. "She never had a chance."

"Nothing can kill her," said Cole.

"Sir, I saw the energy pulse hit, followed by some kind of explosive torpedo."

"I know what you saw," said Cole. "Just keep watching for her signal. That lady is indestructible."

Briggs looked at him as if he'd taken leave of his senses, then shrugged and went back to his computer.

"That was a hell of a hit, Wilson," said Sharon's voice. "I wouldn't get my hopes up."

Before Cole could answer, a familiar female voice came through Briggs's receiver.

". . . and no goddamned motherfucking torpedo is going to slow *me* down!"

Val's image slowly appeared, riddled by static. She was sporting a black eye, blood was trickling down her cheek, the shoulder of her uniform was torn and there was more blood, but she seemed, if anything, more vigorous than usual. "Goddamned shitheel's just lucky he's still on his ship and I can't get my hands on him."

Cole smiled. "That's my girl," he said.

"Hey, Cole, I've got to make way for the repair crews. I'm going up to the top level. There are three Level 4 burners up there. Maybe I'll recruit a crew to man them along the way."

"You're closer to the situation than I am," said Cole. "Do what you think best."

"I'll contact you again after I'm there," she said. Suddenly she looked past the holocam that was capturing her image. "Hey, you! Ever fire a cannon?" Pause. "Well, today's a good day to learn. Get your ass up to the top level."

She broke the connection.

"I'll say it again," said Cole. "Give me fifty like her and I could conquer the galaxy."

"Maybe forty-five," amended Jacovic with one of his very rare smiles.

Cole looked over at Briggs's computer. Forty ships had pulled back after receiving the Teroni's orders, but the battle still raged on around the station.

"Are they positioned the way you want them?" asked Cole.

"Yes," said Jacovic.

"You're sure this is the optimum position?"

"Yes," repeated Jacovic.

"Then let's get back into this fight," said Cole.

"We're strategically placed right now," said the Teroni.

"Yeah, but three thousand ships are fighting on our side right now because *I* decided the Navy wasn't allowed on the Inner Frontier. Maybe they'll look out here and figure out why we pulled back from the battle, but more likely they'll feel like dupes, fighting our battle while we become spectators."

"Why would they think that?" asked Jacovic.

"Because *I* would," answered Cole. "Pilot, coordinate with Mr. Sokolov's and Mr. Moyer's ships. Maybe we can do something with them.

As the *Teddy R* was approaching the station, one of the docking arms broke off, a half-mile-long metallic structure with some fifty ships still attached to it. It floated off into space, clipping an unwary Navy ship along the way and heading out of the battle zone.

"Watch yourself, sir!" came Sokolov's voice.

"What is it?" asked Cole.

"A dead ship almost collided with you. It's getting crowded."

"Where's Moyer?"

"I haven't seen his ship in twenty minutes, sir," said Sokolov.

"I have," chimed in Braxite's voice. "He was hit by friendly fire. I don't know if he survived. He seemed in a bad way, though."

"Have you spotted their flagship?" asked Cole.

"Val took it out as soon as she got to the station, sir."

"So we have three thousand ships with no battle plan, and the enemy has lost their command center," muttered Cole. "This is going to get messy."

And it *did* get messy. It was almost impossible to fire a shot in the vicinity of Singapore Station without hitting *something*, whether friend or foe. The ships, and parts of ships, floated aimlessly around the station, colliding with other ships that were too busy concentrating on the enemy. Soon bodies, first dozens, then hundreds, also began floating through space, spinning crazily when hit by a ship or a laser or pulse blast.

"Hey, Cole!" said a familiar voice. "Get that bottle ready! I'm up to fifteen!"

Cole looked at Val's image. There was so much blood, he couldn't believe that she was still standing.

"I'll get the infirmary ready first," he said. "In fact, there's a medical center on the level below Duke's casino. You'd better get down there while you can still walk."

"You're not getting out of buying me my Scotch that easy!" she bellowed.

"I'll buy it anyway," said Cole. "We just don't want to lose you."

"I'll be standing here long after you and—*shit!*"

"What is it?"

"Seven or eight of the bad guys got into the station somehow!"

"You mean the Navy?" asked Cole.

"Are there any other bad guys around?" she asked, pulling her burner and firing it at someone he couldn't see. She turned to face still more unseen opponents. "Boy, did you dumb bastards choose the wrong station to board!"

The transmission went dead.

"I wouldn't want to be part of that boarding party," said Cole.

"She's remarkable," agreed Jacovic.

"Just be glad she's on *our* side."

The ship shuddered, and Cole was thrown against a bulkhead.

"What the hell was *that?*" he said. "It sure as hell didn't feel like an energy pulse."

"We were broadsided by a class-L Navy ship," announced Briggs.

"On purpose, or derelict?"

"Seems to be a dead one."

"Mr. Odom?"

"Yes, sir?" said the engineer.

"Any damage from that last one?"

"None."

"Not even a dent in the hull?"

"Not with this molecular structure," replied Odom. "They might disintegrate it, but they'll never dent it."

"While I'm thinking of it, how's our ammunition holding out?"

"You've only used about eight percent of it," said Odom. "We've actually fired our weapons very little."

"Okay, thanks." The connection ended. "Has anyone got a count on Navy ships, living or dead?"

"I can't give you an exact count, sir," said Christine. "But we have destroyed or disabled about one hundred and sixty."

"More that half?" said Cole, surprised.

"We *do* outnumber them ten to one," Sharon's voice reminded him. "Or at least we did at the beginning. We've lost about seven hundred ships."

Cole looked at another viewscreen. Like the first, it was filled with live, dead, and dying ships, illuminated every few seconds by pulse and laser bursts and sudden explosions. The tiny bits of debris he saw floating through the area were actually bodies, most of them dead, the rest soon to be dead.

"This isn't the kind of warfare any of us trained for," he said, staring hypnotically at the screen.

"When will it stop?" asked Jacovic.

"When the last of us or the last of them is dead," said Cole.

"And when will it *end*?"

"I just told you."

"I mean, when will the Republic finally leave the Inner Frontier to the people who live here?"

"When they plunder the last world than *can* be plundered," said Cole, "and recruit the last man or woman who can be forcibly pressed into service." He forced a tight smile to his lips. "It *does* bring back all the reasons we're fighting this action."

Suddenly a bulkhead opened up, and David Copperfield crawled out of it, bright pink blood streaming out of what passed for his nostrils.

"What the hell happened to *you*?" asked Briggs.

"I'll tell you what happened," said Cole. He turned to the little alien. "David, how many times have I told you not to hide inside the bulkheads?"

"They were always safe before," said Copperfield.

"We weren't being rammed by derelict ships before," said Cole. He stared at the alien. "Are you badly hurt?"

"No," said Copperfield, shaking his head and simultaneously causing blood to fly in all directions.

"Get down to the infirmary and have them stop the bleeding," said Cole. "After that, you can stay there, come back here, or go to your cabin. But no more bulkheads."

"No more bulkheads," promised Copperfield, heading off to the airlift.

"Bull!" said Cole. "Do you need relief down there?"

"No, sir," said Pampas, replying from the Gunnery section. "There are so many targets we could use some help, but we'll stay here until the battle's over one way or the other."

"Okay, we'll get someone down there right away." He turned to Christine. "Tell Idena Mueller to report to Gunnery."

A huge energy pulse jarred the ship as it was absorbed by the shields.

Odom's image instantly appeared on the bridge. "Sir, we can only take about two more blows of that magnitude before the left forward shield goes."

"You mean buckles?" asked Cole.

Odom shook his head. "I mean becomes totally inoperable. It's not my job to tell you how to run the ship or conduct the battle, but I'd sure try not to get hit on that side again."

"Duly noted," replied Cole. "And thanks."

Domak, who had appropriated the computer in Cole's office, suddenly contacted the bridge.

"Sir," said her image, "I think I've found the spot where the Navy is entering the station."

"Oh?" said Cole. "Where?"

"Not one of the hatches. The Duke booby-trapped them. No, it's an exhaust port on the second of the three human levels. I'm going to enlarge and transmit the image to you."

An instant later her face was replaced by a close-up of the exhaust port. There had been a titanium grate over it, but it had been pulled off and was floating somewhere in space. The hole was large enough for a human body to pass through it, and as Cole stared at it, he was able to discern movement in the exhaust vent's dark interior. He wished he could get word to Val, but her transmission had shorted out when she was preparing to face a party of boarders.

"Can we get a little closer to that vent?" asked Cole.

"If nobody shoots us," answered Wxakgini, putting the ship in motion.

"That's clearly where they're getting in. I want to make sure that no one else can enter the station that way."

Wxakgini maneuvered the ship to within half a mile of the vent. "Any closer and we're not only at risk from enemy fire but from disabled ships," he announced.

"Bull," said Cole, "use the burner, not the thumper, and see if you can seal that exhaust port on the second level."

"I don't see how, sir," answered Pampas. "There was never a door on it, and nothing we have can melt the station's outer shell."

"There are millions of ship parts floating past," said Cole. "Can't you push a door or a piece of a bulkhead against it and melt it? It doesn't have to be pretty, it just has to work until the shooting's over."

"I can't do it with a ship's exterior, sir, but maybe a bulkhead or the inner wall of a corridor . . ."

"Give it a try," said Cole.

Pampas selected what appeared to be the door of a cabin. Working in unison with Idena, they lowered the power on their weapons and nudged it up against the station, edged it into place with an exterior pulse rifle, and then melted it with a laser.

"That's going to have to do, sir," Pampas announced when he'd finished.

"It'll do fine," said Cole.

"Until someone blows it away again," said Briggs.

"No one blew it away the first time," answered Cole. "It's a vent, not a hatch. And I don't think Val's going to leave any survivors to radio back that it's the perfect way to storm the station."

"We've got to do something, sir," said Christine suddenly as she stared at her computer's holoscreen. "Lafferty's men and the volunteers from the station are hitting as many of their own—*our* own—ships as the Navy's."

"I don't know how to call the volunteers off or direct them," said Cole. "At least we can get Lafferty's men to stop. Patch me through to him."

"I can't, sir. Either his computer has been damaged or his communications are out."

"Wonderful," muttered Cole. *Think! How do you organize or call off two thousand men who aren't fighting for you in the first place?* And then it came to him. "Christine, get me the Duke."

The Platinum Duke's image appeared an instant later.

"How are you holding up?" asked Cole.

"So far so good, thanks to our one-woman wrecking machine."

"I need you to do something," said Cole. "I don't know who the hell the station's volunteer defenders are, but they're doing more harm than good. You own the station; you've got to have a record of which ships have taken off since you learned the Navy was approaching. A few of them probably just turned tail and ran, but most of them are involved in the battle. Have your computer sort them out and feed their access codes to the *Teddy R.*"

"It shouldn't take a minute," said the Duke, "half of which will be spent getting to my computer."

He didn't bother breaking the connection. The holoscreen showed an empty chair where he had been for the next twenty seconds, and then he appeared at the desk in his office, giving orders to his computer.

"Here it comes," he announced.

"Got it," said Christine.

"Thanks," said Cole. "Now see if you can get Val to your hospital."

"Why don't you ask for something easy, like conquering Deluros VIII?"

Cole broke the connection. "Christine, can you broadcast my message to all the ships the Duke just gave us?"

"Yes."

"Now." He waited for her to nod that she was ready. "Attention! This is Wilson Cole, Captain of the *Theodore Roosevelt*. We appreciate your intentions, but you're doing as much damage to yourselves as to the enemy. We haven't got time to do this democratically, so I'm designating each ship that's class-J or above as a group leader. I want each leader, accompanied by the thirty closest ships below the level of class-J, to select one target, let your ships know what it is, and home in on it. No side battles, no distractions. If and when you have dispatched that Navy ship, choose another. If you are not a class-J ship and you don't know where one is, wait until you see attack groups forming and attach yourself to one. If any group leader needs tactical advice, now or for the duration of the battle, contact Commander Jacovic. His private channel is being programmed into your ships' computers"—he looked at Christine, who nodded again—"right now."

He ran a finger across his throat, signaling her to break the connection.

"Now get me the Octopus."

The huge man appeared almost instantly.

"I *think* we're winning," he announced. "But there's so much debris and so many dead ships floating around I can't be sure."

"I just gave some basic orders to the two thousand volunteers," said Cole. "Well, maybe thirteen or fourteen hundred now. They're going to choose their targets and attack in force—but there's no rhyme or reason to their choice. It'll be whichever they're closest to. Once they sort themselves out into groups, you and your best-armed ships will be able to tell who they're going after. Let's assume they'll at least neutralize those ships by keeping them busy. I want you to select the best-armed Navy ships that they don't target, and go after them yourselves."

"Give me a minute to see what's available to me," replied the Octopus. "I know a couple of my best ships are dead."

"It'll take more than a minute for the volunteers to organize. They're used to smuggling and stealing and the occasional armed robbery, but most of them have never fought as a military unit. My guess is that right this instant half of them are trying to understand my orders and the other half are arguing with them."

The Octopus laughed. "Well, you wanted to take on the Navy."

"Not really," said Cole. "I just wanted them to leave us alone."

The ship shuddered from another collision, and the communication was broken.

"Mr. Odom, are we okay?"

"Give me a minute to check, sir," said Odom. "That hit the same weakened shield." A brief pause. "Yes, but I really wouldn't advise taking another hit there."

"Thanks," said Cole.

"Hey, Cole!" yelled a familiar voice.

"Someday I'm going to have to teach you how to address your Captain," said Cole.

"Eight men boarded, eight men dead."

"But probably not today," added Cole. "How come I'm not getting a visual of you?"

"Because you've got a weak stomach and a soft heart, and I'm not going to see any medics until this damned battle is over. And I'm up to seventeen ships. Three more and you owe me a bottle of Scotch from Earth."

"I haven't forgotten. Now let me see you."

"You were warned."

Her image appeared.

"Jesus! There's even more blood than before!"

"It matches my hair," she said. Suddenly she smiled. "You should see the other guys."

"I'll take your word for it."

He ended the transmission. "How are we doing?" he asked Jacovic. "Any recognizable groups yet?"

"They're not doing too badly. I wouldn't call them formations, but if you're a Navy ship with two or three cannons and you're being attacked by thirty or forty ships at once, I don't suppose it makes much difference."

Even as he spoke, two Navy ships were blown out of existence, at the cost of fourteen smaller volunteer ships.

"I disapprove of wars of attrition," said Jacovic, "but if we trade seven small ships for every Navy ship, we're going to win this battle."

"There's got to be a way to contact Lafferty's ships and organize them," said Cole.

"We don't have codes for anyone but Lafferty himself, and he's not answering," said Christine.

"There *has* to be—" Suddenly Cole turned to Christina. "Get me the Duke!"

The Platinum Duke's image appeared a few seconds later.

"What is it?" he asked.

"Duke, somewhere on that station is an alien named Dozhin, the one I brought back with me from Piccoli III. We've lost contact with Lafferty. Dozhin's got to know how to contact at least some of the men who came out here with him."

"I'll put out a call for him at once."

"He's about as heroic as David, so make sure he knows that all we want are access codes, that he can stay on the station with you."

"Got it," said the Duke. "Let me get started."

And five minutes later, Christine told Cole that he could now contact seven of the ships in Lafferty's group.

"Assuming they're still in action," added Briggs.

"Let's find out," said Cole.

He made contact with five of the seven ships, and made the same suggestions to them that he'd made to the volunteers.

"That'll work," said one of Lafferty's men. "With Lafferty, Grabowski, and McMullen all dead, we hadn't established a deep enough chain of command, but this will cure that."

"Good luck," said Cole, breaking the connection. He looked around the bridge. "Is there anything else I'm overlooking?"

"I don't think so, sir," said Christine.

"Then to borrow a phrase from the Valkyrie, let's get back to shooting the bad guys."

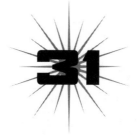

The battle raged on for another five hours. The Octopus had lost more than two hundred and fifty of his ships, Lafferty's men had lost another three hundred, and the volunteers from the station had lost upward of a thousand ships. As nearly as Christine could tell, the Navy had lost close to two hundred eighty ships.

The area around Singapore Station was cluttered with the corpses of dead ships and dead men. Debris floated in all directions, and derelict ships were causing more damage than the weaponry of those ships that remained active. One wounded man collapsed on the firing mechanism of his laser weapon, and as his disabled ship went into a spin the killer beams threatened both sides—and by mutual if unspoken consent, Vladimir Sokolov and a Navy ship combined to blow it up before the unaimed cannon could do any further damage.

"I think we're finally winning!" said Briggs as yet another Navy ship was blown apart.

"How the hell can you tell?" said Cole grimly.

"They can't have twenty ships left," said Briggs.

"And we've lost, what, fifteen hundred ships? Two thousand? To borrow a phrase, another such victory and we are undone."

"Sir!" came Domak's excited voice. "The station! Check your viewscreen!"

Cole looked at the screen, just in time to see a Navy ship plunge into the top level of Singapore Station. It vanished in a spectacular flare of light.

"It's a little late in the game for kamikazes, isn't it?" said Christine.

"Val's in there," said Cole. "So are the Duke and maybe forty thousand others. Mr. Odom, can they break it open with that tactic?"

Odom's image appeared. "I very much doubt it. I inspected the station when I was trying to position its defenses, and its outer walls are built to withstand meteors and comets."

"You're sure?"

"Yes, sir."

"Thanks," said Cole as Odom's image vanished. "That means we won't have to try to englobe the station and bear the brunt of the suicide attacks."

"It would be exceptionally difficult anyway," said Jacovic. "It's seven miles long, and it has a lot of corners."

"There goes another Navy ship," noted Christine.

"That's twenty-seven!" said Val, her bloody face floating just in front of the largest viewscreen. "I don't suppose you're paying a bounty on these things."

"You're already getting your Scotch," said Cole. "I'll toss in your hospital charges."

"I never saw anyone make such a fuss over a few nicks and scratches," said Val. "When we take out another half-dozen Navy ships, I think I'll come back to the *Teddy R*. Too much garbage floating around here for me to get in many clean shots."

"Stay where you are," ordered Cole. "We can't protect you from the Navy *and* the debris."

"How's my protégé doing down in Gunnery?"

"Bull? He's doing fine."

"He'd better be. Tell him I've got my eye on him." She uttered a string of obscenities. "All I can see from here are bits and pieces of dead ships. I can't get a clear shot. I'm going to go borrow some of the

Duke's drinkin' stuff and see if some of this crap has floated away by the time I get back."

The transmission went dead.

"Thank God she's on *our* side!" said Christine.

"Twenty-seven!" added Briggs. "She's really something!"

"Sir?" came Vladimir Sokolov's voice. "I've just taken a major hit. I'm unharmed, but all my controls have gone dead. The ship's in a slow spin; I think it'll bounce off the station in about two or three minutes."

"Is your emergency life-support system working?" asked Cole.

"No, sir. I'm in my space suit. With my auxiliary air supply, I'm good for eight or nine hours. I think that—"

The transmission ended in midsentence.

"Mr. Briggs, have your computer track his ship. I want to make sure we can pick him up before he's out of air."

"Yes, sir."

"Got five of them englobed!" said the Octopus. "Take a look, Cole!"

There was a blinding explosion.

"Shoot *my* son, will you?" yelled the Octopus. A triumphant smile spread across his face as his image vanished.

"Christine, how many of them are left?" asked Cole.

She checked her computer, then turned to him with a surprised expression. "Nine, sir."

"You're sure?"

"Pretty sure." Suddenly she smiled. "We're actually going to win, aren't we, sir? We're actually going to beat the Navy!"

"Until the next time," said Cole.

"You don't seem very elated," she noted.

"You're counting *their* dead," replied Cole. "I'm counting *ours*."

He turned back to the battle at hand. Six Navy ships were under heavy bombardment. He tried to find the other three, but there was so much junk floating around that he couldn't spot them. Then he saw an explosion and knew that *somebody* had spotted one of them.

Another ten minutes passed, and five more Navy ships were blown apart.

"They've got guts, I'll give them that," said Briggs about the last three Navy ships. "They have to know they haven't got a chance, but they're not retreating."

One of the Navy ships fired, and two of Lafferty's ships vanished.

"They're still dangerous," noted Jacovic.

"They're not the problem," said Cole. "If killing one ship cost two million people on Braccio II their lives, what kind of retribution will the Republic be planning for *this?*"

"Another one down, sir," reported Briggs. "Only two left."

The Octopus had one englobed in a matter of seconds, and then there was only one Navy ship left. Lafferty's ships instantly swarmed over it, shattering it into a million pieces.

"It's over," said Cole to Christine. "Pass the word to cease fire."

"Yes, sir."

"Mr. Briggs, see if you can pinpoint their flagship. If it's still intact, we ought to be able to extract some of their codes. It might help us the next time."

"Will there *be* a next time?" asked Briggs.

Cole merely stared at him, and finally Briggs turned nervously to his computer. After a couple of minutes he announced that he had found the flagship, which had been taken out of action in the first few minutes of battle.

"Pilot, get the coordinates from Mr. Briggs and take us there. We may have to enter the ship to get everything we want."

They reached it in another minute.

"Sir," said Domak's voice. "Before you board it, there's still someone alive on it."

"Christine, can you get me a visual of their bridge?"

"I'll try, sir," she said, giving her computer a number of commands. "It will be difficult, since their transmitter has been disabled. But . . . Ah! Here it comes, sir."

Suddenly they saw the bridge of the Navy's flagship. It was littered with bodies. Five Men, a Molarian, a Mollutei, and a Polonoi lay at awkward angles, drenched in blood.

"Where's the—?" began Cole, and then he saw him.

It was a young ensign, his face bleeding, his left arm held at an impossible angle, his tunic shredded, his torso covered with still more blood.

"Come on!" said the ensign, and now Cole could see that his right eye was swollen shut. "Where are you?" He held his sonic pistol in a shaking hand.

Jesus! thought Cole. *He's so young. He could be Rachel's kid brother. Or Chadwick's. He's in agony, he's got to be scared, he's got to know it's all over, that the Navy lost—but he's not backing off.*

Cole couldn't take his eyes off the young man. *He's not going to back up a step.* He remembered the first thing he learned when he himself had first joined the Navy: "Surrender is not in our lexicon."

And then he realized: *That's not Rachel's brother. That's* me *twenty years ago.*

"Go home, kid," said Cole at last.

"Who said that?" demanded the ensign.

"You've got a shuttle that's working. If you'll drop your weapon, I'll send a medic over to patch you up. Then get the hell out of here. I'll guarantee you safe passage home."

The young man whirled around, still trying to spot Cole. As he spun he fell heavily to the deck. It forced an inadvertent howl of pain from him. His pistol flew halfway across the bridge. He started painfully crawling toward it, but lost consciousness halfway there.

"Rachel?" said Cole.

Her image appeared. "Yes, sir?"

"Take our doctor onto the *Kermit* and get over to the flagship. You'll find a young man there. Have him patched up, put him in his own shuttle, feed in Chambon V's coordinates, and send him on his way."

"Yes, sir."

Cole turned back to his own crew. "All right. Let's round up our people and start repairing our damages. The shooting's over."

For the time being, he added silently.

A week had passed.

The bodies—those that remained intact and identifiable—were rounded up and buried in a mass grave on Durstan IV, the nearest oxygen world.

The Duke offered free drinks for a week to anyone who had been involved in the fighting, but furiously ended the policy within a day when eleven thousand men, women, and aliens showed up, each claiming to have been aboard one of the ships.

Aboard the *Teddy R*, Cole called a meeting, not just of his senior staff, but of every member of the crew. Christine transmitted his words and image to every corner of the ship, and signaled him when it was completed.

"Paul had his revelation at Tarsus," began Cole. "I had mine last week, when I saw a brave young man refuse to surrender aboard the Navy's flagship. He knew that the battle was lost, that he was the only survivor on his ship, possibly the only survivor from a fleet of three hundred ships. He had been badly injured hours earlier, but he wasn't going to surrender his ship to what he had been told was the enemy." Cole paused. "I found myself admiring that young man. He didn't know what happened on Braccio II. He didn't know about any of the Navy's abuses. If he attacked a world, it was because commanders he trusted told him that world deserved to be attacked. I am sure he was told that he was coming to Singapore Station to avenge a heinous surprise attack on the Navy.

"As I looked at that young man, I realized that *he* was not the enemy. He was doing exactly what every one of us did for years: He was following orders because he believed in the rightness of those orders."

Cole looked from Jacovic to Christine to Val, and then to those of the crew who had crowded onto the bridge.

"Just as that young man was not the enemy, the Navy is not the enemy." He saw a few puzzled expressions. "The Navy is the *tool* of the enemy. I suppose I've known it all along: The enemy is the Republic. I didn't issue my ultimatum to keep out of the Inner Frontier to the Navy; I issued it to the Republic.

"Well, it didn't work. They came here to punish us for our audacity, and while we were fortunate enough to win this time, they won't allow it to stand. They'll be back, which is what we have to discuss. We can either stay where we are, and fend off each attack against greater and greater odds until we lose—or we can carry the battle to *them*."

"To the Republic?" asked Pampas.

"To Deluros VIII itself," answered Cole.

"Well, goddamn!" said Val. "It's about time!"

"At the risk of disappointing the Valkyrie, this will not be a frontal assault," said Cole. "How could it be? I am asking you to go up against the most powerful entity in the history of the galaxy. Even Christine's computer couldn't dope out the odds against us. So anyone who wants to stay out here has one Standard day to take their gear and move it to the station."

"Have you spoken to the Octopus?" asked Rachel.

"He's with us. So are Lafferty's men, of course. We won't be just one ship. We're going to organize the Inner Frontier, and we'll pick up still more support within the Republic itself."

"The Republic," repeated one of the men dully.

"The Republic," replied Cole. He waited for more questions from his stunned crew. There weren't any. "All right," he said. "This meeting is over. You have one Standard day to make your decisions."

The meeting dispersed, and he went down to the mess hall for some coffee, where he was joined by Sharon.

"You don't pick small targets, I'll give you that," she said.

"This target picked itself," he said. "I served it loyally for most of my life." He grimaced. "Makes me feel like a damned fool."

"Let's see how much smarter you feel when we're facing three million warships."

Suddenly he smiled. "Three thousand, three million—when you're our size, what's the difference?"

"I think that's what I meant," she said, returning his smile. Suddenly the smile vanished. "Do you really think we have a chance?"

"Everyone's got a chance."

"But against the *Republic*!"

"Ever hear of St. George?"

"Yes," said Sharon. "Why?"

"Think you'd have heard of him if he'd fought a dragonfly?"

"He had armor and an enchanted sword."

"We've got the *Teddy R*," replied Cole. "I'll settle."

APPENDIXES

Appendix One

THE ORIGIN OF THE
BIRTHRIGHT UNIVERSE

I t happened in the 1970s. Carol and I were watching a truly awful movie at a local theater, and about halfway through it I muttered, "Why am I wasting my time here when I could be doing something really interesting, like, say, writing the entire history of the human race from now until its extinction?" And she whispered back, "So why don't you?" We got up immediately, walked out of the theater, and that night I outlined a novel called *Birthright: The Book of Man*, which would tell the story of the human race from its attainment of faster-than-light flight until its death eighteen thousand years from now.

It was a long book to write. I divided the future into five political eras—Republic, Democracy, Oligarchy, Monarchy, and Anarchy—and wrote twenty-six connected stories ("demonstrations," *Analog* called them, and rightly so), displaying every facet of the human race, both admirable and not so admirable. Since each is set a few centuries from the last, there are no continuing characters (unless you consider Man, with a capital *M*, the main character, in which case you could make an argument—or at least, *I* could—that it's really a character study).

I sold it to Signet, along with another novel, titled *The Soul Eater*. My editor there, Sheila Gilbert, loved the Birthright Universe and asked me if I would be willing to make a few changes to *The Soul Eater* so that it was set in that future. I agreed, and the changes actually took less than a day. She made the same request—in advance, this time—for the four-book Tales of the Galactic Midway series, the four-book Tales of the Velvet Comet series, and *Walpurgis III*. Looking back, I see that only two of the thirteen novels I wrote for Signet were *not* set there.

When I moved to Tor Books, my editor there, Beth Meacham, had a fondness for the Birthright Universe, and most of my books for her— not all, but most—were set in it: *Santiago, Ivory, Paradise, Purgatory, Inferno, A Miracle of Rare Design, A Hunger in the Soul, The Outpost,* and *The Return of Santiago.*

When Ace agreed to buy *Soothsayer, Oracle,* and *Prophet* from me, my editor, Ginjer Buchanan, assumed that of course they'd be set in the Birthright Universe—and of course they were, because as I learned a little more about my eighteen-thousand-year, two-million-world future, I felt a lot more comfortable writing about it.

In fact, I started setting short stories in the Birthright Universe. Two of my Hugo winners—"Seven Views of Olduvai Gorge" and "The 43 Antarean Dynasties"—are set there, and so are perhaps fifteen others.

When Bantam agreed to take the Widowmaker trilogy from me, it was a foregone conclusion that Janna Silverstein, who purchased the books but had moved to another company before they came out, would want them to take place in the Birthright Universe. She did indeed request it, and I did indeed agree.

I recently handed in a book to Meisha Merlin, set—where else?— in the Birthright Universe.

And when it came time to suggest a series of books to Lou Anders for the new Pyr line of science fiction, I don't think I ever considered any ideas or stories that *weren't* set in the Birthright Universe.

I've gotten so much of my career from the Birthright Universe that I wish I could remember the name of that turkey we walked out of all those years ago so I could write the producers and thank them.

Appendix Two

THE LAYOUT OF THE BIRTHRIGHT UNIVERSE

The most heavily populated (by both stars and inhabitants) section of the Birthright Universe is always referred to by its political identity, which evolves from Republic to Democracy to Oligarchy to Monarchy. It encompasses millions of inhabited and habitable worlds. Earth is too small and too far out of the mainstream of galactic commerce to remain Man's capital world, and within a couple of thousand years the capital has been moved lock, stock, and barrel halfway across the galaxy to Deluros VIII, a huge world with about ten times Earth's surface and near-identical atmosphere and gravity. By the middle of the Democracy, perhaps four thousand years from now, the entire planet is covered by one huge sprawling city. By the time of the Oligarchy, even Deluros VIII isn't big enough for our billions of empire-running bureaucrats, and Deluros VI, another large world, is broken up into forty-eight planetoids, each housing a major department of the government (with four planetoids given over entirely to the military).

Earth itself is way out in the boonies, on the Spiral Arm. I don't believe I've set more than parts of a couple of stories on the Arm.

At the outer edge of the galaxy is the Rim, where worlds are spread out and underpopulated. There's so little of value or military interest on the Rim that one ship, such as the *Theodore Roosevelt*, can patrol a couple of hundred worlds by itself. In later eras, the Rim will be dominated by feuding warlords, but it's so far away from the center of things that the governments, for the most part, just ignore it.

Then there are the Inner and Outer Frontiers. The Outer Frontier is that vast but sparsely populated area between the outer edge of the Republic/Democracy/Oligarchy/Monarchy and the Rim. The Inner Frontier is that somewhat smaller (but still huge) area between the inner reaches of the Republic/etc. and the black hole at the core of the galaxy.

It's on the Inner Frontier that I've chosen to set more than half of my novels. Years ago the brilliant writer R. A. Lafferty wrote, "Will there be a mythology of the future, they used to ask, after all has become science? Will high deeds be told in epic, or only in computer code?" I decided that I'd like to spend at least a part of my career trying to create those myths of the future, and it seems to me that myths, with their bigger-than-life characters and colorful settings, work best on frontiers where there aren't too many people around to chronicle them accurately, or too many authority figures around to prevent them from playing out to their inevitable conclusions. So I arbitrarily decided that the Inner Frontier was where *my* myths would take place, and I populated it with people bearing names like Catastrophe Baker, the Widowmaker, the Cyborg de Milo, the ageless Forever Kid, and the like. It not only allows me to tell my heroic (and sometimes antiheroic) myths, but lets me tell more realistic stories occurring at the very same time a few thousand light-years away in the Republic or Democracy or whatever happens to exist at that moment.

Over the years I've fleshed out the galaxy. There are the star clusters—the Albion Cluster, the Quinellus Cluster, a few others. There are the individual worlds, some important enough to appear as the title of a book, such as Walpurgis III, some reappearing throughout the time periods and stories, such as Deluros VIII, Antares III, Binder X, Keepsake, Spica II, and some others, and hundreds (maybe thousands by now) of worlds (and races, now that I think about it) mentioned once and never again.

Then there are, if not the bad guys, at least what I think of as the Disloyal Opposition. Some, like the Sett Empire, get into one war with humanity and that's the end of it. Some, like the Canphor Twins (Canphor VI and Canphor VII), have been a thorn in Man's side for the better part of ten millennia. Some, like Lodin XI, vary almost daily in their loyalties depending on the political situation.

I've been building this universe, politically and geographically, for a quarter of a century now, and with each passing book and story it feels a little more real to me. Give me another thirty years and I'll probably believe every word I've written about it.

Appendix Three

CHRONOLOGY OF THE BIRTHRIGHT UNIVERSE

Year	Era	World	Story or Novel
1885	A.D.		"The Hunter" (*Ivory*)
1898	A.D.		"Himself" (*Ivory*)
1982	A.D.		*Sideshow*
1983	A.D.		*The Three-Legged Hootch Dancer*
1985	A.D.		*The Wild Alien Tamer*
1987	A.D.		*The Best Rootin' Tootin' Shootin' Gunslinger in the Whole Damned Galaxy*
2057	A.D.		"The Politician" (*Ivory*)
2988	A.D. = 1 G.E.		
16	G.E.	Republic	"The Curator" (*Ivory*)
264	G.E.	Republic	"The Pioneers" (*Birthright*)
332	G.E.	Republic	"The Cartographers" (*Birthright*)
346	G.E.	Republic	*Walpurgis III*
367	G.E.	Republic	*Eros Ascending*
396	G.E.	Republic	"The Miners" (*Birthright*)
401	G.E.	Republic	*Eros at Zenith*
442	G.E.	Republic	*Eros Descending*
465	G.E.	Republic	*Eros at Nadir*
522	G.E.	Republic	"All the Things You Are"
588	G.E.	Republic	"The Psychologists" (*Birthright*)

616	G.E.	Republic	*A Miracle of Rare Design*
882	G.E.	Republic	"The Potentate" (*Ivory*)
962	G.E.	Republic	"The Merchants" (*Birthright*)
1150	G.E.	Republic	"Cobbling Together a Solution"
1151	G.E.	Republic	"Nowhere in Particular"
1152	G.E.	Republic	"The God Biz"
1394	G.E.	Republic	"Keepsakes"
1701	G.E.	Republic	"The Artist" (*Ivory*)
1813	G.E.	Republic	"Dawn" (*Paradise*)
1826	G.E.	Republic	*Purgatory*
1859	G.E.	Republic	"Noon" (*Paradise*)
1888	G.E.	Republic	"Midafternoon" (*Paradise*)
1902	G.E.	Republic	"Dusk" (*Paradise*)
1921	G.E.	Republic	*Inferno*
1966	G.E.	Republic	*Starship: Mutiny*
1967	G.E.	Republic	*Starship: Pirate*
1968	G.E.	Republic	*Starship: Mercenary*
1969	G.E.	Republic	*Starship: Rebel*
1970	G.E.	Republic	*Starship: Flagship*
2122	G.E.	Democracy	"The 43 Antarean Dynasties"
2154	G.E.	Democracy	"The Diplomats" (*Birthright*)
2239	G.E.	Democracy	"Monuments of Flesh and Stone"
2275	G.E.	Democracy	"The Olympians" (*Birthright*)
2469	G.E.	Democracy	"The Barristers" (*Birthright*)
2885	G.E.	Democracy	"Robots Don't Cry"
2911	G.E.	Democracy	"The Medics" (*Birthright*)
3004	G.E.	Democracy	"The Policitians" (*Birthright*)
3042	G.E.	Democracy	"The Gambler" (*Ivory*)
3286	G.E.	Democracy	*Santiago*
3322	G.E.	Democracy	*A Hunger in the Soul*
3324	G.E.	Democracy	*The Soul Eater*

3324	G.E.	Democracy	"Nicobar Lane: The Soul Eater's Story"
3407	G.E.	Democracy	*The Return of Santiago*
3427	G.E.	Democracy	*Soothsayer*
3441	G.E.	Democracy	*Oracle*
3447	G.E.	Democracy	*Prophet*
3502	G.E.	Democracy	"Guardian Angel"
3504	G.E.	Democracy	"A Locked-Planet Mystery"
3504	G.E.	Democracy	"Honorable Enemies"
3719	G.E.	Democracy	"Hunting the Snark"
4375	G.E.	Democracy	"The Graverobber" (*Ivory*)
4822	G.E.	Oligarchy	"The Administrators" (*Birthright*)
4839	G.E.	Oligarchy	*The Dark Lady*
5101	G.E.	Oligarchy	*The Widowmaker*
5103	G.E.	Oligarchy	*The Widowmaker Reborn*
5106	G.E.	Oligarchy	*The Widowmaker Unleashed*
5108	G.E.	Oligarchy	*A Gathering of Widowmakers*
5461	G.E.	Oligarchy	"The Media" (*Birthright*)
5492	G.E.	Oligarchy	"The Artists" (*Birthright*)
5521	G.E.	Oligarchy	"The Warlord" (*Ivory*)
5655	G.E.	Oligarchy	"The Biochemists" (*Birthright*)
5912	G.E.	Oligarchy	"The Warlords" (*Birthright*)
5993	G.E.	Oligarchy	"The Conspirators" (*Birthright*)
6304	G.E.	Monarchy	*Ivory*
6321	G.E.	Monarchy	"The Rulers" (*Birthright*)
6400	G.E.	Monarchy	"The Symbiotics" (*Birthright*)
6521	G.E.	Monarchy	"Catastrophe Baker and the Cold Equations"
6523	G.E.	Monarchy	*The Outpost*
6599	G.E.	Monarchy	"The Philosophers" (*Birthright*)
6746	G.E.	Monarchy	"The Architects" (*Birthright*)

6962	G.E.	Monarchy	"The Collectors" (*Birthright*)
7019	G.E.	Monarchy	"The Rebels" (*Birthright*)
16201	G.E.	Anarchy	"The Archaeologists" (*Birthright*)
16673	G.E.	Anarchy	"The Priests" (*Birthright*)
16888	G.E.	Anarchy	"The Pacifists" (*Birthright*)
17001	G.E.	Anarchy	"The Destroyers" (*Birthright*)
21703	G.E.		"Seven Views of Olduvai Gorge"

Novels not set in this future

Adventures (1922–1926 A.D.)
Exploits (1926–1931 A.D.)
Encounters (1931–1934 A.D.)
Hazards (1934–1939 A.D.)
Stalking the Unicorn ("Tonight")
Stalking the Vampire ("Tonight")
Stalking the Dragon ("Tonight")
The Branch (2047–2051 A.D.)
Second Contact (2065 A.D.)
Bully! (1910–1912 A.D.)
Kirinyaga (2123–2137 A.D.)
Kilimanjaro (2235–2241 A.D.)
Lady with an Alien (1490 A.D.)
A Club in Montmartre (1890–1901 A.D.)
Dragon America: Revolution (1779–1780 A.D.)
The World behind the Door (1928 A.D.)
The Other Teddy Roosevelts (1888–1919 A.D.)

Appendix Four

SINGAPORE STATION SCHEMATIC

By Deborah Oakes

1. Main Station—In this view, looking down from above, you can view the four interlocking standard atmosphere levels of the station.

2. Main Commercial Docks—One of the newer additions to the station, this structure can dock almost three hundred ships simultaneously. Like all the station's docks, it is an independent structure that maintains a position on the main station and is tied to it only through the monorail and magnetic induction cargo systems.

3. Bulk Cargo Docks—This is the main cargo-sorting dock for the station—cargos can be transshipped here without entering the station.

4. Domestic Cargo Dock—Most cargos intended for consumption on the station enter at this dock.

5. Magnetic Induction Cargo System—All cargo within the station and all cargo transshipped at Singapore Station travels via cargo pods on this transit system.

6. Methane Docks—These two docks service the large ships belonging to the methane breathers.

7. Direct Dock—Methane Habitat—For the comfort and safety of

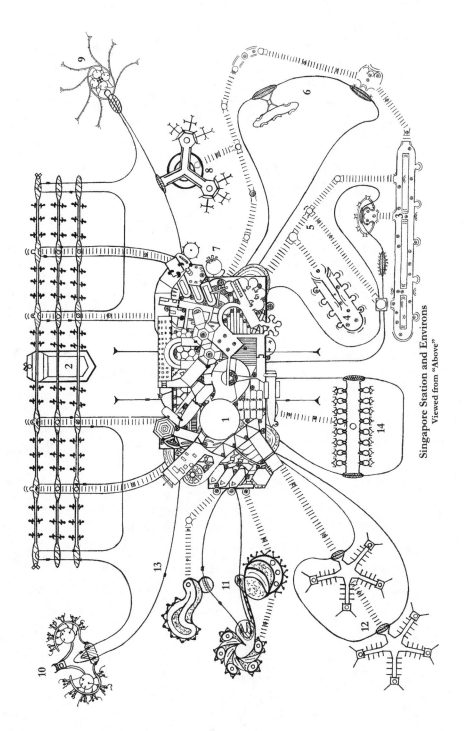

Singapore Station and Environs
Viewed from "Above"

passengers, the newest methane habitat boasts two direct dock ports for passenger ships.

8. Private Docks—As on any station, the wealthy can command private facilities on Singapore Station. This dock services only private vessels.

9. Large Ship Refueling Station—Large ships, mainly freighters, visit this dock only for refueling—no cargo is handled here.

10. Standard Ship Refueling Station—This dock refuels most small- to medium-sized ships.

11. Chlorine Docks—These three docks, cannibalized from three stations with chlorine atmospheres that now form part of the chlorine breathers' Level 6, service the chlorine level directly.

12. Company Docks—These standard atmosphere docks are dedicated to companies that maintain a presence on Singapore Station.

13. Monorail System—The monorail system, built with incredibly tough monofilament, provides the primary transportation and connection between the Main Station and its many outlying docks.

14. Ammonia Dock—This dock is dedicated to the ammonia habitats and is maintained with a basic ammonia atmosphere. Due to the wide variety of ammonia/gas atmospheric mixtures, all ammonia habitats also possess direct docking ports.

15. Level 7 Direct Dock Port—This port is one of four on the airless Level 7. The four independent ports lead to four staging chambers that can be supplied with any atmosphere. Each chamber in turn leads to an airlock, and from there into the main negotiation level.

16. Methane Habitat—This is the newer and larger of the two methane habitats attached to Singapore Station. The direct docking ports for the methane ships are on this habitat.

17. Original Methane Habitat—This is the original methane station attached to Singapore Station. It functions now mainly as a com-

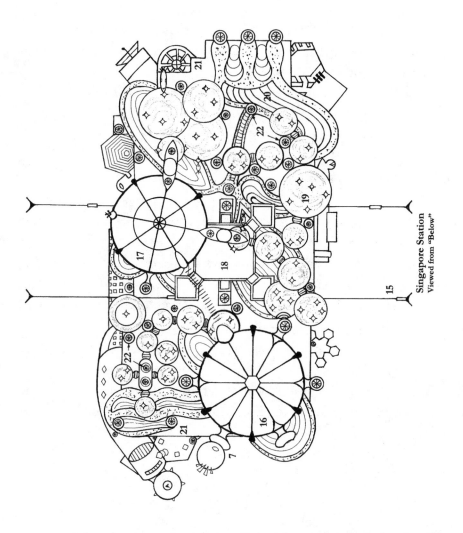

Singapore Station
Viewed from "Below"

mercial and cargo center, being linked by magnetic induction to the newer methane habitat and by two special docking ports to the ammonia habitats.

18. Airless Level 7—This is the airless negotiation level of the station. It is configured with four independent docks and two direct accesses to the transportation level. All dock accesses have inde-

pendent staging areas capable of operating at any known atmospheric conditions, linked by airlocks to the main airless negotiation chambers.

19. Ammonia Habitats—The ammonia habitats form Level 8 of Singapore Station. They are linked in chains, to allow transitions in atmosphere composition. They have the most direct links to the methane habitats and have many small ships constantly moving between habitats.

20. Level 6—The interlinked chlorine breathing habitats form Level 6 of Singapore Station. They are identified by their unique, curved architecture.

21. Transportation Level 5—This deck houses the lift shaft, monorail, and cargo systems. All levels have connections to this level. This level grows as Singapore Station adds additional stations to its total tonnage. It can be seen most clearly in the view from below the station, since the nonstandard atmospheric levels are more porous.

22. Lift Shafts—These are the external lift shafts connecting levels to the transportation level. Each standard atmosphere level has additional internal lift shafts.

Appendix Five

KERMIT SHUTTLE SCHEMATIC

By Deborah Oakes

The *Kermit* Shuttle from the *Theodore Roosevelt*

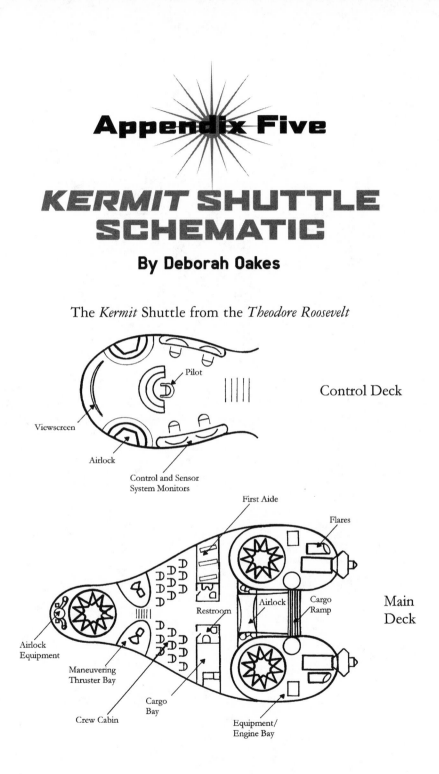

Control Deck

Pilot

Viewscreen

Airlock

Control and Sensor
System Monitors

First Aide

Flares

Airlock

Cargo
Ramp

Restroom

Main
Deck

Airlock
Equipment

Maneuvering
Thruster Bay

Crew Cabin

Cargo
Bay

Equipment/
Engine Bay

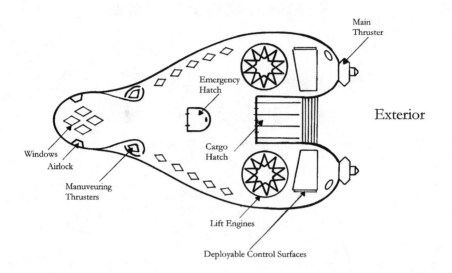

Main
Thruster

Emergency
Hatch

Exterior

Cargo
Hatch

Windows
Airlock

Manuveuring
Thrusters

Lift Engines

Deployable Control Surfaces

Appendix Six

MILITARY SCIENCE FICTION

A BRIEF HISTORY

By Mike Resnick

t's perfectly natural to wonder what the future of warfare will be. We already have the capacity to destroy almost all life on Earth; what weaponry will we use a millennium from now (if we're still here, that is)? How can we negotiate a cease-fire with an enemy that inhales ammonia, excretes bricks, and smells colors? What kind of collateral damage are you looking at when you can obliterate entire planets in seconds? What does a war do to your economy when it's being waged five thousand light-years away?

That's where science fiction comes in.

Stories of interstellar warfare go back to 1859, and of course everyone's read or at least heard of H. G. Wells's *The War of the Worlds*, but for all practical purposes, military science fiction as a viable and popular category began with the works of E. E. "Doc" Smith.

Doc, who was a superstar back in the 1930s and early 1940s, was sought after by editors and beloved by fans. His first series was the Skylark series, in which two young men go off to see the galaxy and get into more trouble than anyone could anticipate. (Years later Harry Harrison did a hilarious and loving parody of the series with his *Star Smashers of the Galaxy Rangers*.) The Skylark books—there were three in the early and mid-1930s and a fourth three decades later—established Doc's reputation, but it was the Lensman series that put him in orbit.

This series consisted originally of *Galactic Patrol*, *The Gray Lensman*, *Second Stage Lensman*, and *Children of the Lens* (the two prequels—*Triplanetary* and *First Lensman*—were written, one from scratch and one to conform to the series' history, after the main story, contained in these four, was completed). Kimball Kinnison and his fellow Lensmen, a trio of very different, distinct, and memorable aliens, think they are battling against the empire of Boskone—but after a couple of books it is revealed that this is nothing less than the ultimate battle of Good versus Evil for control of the galaxy—kind of a high-tech Lord of the Rings on an infinitely greater scale. Sure, it was space opera, but it was *military* space opera. There are space battles, and englobements, and ships are always "matching intrinsics" (whatever that means), and when Kinnison isn't leading vast numbers of ships into battle, he's a covert agent operating alone on alien worlds, and it's a lot of rip-roaring fun.

Doc Smith reigned supreme in the 1930s, but he had a lot of competitors. It was said that Jack Williamson and Edmond Hamilton worked in tandem, one destroying the solar system on odd-numbered months, the other doing it on even-numbered months (and both defending it just as vigorously on months they weren't destroying it). Williamson produced a series that was every bit as popular as the Skylark series; the books include *The Legion of Time*, *One Against the Legion*, and *The Legion of Space*. Hamilton wrote the Interstellar Patrol series and then, in a relatively brief time, churned out more than twenty *Captain Future* novels for the magazine of the same name.

These all appeared in the days of the beloved old half-cent-a-word (or sometimes less) pulp magazines. The covers usually featured gorgeous maidens in varying states of undress (nothing you can't see on a beach today, but wildly erotic for teenaged readers of sixty and seventy years ago), and these ladies were invariably being accosted by BEMs (Bug-Eyed Monsters, for the uninitiated), who seemed more intent on eating their clothes than eating *them.*

Well, everything matures, even science fiction. Which is not to say that it outgrew military science fiction any more than the governments of Earth have outgrown military adventurism—but the stories became a bit more mature. A. E. van Vogt took a run at the category with *The War against the Rull*, and others also tried their hands at it—most notably the team of Cyril M. Kornbluth and Judy Merril, who as Cyril Judd wrote *Gunner Cade*—but the world was just recovering from its second "war to end all wars" in two decades, and while military science fiction still appeared in the 1940s and early 1950s, it wasn't quite as popular as Doc and the boys had made it a decade earlier. (Though the Lensman series itself lasted through 1948—but then, it *was* the Lensman series, long-running and much cherished.)

As we got a little farther from World War II, and the Korean War proved to be less cataclysmic and of shorter duration, military science fiction came back with a vengeance—and with considerably more sophistication. Gordon R. Dickson created the Dorsai and got three decades of outstanding stories from those interstellar mercenaries. There were other fine military science fiction novels in the 1950s—H. Beam Piper's *Uller Uprising* comes to mind—but it was at the end of the decade that science fiction finally produced a true military classic: Robert A. Heinlein's *Starship Troopers*, which to this day remains his most discussed novel. (Pay no attention to the big-budget film, which should have been titled "Ken and Barbie Go to War.") Heinlein not only gave us a war but also a lot to think about, including the suggestion that only those who have served in the military should have the right to vote. A lot of the book concerned the schooling of young troopers, and the philosophy conveyed in those classroom lectures remains controversial half a century later.

Also in the 1950s, C. S. Forester's Horatio Hornblower resurfaced in science fiction guise, in the works of A. Bertram Chandler's Admiral John Grimes. Chandler himself had spent most of his adult life aboard ships, had been master of an aircraft carrier, and had spent many years as captain of a merchant ship, so his works had a great sense of verisimilitude to them. He got a good quarter of a century's worth of tales from his Hornblower updates, and he wasn't the only one.

David Feintuch, who died only ten years after winning the John W. Campbell Memorial Award for Best New Science Fiction Writer in 1996, created his own military series science-fictionalizing the Hornblower stories, writing seven books about the adventures of Nicholas Seafort.

But it remained for David Weber, creator of Honor Harrington, who is kind of a female science fiction analog to Hornblower, to put a military series on the *New York Times* best-seller list—and do it again and again.

Now, while all this was going on, we were fighting a very long, very brutal, and very unpopular war in Vietnam—and suddenly some military science fiction began taking on a new shape and philosophy. The first to make a major impact was David Drake, with his Hammer's Slammers series. It was military, it was science fiction, it was exciting, but it also showed some of the less glorious consequences of war.

Another Vietnam vet with a new take on military science fiction was Joe Haldeman, whose novel *The Forever War*, which won the Hugo and the Nebula in 1976, was viewed by many as a rebuttal to Heinlein's *Starship Troopers* (the only previous military novel to win the Hugo).

And for the past three decades, just about every type of military fiction has made its way into print, as the subgenre has increased in popularity. Jerry Pournelle gave us *The Mercenary* and *A Spaceship for the King*; Elizabeth Ann Scarborough won a Nebula for *The Healer's War*; Fred Saberhagen produced his popular Berserker series; John Steakley's *Armor* was clearly inspired by *Starship Troopers*; Piers Anthony came up with his Bio of a Space Tyrant series; Keith Laumer wrote the Bolo series; Walter Jon Williams gave us *Dread Empire's Fall*; Barry Malzberg first made a name for himself with *Final War*; Orson Scott Card copped every award the field had to offer with *Ender's Game*, in which a brilliant young boy is basically fooled into winning a war; Larry Niven gave us his Man-Kzin War series; David Drake added the Northworld series to his already impressive military credentials; Bob Asprin wrote the Phule's Company series; Elizabeth Moon produced the Sarrano Legacy and Vatta's War series; C. J. Cherry's *Downbelow Station* was a Hugo winner; Harry Turtledove and Eric Flint are both masters of alternate history, and especially alternate military history; G. Harry Stine came up with his Warbots series; John Ringo has recently been reaping huge sales with his military fiction, most notably *Council Wars* and his Legacy of the Aldenata series; John Scalzi had a unique take on the military in *Old Man's War* and *The Ghost Brigades*. And some fifty novels into my science fiction career, I added the Starship series to the canon.

Military science fiction, by the way, doesn't exist only in novels. Jerry Pournelle edited a series of nine anthologies under the title of *There Will Be War*; there was an anthology of Bolo stories created after Keith Laumer's death; and David Drake and Bill Fawcett's Fleet anthologies ran for six volumes.

This survey, I should note, barely scratches the surface. Just about every publisher has military science fiction out there on the racks, which they wouldn't continue to do if there wasn't a ready audience for it, and Baen Books in particular has come to be identified with some of the most popular titles and authors in the subgenre.

I suspect one reason for military science fiction's enduring popularity is that science fiction has traditionally appealed to young readers—and where do we get our youthful readers these days? They watch *Star Wars*, which abounds in space battles, or *Star Trek*, which concerns the voyages of a military ship, and when they decide it's time to read some science fiction, they want to read the type of story they're used to.

Does military science fiction glorify war?

Well, some of it does.

Does it show you the horrors of war?

Some of it does that, too.

The tactics?

Yeah, some.

The nobility, the bravery, even the cowardice?

Yes, a lot of it does, or tries to.

The burdens of leadership?

Sure, some of it.

Which is just as it should be. *From Here to Eternity* and *The Naked and the Dead* and *Battle Cry* and *The Caine Mutiny* and *Catch-22* aren't interchangeable. They're all about aspects of one country's military during a particular war that lasted four years, but each had a totally different take on it and a completely different purpose.

And it's the same with military science fiction, a subgenre that can encompass *Starship Troopers*, *Hammer's Slammers*, *The Forever War*, the Honor Harrington stories, *A Spaceship for the King*, *Old Man's War*, and the adventures of the *Theodore Roosevelt* and its crew.

ABOUT THE AUTHOR

L ocus, *the trade journal of science fiction, keeps a list of the winners of major science fiction awards on its Web page. Mike Resnick is currently fourth in the all-time standings, ahead of Isaac Asimov, Sir Arthur C. Clarke, Ray Bradbury, and Robert A. Heinlein. He is the leading award-winner among all authors, living and dead, for short science fiction.*

* * * * * *

Mike was born on March 5, 1942. He sold his first article in 1957, his first short story in 1959, and his first book in 1962.

He attended the University of Chicago from 1959 through 1961, won three letters on the fencing team, and met and married Carol. Their daughter, Laura, was born in 1962, and has since become a writer herself, winning three awards for her romance novels and the 1993 Campbell Award for Best New Science Fiction Writer.

Mike and Carol discovered science fiction fandom in 1962, attended their first Worldcon in 1963, and more than fifty science fiction novels into his career, Mike still considers himself a fan and frequently contributes articles to fanzines. He and Carol appeared in five Worldcon masquerades in the 1970s in costumes that she created, and they won four of them.

Mike labored anonymously but profitably from 1964 through 1976, selling more than two hundred novels, three hundred short stories, and two thousand articles, almost all of them under pseudonyms, most of them in the "adult" field. He edited seven different tabloid newspapers, and a trio of men's magazines as well.

In 1968 Mike and Carol became serious breeders and exhibitors of collies, a pursuit they continued through 1981. During that time they bred and/or exhibited twenty-seven champion collies, and they were the country's leading breeders and exhibitors during various years along the way.

This led them to purchase the Briarwood Pet Motel in Cincinnati in 1976. It was the country's second-largest luxury boarding and grooming establishment, and they worked full-time at it for the next few years. By 1980 the kennel was being run by a staff of twenty-one, and Mike was free to return to his first love, science fiction, albeit at a far slower pace than his previous writing. They sold the kennel in 1993.

Mike's first novel in this "second career" was *The Soul Eater*, which was followed shortly by *Birthright: The Book of Man*, *Walpurgis III*, the four-book Tales of the Galactic Midway series, *The Branch*, the four-book Tales of the Velvet Comet series, and *Adventures*, all from Signet. His breakthrough novel was the international best seller *Santiago*, published by Tor in 1986. Tor has since published *Stalking the Unicorn*, *The Dark Lady*, *Ivory*, *Second Contact*, *Paradise*, *Purgatory*, *Inferno*, the double *Bwana/Bully!*, and the collection *Will the Last Person to Leave the Planet Please Shut Off the Sun?* His most recent Tor releases were *A Miracle of Rare Design*, *A Hunger in the Soul*, *The Outpost*, and *The Return of Santiago*.

Even at his reduced rate, Mike is too prolific for one publisher, and in the 1990s Ace published *Soothsayer*, *Oracle*, and *Prophet*; Questar published *Lucifer Jones*; Bantam brought out the *Locus* best-selling trilogy of *The Widowmaker*, *The Widowmaker Reborn*, and *The Widowmaker Unleashed*; and Del Rey published *Kirinyaga: A Fable of Utopia* and *Lara Croft, Tomb Raider: The Amulet of Power*. His current releases include *A Gathering of Widowmakers* for Meisha Merlin, *Dragon America* for Phobos, *Lady with an Alien*, *A Club in Montmarte*, and *The World behind the Door* for Watson-Guptill, and *The Alternate Teddy Roosevelts* and *Kilimanjaro* for Subterranean Press.

Beginning with *Shaggy B.E.M. Stories* in 1988, Mike has also become an anthology editor (and was nominated for a Best Editor Hugo in 1994 and 1995). His list of anthologies in print and in press totals forty-eight, and includes *Alternate Presidents*, *Alternate Kennedys*, *Sherlock Holmes in Orbit*, *By Any Other Fame*, *Dinosaur Fantastic*, and *Christmas Ghosts*, plus the recent *Stars*, coedited with superstar singer Janis Ian, and *The Dragon Done It*, coedited with best seller Eric Flint.

Mike has always supported the "specialty press," and he has numerous books and collections out in limited editions from such diverse publishers as Phantasia Press, Axolotl Press, Misfit Press, Pulphouse Publishing, Wildside Press, Dark Regions Press, NESFA Press, WSFA Press, Obscura Press, Farthest Star, and others. He recently served a stint as the science fiction editor for BenBella Books, and in 2006 he became the executive editor of *Jim Baen's Universe.*

Mike was never interested in writing short stories early in his career, producing only seven between 1976 and 1986. Then something clicked, and he has written and sold more than two hundred stories since 1986, and now spends more time on short fiction than on novels. The writing that has brought him the most acclaim thus far in his career is the Kirinyaga series, which, with sixty-seven major and minor awards and nominations to date, is the most honored series of stories in the history of science fiction.

He also began writing short nonfiction as well. He sold a four-part series, "Forgotten Treasures," to the *Magazine of Fantasy and Science Fiction*, was a regular columnist for *Speculations* ("Ask Bwana") for twelve years, currently appears in every issue of the *SFWA Bulletin* ("The Resnick/Malzberg Dialogues"), and wrote a biweekly column for the late, lamented GalaxyOnline.com.

Carol has always been Mike's uncredited collaborator on his science fiction, but in the past few years they have sold two movie scripts— *Santiago* and *The Widowmaker*, both based on Mike's books—and Carol *is* listed as his collaborator on those.

Readers of Mike's works are aware of his fascination with Africa, and the many uses to which he has put it in his science fiction. Mike and Carol have taken numerous safaris, visiting Kenya (four times), Tanzania, Malawi, Zimbabwe, Egypt, Botswana, and Uganda. Mike edited the Library of African Adventure series for St. Martin's Press and is currently editing *The Resnick Library of African Adventure* and, with Carol as coeditor, *The Resnick Library of Worldwide Adventure* for Alexander Books.

Since 1989, Mike has won five Hugo Awards (for "Kirinyaga," "The Manamouki," "Seven Views of Olduvai Gorge," "The 43 Antarean Dynasties," and "Travels with My Cats") and a Nebula Award (for "Seven Views of Olduvai Gorge"), and has been nominated for thirty-one Hugos, eleven Nebulas, a Clarke (British), and six Seiun-sho (Japanese). He has also won a Seiun-sho, a Prix Tour Eiffel (French), two Prix Ozones (French), ten HOMer Awards, an Alexander Award, a Golden Pagoda Award, a Hayakawa SF Award (Japanese), a Locus Award, three Ignotus Awards (Spanish), a Xatafi-Cyberdark Award (Spanish), a Futura Award (Croatian), an El Melocoton Mechanico (Spanish), two Sfinks Awards (Polish), and a Fantastyka Award (Polish), and has topped the Science Fiction Chronicle Poll six times, the Scifi Weekly Hugo Straw Poll three times, and the Asimov's Readers Poll five times. In 1993 he was awarded the Skylark Award for Lifetime Achievement in Science Fiction, and both in 2001 and in 2004 he was named Fictionwise.com's Author of the Year.

His work has been translated into French, Italian, German, Spanish, Japanese, Korean, Bulgarian, Hungarian, Hebrew, Russian,

Latvian, Lithuanian, Polish, Czech, Dutch, Swedish, Romanian, Finnish, Danish, Chinese, and Croatian.

He was recently the subject of Fiona Kelleghan's massive *Mike Resnick: An Annotated Bibliography and Guide to His Work*. Adrienne Gormley is currently preparing a second edition.